7

To Harlow Writers'
Workshop

from

Leslie Tate

Leslie Tate is a full-time novelist and poet. He has taught English to asylum seekers and university students; has a MA in creative writing and is the author of two poetic, character-led novels. They portray modern relationships in different eras.

'Frontliners' deals with urban feminist-led relationships in the 80s/90s.

'Aphrodite's Children', his debut, recreates the wildness of the 60s.

Leslie often gives readings combining poetry, prose and commentary, and has appeared at Hackney Empire, Goldsmiths College, libraries and bookshops, U3As and writing festivals. Believing in passionate complexity, he writes from head and heart about love, authenticity, generational change and matters of soul.

www.leslietate.com

FRONTLINERS

By the same author

Aphrodite`s Children (Vanguard Press), 2009,
ISBN 978 1 843865 04 9

Leslie Tate

FRONTLINERS

Vanguard Press

Vanguard Press is an imprint of
Pegasus Elliot MacKenzie Publishers Ltd.
www.pegasuspublishers.com

First Published in 2011

Vanguard Press
Sheraton House Castle Park
Cambridge England

Printed & Bound in Great Britain

Dedication

To Sue

Acknowledgments

The cover image is an original artwork created by Maria Emilov (www.mariaemilov.net) in response to reading *Frontliners*

CHAPTER ONE

It was Friday afternoon and Richard Lawrence had taken himself off beyond the lawn and the shadow of the house to sit out on concrete at the far end of the garden. With a wineglass close to hand Richard was dividing his attention between two book collections, marking and transferring from one pile to the other. As he checked and sampled his eyes moved quickly, searching and comparing, forward and back. At one page, a fold-out, he paused, weighing up evidence; at another he smiled; a couple he reread – for most he remained expressionless.

He wondered if now, at last, after talking and trying and so much wasted effort, he'd finally had enough.

A cloud dimmed the sun and for a while he looked off, grey-eyed, abstracted, examining the house. Dream-vague and wishful, he was searching into thought. When the cloud passed over he pushed up in his chair, nodded and read a few more pages. As he checked back on comments he rolled up a sleeve, glanced at his watch, then pressed in closer, bending to his work. Flicking over pages, he recorded marks. High-cheeked and definite with quick, attentive glances and firm-set lips, he was on task.

He'd really had enough. Enough for anyone.

From time to time he put aside his schoolbooks, closed his eyes and angled back his head, directing forward to the mid-May sun. Then he was himself. A boy grown to man: not too old, not too young. Actorly as well; thirtyish, with presence. At other times he gazed both ways, sighting the back gardens while taking in the sounds of birds on branches, dishes clashing, TV announcements, children crying. Occasionally he rose, topped up his glass from an unstoppered bottle, and stood tall beside the fence examining the climbers while absorbing scent from a newly-opened rose. A plane passed over as he sampled wine.

Glancing skyward, he yawned, stretched, then refilled his glass. Returning to his chair he placed his drink on concrete, then, spreading both hands, fingered-combed his hair. Layered from the front, it was mouse-brown, cheek-length and slightly girlish. A dog barked, a window slid up and a radio sounded. When a woman called out he frowned, looked back at the house, then settled in his seat and picked up his ballpoint. Holding it sideways, cigarette-wise, he paused, swigged another mouthful then reached to the floor and scooped up a blue-bound jotter which he'd stowed beneath the chair. He opened, thumbed through the pages, shifted round his pen and stared into white.

Enough was enough. Enough, and too much.

In the house three doors away Vanessa Lawrence was talking with her dear friend Ruth.

"He's OTT," she said, sipping at her tea.

Her host, who was wedged in with cushions at one end of the sofa, nodded. "Mine's the same."

Vanessa smiled. "Doug? Surely not. He's more monkish."

"Can be fiery."

"Ah, but Richard—" Vanessa paused. There was so much she could say.

Ruth leaned forward and blinked. Her face, which was long and narrow, was flushed with awareness. Wearing a belted dress and open-toed sandals, she held herself at an angle, sidelong, with a *why-me* expression. With her slightly watery eyes, red-blotched neck and freckled shoulders, she looked like a tourist just off the beach.

"He's obsessive," Vanessa continued. "Music, writing, the latest theory – it's all about him: his opinions. And each new one's the best, the most important, so nothing else matters."

Her friend tut-tutted.

Vanessa eyed her tea. Thinking, deliberating, she was giving out.

"The men's club," she said, speaking slowly. "They're not like us."

16

Ruth raised her fingers to signal behind her head. "Bloody Martians," she called, pulling a face.

Vanessa laughed. Again she eyed her tea. Her gaze was assured, mixed with surprise.

"I do wonder sometimes," she added, speaking more quietly. "Richard's so driven. It's all about what he calls *thinking straight* – which means, as far as I can see, putting things in boxes, labelling, having his own way. And whatever he's into, it's that and that only. Day and night, nothing else matters. He's what you call *hyper*. Life for him is one long campaign."

Shaking her head, she took a sip of tea.

Ruth, agreeing, settled into silence.

As Vanessa drank, she kept up her talk – but now more random: half-chatty, half-reflective. There was something watchful – even self-regarding – in her well-rounded vowels and stretch on the sofa. With her large eyes and firmed-up mouth, it seemed she'd things in hand. She belonged – at least in imagination – to those well-born ladies whose understated gestures, full of hidden meanings, are references off.

"There are things I could tell…" she said, echoing her own thoughts.

Lapsing into quiet, her expression flattened. She adjusted her hold on the teacup. Gazing, she sighed.

She was measuring and comparing: a level and how much remained. The first taste and after. And how talking with Ruth always brought it out. Framed and examined, seen in perspective, the truth served up. And the images – still-life – held between fingers, the time-lapse and memories, the otherness.

They'd been looking at photos in a frayed black album. It lay discarded now on a low-level table with a double page on show. The pictures, snapshots mainly (dated and captioned with fixed and public smiles) were arranged, it seemed, to illustrate aspects of two contrasting states. On one side a wedding with Ruth in white and Doug by her side (with, below it, a passport-sized cameo of an upstanding Richard, boyish and smiling, offering a toast), on the other side a beach-shot of children squatted, guzzling ice cream. With the women, now older, working as a twosome, cleaning and wiping and directing to the tent. And, next step in the series, the children facing camera, seated under canvas, finger-licking chocolates and sipping fizzy drinks. While outside (pictured last) were the open-air husbands, one testing and tying up flaps, the other checking pegs. Both seemed distant, absorbed in activity, their minds set on actions, ignoring the rain.

On the upstairs landing there was a scuffle, followed by a thump, a squeal and a door clicking shut.

Ruth eyed the ceiling as if it might cave in. "What on earth d'you think is going on up there?"

Vanessa blinked, unhanding her cup. The answer she gave seemed to come from a long way off. *Something* she supposed.

"A death, I should imagine," replied Ruth, grinning.

A child appeared at the doorway. He was thin and taut, high-cheeked, serious, with round brown eyes and a girl-smooth complexion.

"Stephan," said Vanessa shifting forward, "what's wrong?"

"They locked me out," he said, breathing quickly.

"Locked you out?"

Nodding, he threw himself forward over chair arm and lap.

His mother pulled a face. "Oh dear, I'm sure they don't mean it." She began to rub his back.

"They did."

"Well it's over now."

"They have to let me in."

"I'm sure they will."

His nostrils flared as he pulled back upright. "You tell them."

"I can try."

The boy began to push.

"All right, lovey. Don't get angry."

"*You* tell them."

"All right."

"*Tell* them."

"I will."

"*You tell them.*"

"Yes, yes."

"Go on then."

18

He pushed and arm-pinched her to upright. "Stephan, don't hurt," she said as he herded her to the stairs.

Appearing on the landing, a girl called his name.

Vanessa looked up. "Charlotte," she cried, "let him in."

Her daughter considered. Two large brown eyes gazed into space. "He's not nice. He says bad things."

"Never mind, lovey, just let him in."

The girl stood doubtful.

Ruth appeared, calling encouragement from just inside the door. Vanessa appealed, patting Stephan lightly on the back. The boy stood head down, concentrated, apparently resigned to whatever might follow. A sense of obligation hung in the air.

Charlotte gazed, without saying anything. Her look was fixed. Her eyes, like her mother's, were round, large and vaguely inquisitorial. Finally she moved back and away, allowing access. "Only if he's nice," she cautioned.

Stephan, after some hesitation, climbed to the landing, paused to look back, then threw out a challenge as he headed for the door.

"Don't!" she shrieked, lunging forward. There was a thump, a scuffle and shouts of protest as the two disappeared higher, fighting for advantage.

"Please. Children," Vanessa sighed and took two steps up, requesting calm. Ruth stood behind, calling instructions.

Upstairs the protests slackened and a door opened. Two more voices joined in, followed by giggles, then silence.

Vanessa remained poised, head to one side. Like a back row spectator she was straining to understand. "You think they're OK?" she asked, turning to her friend.

Ruth shrugged, saying nothing.

"Should we go and see?" added Vanessa, descending to the hallway.

"Best not."

"You think they're safe?"

"As much as can be expected."

"I feel we ought to be *doing* something."

"Then call in Sir Richard," Ruth said sardonically, "*he'll* sort 'em out."

"God forbid."

They entered the lounge, shaking their heads. As they settled on the sofa, adjusting cushions, a shout went up from the room overhead.

Vanessa caught her breath.

"Don't worry," said Ruth, "it's a computer game. Latest thing."

Grinning, she offered more tea. When Vanessa nodded, she topped up and stirred. Her mouth set firm as her eye caught the album. She pointed to the picture of children eating, huddled against rain. Woman to woman, an understanding passed.

"Kids."

"Husbands."

It had seemed to Vanessa, when she'd first met Richard, that he kept himself apart. He was tall and rather visible, which made him count, but his manner wasn't smooth (her friends called him *different*) and he certainly wasn't easy or trendy or simple to get on with. But he did act teacherly, wording what he said carefully, with weight, and giving off an air of something measured. Because he aimed, he'd once said, to work at what he did – delivery, pitch and (surprising in someone who was, like her, barely twenty-one) a sense of real purpose, an engagement.

And what made for difference was the wildness, the little boy, the joker underneath. With above that the performer, the speaker, the man who registered, holding himself separate as he checked on fact or opened up a gap between himself and fellow students through careful choice of language and what she called *edge*. He'd position and shape and register and first-time definition.

And for her he was special – unusual, uncomfortable – and really quite different.

They'd met on training: PGCE, London, 1982 – both young, seeking experience. For her, a teaching course was a way of giving back. It opened into life (street life, the actual, the real and present thing), a window on the world. It also offered style, engagement and a break with parents. For Richard it was more ad lib, a try-out and gap-fill, a way of killing time.

At a presentational seminar she'd talked and passed comment, expounding on Illich, Holt and how schools fail. Her voice was a signal, poised and definite. Raised-up and plummy, offered without blushes, it marked her out. To Richard her interventions were of interest – almost stately – delivered clear, for all to admire. Long-faced and abstract, he thought she'd a head – a body too – and held herself tall with long lines and curves and a well-meant expression. She was at centre, talking to impress. And her words came slowly, pausing between phrases, with a hint of something hidden, a glitch or drama, a punch line held back.

When the seminar ended those who remained adopted her suggestion that they went for a drink. They were young and bright and willing and accepted without question. She'd established a following. As she led off down the pavement Richard held back, refusing to be drawn. His jaw was set, eyes to the ground. He'd turned and gone against. Wasn't much impressed. Didn't like her assumptions, her *this is so* manner, her airs and graces.

In the bar (which was steps down to a basement, with fluted columns and pyramid-folded cards positioned on stone-grey tables) he kept a careful distance, minimised, put himself away. Choosing a corner he sat off separate, concealed behind a pillar. As critic and observer, he wasn't taken in.

At one point he'd passed close, on his way to the toilet, and heard her giving forth. She was talking, it seemed, about political parties. She knew a few names, had inside and knowledge, was up on gossip and who was knocking who. When he returned she'd moved on to fashion, galleries and living in the city. As he walked to his seat he felt her inspection and the lift in her voice, the words pushed out, aimed at him.

"Some do, some don't," she said airily.

"And some teach?" came back, as if on cue, from a short-haired friend called Bess.

"Or worse," she replied, dryly.

Richard, having reached his table, refused to be drawn. He remained seated by the pillar, purposed now. He'd listen, gather evidence, plot what he could say. The more she talked the more he had her measure. And as the afternoon wore on he felt a strange kind of flutteriness, an overlap, mixed in with irritation and an air lump of tightness, getting larger.

When the others had departed, leaving just them – both held back by unfinished business: a drink to drain, tickets, money, clothes to gather – he resolved to say something, shrugged on his jacket, and went up and spoke. "So what d'you think of the course so far?"

She examined him slowly, smiling without warmth: "What do *you* think?"

He considered, standing at the corner of her table: "The usual crap."

She gazed off, unmoved: "That's it, is it?"

"How d'you mean?"

"It's worth four letters."

"It will be when we get to teaching and find what we've done is useless."

Vanessa continued gazing. Her long thin fingers, extended on the table, were fidgeting with a mat. "It rather depends..." she said slowly, then stopped.

"Of course we've all read the theory," he said dismissively. "For what good that'll do."

She pushed her way up, cool and self-contained. With her large brown eyes and quizzical features she was facing him down. "So I take it," she said, affecting nonchalance, "you'll be leaving."

"What?"

She turned and began to move towards the door.

"You going to explain?" he asked quietly, closing to her shoulder.

"Isn't it obvious?"

She stopped at the steps that led up to the street. She was regarding him now as if he'd just arrived. "If you really think it's crap," she said slowly, "then you know what to do."

"Not sure I'm with you."

"I think it's called the honourable thing."

"What – fall on my sword?"

She laughed, sardonically. "I shouldn't bother. It might not do the job."

Richard snorted: "I've offended?"

She narrowed her eyes: "Criminals offend."

"Bring back hanging. It didn't do me any harm."

She pulled a face.

"You think that's tasteless?" he asked, goadingly.

"Just silly."

Stepping back, he waved her to the door: "Have it your way."

Vanessa detached and climbed towards street level. As she reached the frame she glanced back quickly with an expression of distaste. "I will," she said calmly, stopping at the threshold to button up her jacket.

"Then don't let *me* stop you."

She smiled to herself, "Do you imagine you could?"

He grimaced. "If I had to."

"But you'd rather talk and swear and make protestation."

"Oh bloody hell, yes."

She laughed, without humour. It seemed, as she turned into the street, he'd had the final say.

Richard withdrew, re-entering the café. It was bare now and quiet, with plates and glasses stacked on tables, discarded newspapers and drip stains over grey. The chairs were pushed back, there were coins on tables, unused cutlery, side plates with slops and a litter of tissue-scraps – all of which the waiters were clearing, collecting, straightening, wiping over.

He idled by a pillar, marking time. He wanted to stay low. To step back and away, allow for what had happened. Because inwardly he was himself. Surprised, really, to feel this way. Part of him was calm, proud and satisfied at having stood his ground, another part was amazed – at his sudden sharp insistence – and another part focused on what he'd done wrong. But mostly he was himself: alert, observant and distanced off. He wanted closure.

He'd just checked the time and turned toward the door (imagining her pique, the talk with gestures, the version given, protesting to her friends) when his hand brushed the chair back, catching on plastic. Cool-edged and slack, its feel was soft. Withdrawing, he looked down. What he saw made him wince. On the post-end, suspended, was a creamy-yellow handbag which he knew, or reckoned, could only have one owner and had been left there, he suspected, as a quiet kind of signal, something with aim and intention to make him feel obliged.

He swore beneath his breath. Hoping he'd mistaken he checked an outside flap. Her name was there: *Vanessa Quinton* stitched into liner. Words went through his head: excuses, alibis, with time and place and movements reconstructed. Whichever way he played it: damned both ways. Imagining his arrest, he tugged at the handle, paused to examine, before lifting from below. Light and rather fem, it marked him out. With the bag to his chest he climbed to the exit, wondering what to do. He imagined her observing, just beyond the doorframe; charted his actions, had his words prepared, he even *expected*. This, he thought was strange, as if he might want it, plotting intervention as teller and protagonist, was writing as he watched. He could feel his own excitement, the shift and the exposure, as he levelled to the door.

Emerging, he blinked and looked both ways.

The afternoon was mild with sunspots on buildings, birds on ledges and people walking coatless. To his left there was traffic, queued right back. Both sides stationary, mainly commercial, with taxis, a large white bus, cars between vans and the odd containerised lorry. To his right was a split-level office block and a one-way street, a channel for cyclists and walkers. Set back behind the block was a small rectangular park, half-screened by railings and trees. The trees were green-yellow and pre-autumnal. Already the shadow of the building was touching their lower branches.

No Vanessa.

He peered back at the traffic, checking for gaps. Scrutinised for passengers. He recalled her hair – long, dark and centre-parted

– looked for jeans with a purple jacket, scanned along pavements by shop fronts and entrances. He flashed back for a moment to picture how she stood (tall and precise with an element of throwaway, long-faced and inward with a languid kind of smile) and began to search harder, fearing he'd not find her, that he'd be left hanging with her property to account for, a sense of being burdened, and a need for explanation next time they met.

No sign of Vanessa.

Looking straight ahead, he focused in on a paved square. It was crisscrossed by pedestrians and grazing pigeons. In the centre was a statue, blackened by grime, of a long-robed man with a book in his hand. Behind was the glass and metal entrance to a steel-arched station.

Still no Vanessa.

Feeling the bag press against his chest, he turned a half-circle to scan to the end of a narrow walled-in lane. This time he was careful, examining every walker for something familiar, a movement or gesture, aspects of her presence, concealed within the crowd. Perhaps, he thought, it was all in the looking. A matter of approach. He'd just begun to wonder if in fact he'd seen her but simply not noticed. Maybe she was watching or calibrating his performance, reading how he thought. He'd even imagined the maze-like pleasure she must get from giving him the run-around, seeing him discomforted, leading him on. His rebuttal was in process (from casual dismissal, dead set and careless, to looking straight through her as if she wasn't there) when a movement caught his eye. Turning towards the station, he heard his name called and saw her approaching, waving and greeting, pointing to her bag.

"You picked it up."

Richard acknowledged, trying to read her mood.

"I must have left it. I never thought—"

He held out the bag.

"It's a relief," she continued. "Thank you."

In his mind he heard it, registering the shift.

"No problem," he said, managing a smile.

"Well I'm grateful," she said, "I was looking everywhere."

"All part of the service."

"But you could've left it. You might have been tempted. After—"

Their eyes met in a second's understanding. Richard smiled: "Well, I didn't."

Vanessa paused. "I suppose..." she began, furrowing her brow. Her words hung fire while she stared off down the street.

Richard found himself looking with her. "You were wondering?" he asked.

She looked round vaguely. A slackness had descended, a pause, a sighting and a look-around. It was as if they were dancers preparing for the show.

"I don't know. Maybe..."

Richard took a breath. He could see her watching, awaiting developments. They'd something to catch up on.

"Shall we walk?" he asked suddenly.

Vanessa showed willing. "Hmm. The river," she said, nodding downhill to a lane beside the station. It was decided; a mood had taken over; together they set out.

They passed into shadow, pacing quietly with a hand's space between them, crossing the road to reach a sweep of pavement which ran along the front of a tall row of shops. The row was irregular with worn-down frontages, part-wood, part-brick, with fruit crates outside and window stickers displayed at all angles. The doorways led in to tiles and bare boards, dried-out plants and dark, cavernous, piled-up interiors. They walked and observed, saw themselves reflected; they checked and explored and played at being tourists. At one, a bookshop, Vanessa paused, pointing to a photo which showed a thin-faced man peering from the cockpit of an open-topped biplane. She explained he was her cousin Vaughan, a well-known aviator, whose stunts had brought him fame. In answer to Richard's questions she shrugged one shoulder. In truth, she said, she hardly ever saw him. She added that when she did (glancing skyward as if to spot his plane) he wasn't that easy.

Richard laughed. "Behind the image. The man's not so nice." He stared at the book cover holding to a grin, then suggested they move on. When Vanessa nodded his voice tone softened: "Well, presumably he can fly. That part's not managed."

"Yes," she said. "And he is a character."

"Peter Pan?"

She smiled, "I do wonder sometimes."

They walked to the row end, emerging at a gateway flanked by railings. It led in to a small public garden. On the other side, rising in tiers, the steel-grey station closed off the sun. Turning through the gates they followed a path which wound through a shrubbery. They were talking now in snatches, exchanging observations as if they were the owners inspecting their patch. They had their favourite colours, knew most plant names, were aware of other walkers, had the river now in sight. Everything amused them, everything was a show.

"Do you walk a lot?" he asked, as they passed out through a gate and faced across a busy main road, looking to the river.

"This way, yes," she confirmed, pointing to a bridge with a walkway to the side. "It's exercise. My route, here and back. To my flat," she said, pausing between phrases to scan the road, then crossing quickly.

Richard followed. In both directions the vehicles were queued up, windows down, waiting for the lights. He walked between bumpers, eyeing her waist glimpsed between the half-length jacket and long-strapped handbag. Below and beside it her hips moved smoothly, shifting in an arc. She'd set off, he imagined, to avoid any further questions.

At the far side of the road Vanessa veered right. She led pointing forward to open-framed steps. They rose like a fire escape, turned halfway and connected side-on to the rail bridge. She pointed, but her words were lost, drowned out by a lights-change and the traffic roar that followed. Richard nodded, Vanessa took the railing, and they climbed the metal steps to the walkway. It ran out over water, divided from the trains by cross-barred girders.

They stopped at the centre to gaze upstream. The sun had now declined and the buildings by the water were already part-shaded. Behind them, higher, light fell in patches on walls and tiles, while higher still the domes and office blocks were bathed in ochre-yellow brightness. On one building, halfway up, a window glinted. Beside it, where columns rose to a carved stone pediment, a gull was circling and a collection of flags rippled in the breeze.

As they watched a pleasure boat appeared. It approached, skirted a line of tied-up barges, gave a toneless hoot, and passed beneath the bridge. The barges continued knocking and jostling afterwards, shunting like freight.

"Ships in the night," said Richard. He'd spread both hands on the walkway railing. It was flat, studded with bolt heads and hollow underneath.

"You wonder what the barges are carrying," said Vanessa, looking down.

Richard peered through struts at their tarpaulin-ed decks. "Dirty British coaster…"

"Ah… we did that one at school."

He nodded.

"And you have the words by heart?"

Richard frowned. "Not sure. But I know it ends with cheap tin trays."

"You enjoyed it?"

"Would've done. If it wasn't for the teaching."

She paused, looking down. "You remember how they did it?"

"Don't I just."

She pulled back from the railing. "We have to do better. Improve. Find another way." She was speaking now with an offhand assurance, gazing past him as if he was only half there. "I read somewhere that teaching is about power-sharing. Knowing when to lead and when to step back. The book called it signposting. It's all about building skills, finding what works, then bowing out."

He laughed. "But is it that easy?"

Vanessa thought so. It was, she said, what their course was about. Opening doors. Learning new methods. Making the difference.

Richard shook his head. He just couldn't buy that. "They want to fit us," he said thoughtfully. "Line us up. All in one mould. The university knows best. Big Brother professors with nothing better to do. It's a kind job creation scheme: only dyed-in-the-wool academics need apply."

"You think so?"

He nodded. "It's what they call *process*. They think they're counsellors or something. Always batting it back. 'And how do you *feel* about that? Isn't that rather *directive*? Are you *sure* of that?' It's a power game really. They keep us dangling till we see it their way."

Vanessa stared off towards the far end of the bridge. She'd heard and understood, knew just what he meant. She pictured their tutor: a soft-voiced woman whose frequent pauses were (she thought) designed for effect. Long-held stares and ironic deliberations, a sense of things expected, of traps and evasions and laid-out sequence, of hoops to jump.

"Leading from behind," she said, surprising herself.

Richard nodded. It all seemed to fit. Her words, his, and suddenly they were *talking* – not just sparring but offering, responding, analysing experience and adapting what they said. The bridge, the river, something in the air (or maybe earlier: the handbag, the walkout, the faces in the garden) – whatever it was, a viewpoint had opened. She wasn't what he thought. They'd found common ground.

"Yes," he said quietly, "but we don't have to play that game."

As he spoke, a far-off shiver ran along the bridge. Beginning low, the sound moved round and out, advancing with a shudder and a bottom-heavy lurch. It drummed and became firmer, harder, shifted up, then moved to a percussive rattle and a slow, bumping weight of metal on metal. Sound filled the air, moving and tracking like a heavy hinged door.

"Pullman," he mouthed as the engine passed by, dragging behind it a long line of carriages. Each was flashed purple, with curtains in the windows and self-absorbed faces behind tinted glass.

Picking up speed, the train cleared the bridge. The sound went with it, dropping to a murmur as the last retreating carriage curved off between buildings.

"OK," said Richard. "It's gone." Suddenly he smiled. "So now, in the words of the song: *should I go or should I stay?*"

Before she could answer a second train appeared, this time incoming, and the bridge began to shake. As the noise level rose, Vanessa ducked forward. Her eyes scanned the walkway in search of a reply. "Stay if you like," she said quietly. When Richard didn't answer she pointed forward. "Stay…" she repeated, louder. When he raised both hands, pleading deafness, Vanessa shouted. As the train roar closed, she said it once again (mouthing quietly, just between themselves) pointed, then led off smiling to the bridge end, the steps down and the walk towards her flat.

"It isn't much," said Vanessa when they arrived at the door.

They'd walked the quickest route, cutting down streets with office blocks and flats, passing through a tunnel (with above them the railway, thundering, and on one side a wall with shoulder-level doorways, on the other side pits and chambers in what looked like a dig). They'd emerged up a ramp, traversed an estate, a rundown shopping mall, a park with asphalt paths and unplanted borders, continuing along a high-kerbed road, with houses in blocks, fences with gaps, long unkempt gardens and concrete steps fronting peeling doorways.

Her block, she'd told him, was shared. It was three stories high with a bay at the front and a path leading round to an entrance with lights above. There were bells with name slips which he glanced at as she opened. They were handwritten, faded, almost illegible. As they entered he saw a carpeted lobby, woodchip wallpaper, doors both sides and a staircase straight ahead. It smelt of cooking and polish.

"The downstairs used to be a surgery," Vanessa said, leading up. "A dentist's, I think."

The stairs were wide, turning once, again at a landing with more doors off, narrowing at the top to a ladder-like ascent, rising to a bare-walled square, a skylight and a white-and-blue door.

"Chez nous," she announced, then proceeded to unlock.

The apartment they entered was a converted loft. Set within the eaves, it was long and spacious. Running the length of the back extension, it had a central corridor with four doors off and, beyond that, a kitchen side-on to a large, L-shaped lounge.

"My nest," she said with irony, leading through.

He noticed the shoes lined on a rack, the clothes on chair backs, the artworks and posters pinned on doors. A string across an arch held postcards and photos; glass and ceramics occupied the shelves. There were transfers on the windows, stickers on the fridge and piles of worksheets and files scattered all over.

She offered tea or coffee. When she'd brewed they settled, Vanessa at the centre of a two-seater sofa, Richard at an angle, sat forward on a chair.

He was calculating privately, turning over phrases, reckoning what to say. To be here and facing (and not just facing but in agreement, somehow, clicked in and focused, sharing space) – it made him wonder, really, just what was happening, whether he should say something and how far it might go. Though he also felt he'd rather not put that kind of weight on it, that this was far enough. Anything further might prove difficult.

"I like your flat," he said, smiling. He glanced round quickly, to avoid putting pressure. In himself, he was admiring. Her long lean body, visible in outline, was there on view.

"It's a tip," she answered, wrinkling up her nose. "I try, but things go all over. You'd think it had gremlins, messing up the place."

Richard shrugged. He mentioned the words *interesting* and *choice*, leading on to a poster he could see displayed on the door. Waving, he named it. Film clips... Russian... Expressionist. With scenes from Eisenstein which he recognised by shots from the Odessa steps. They were surrounded by a collage of guns and cornfields and people running. There were raised fists, a picture of

Lenin and an outside border of flags and tractors with words in Cyrillic.

He wanted to know about her politics. Vanessa smiled. She had some, yes.

"Politics, capital P. Your beliefs."

"Ah, my Personal manifesto. Now let's see… Should it be *The People*? Or *Popularist*? Maybe *Proleteriat*?"

Expressionless, Richard shook his head: "Aka Posturing."

She laughed, a full-mouthed show. It came out quickly, in a rush. Richard realised that she'd intention.

He checked back on her opinions, what she really liked. His words were chosen carefully.

"I'm a believer in style – all styles," she said when asked about revolutionary art, "especially the ones who had it."

"Anyone with attitude," she added when pressed for names.

"Groucho?" she countered when asked about Marx.

And she looked as she talked, levelling her expression, watching, examining, taking in his interest.

For Richard it was simple. He knew the conventions, had been with other girls, understood the score. To be here drinking coffee (invited, asked in, access freely given) – well, wasn't that a signal? She'd chosen, showed herself willing, or at least she'd requested. And whatever happened now, they'd established permission.

At one point in the evening they stood at the window observing the garden and the blocks beyond (side by side, their bodies nearly touching, watching the lights appearing in windows, the glimpsed interiors and the drawing of the blinds). They stood, aware of the physical, yet pleased to take it slowly, to profit by delay. There was time yet, and opportunity. Later, at Vanessa's suggestion, they sampled bits of salad folded into pitta bread, adding in cheese, thin-sliced ham and a collection of dips. They talked through the meal of places to visit, projected journeys, their lives in prospect, two years, five, ten: where they'd like to be. Both were against settling, wanted experience, had much to explore. They were world citizens.

Afterwards, when they'd moved back to the lounge, he offered to wash up.

Vanessa pulled a face. She'd rather he left it.

"Well… I ought to do my bit."

"No, no. I'll do it."

Richard smiled. He wanted reasons.

"It's the least I can do."

He blinked: "What for?"

"What I owe."

"What you *owe*?"

"Hmm. For what happened."

"Ah, you mean the handbag." He shrugged: "Anybody would've done the same."

"Well, I'm grateful you did."

"No trouble." He laughed. "If that's all it takes—"

Vanessa shook her head. "But just imagine. If you hadn't…"

"OK. But you don't *owe* me."

"Oh yes I do."

Richard shook his head. "The other way round. I took against. Pigeonholed you. I shouldn't have done that."

Colouring slightly, she smiled. "Takes two. I thought the same."

"And now…" he said, breaking off as the words of the song *What now my love* sounded in his head.

She smiled and offered drinks.

Richard declined. "I think," he said slowly, "I'd better get going."

"You're leaving?"

He angled his head to one side, "What else?"

She sucked in her breath. "It would be nice…"

Between them now there were thoughts and suggestions, hidden implications, a balance to be struck.

"I suppose…" he said, indicating the door. "You see, I don't want you to get me wrong." Suddenly he rallied: "OK, it's simple. I'll stay, if you're willing, but we play it by ear. There's nothing *required*."

She smiled. Of course, she said, it was always like that.

"In any case," he continued, "I think I'd like—"

Vanessa half-closed her eyes. A silent invitation hung between them.

Richard realised suddenly that whatever he said, or intended, didn't really matter. He was here and now, simple as that. From rival to visitor (and now, it seemed, a more-than-welcome guest), he'd entered, fitted, settled in to join her.

"But then," he added slowly, in dialogue with himself, "that's just theory. The stuff of books."

Vanessa nodded. Together they'd engaged.

He moved to where she sat. Angled on the sofa, her body was long and slim and her face was smiling. He touched her on the arm, lightly, with purpose. As he lowered to her side his hand found hers. Squeezing gently, he paused and examined. There were of course words: soft words, slow words, words of approbation. And also those words that passed beneath breath, heard but not said, half-thought or silent, the words that now guided – underthoughts and promptings, flesh-touch expressions. And the one word that remained, the *feel* word, smiling, as they closed together and, working together with calm and willing movements, absorbed each other in a long-held kiss.

When he left next morning he could hear her voice tones running in his head. Offhand but warm, they were delivered as given, with attention, on the level. Closing the front door he heard, or imagined, her words on waking, exchanges and jokes, their goodbyes on the stairs. As he turned down the street the birds were singing and the traffic was picking up. Glancing at his watch, he smiled. This early, and the airfresh brightness was something he walked through, a close and steady presence, a spotlight in his head. The city, which was stirring, had its own sounds and rhythms, tide flows, divergences, openings, closures and unsuspected corners.

Crossing the park, he retraced his steps. As he paused and looked at a junction between paths, Richard smiled. He stepped out onto grass, continuing forward with the sun to his right.

Moving smoothly, his awareness played across light and shadow. At the end of the grass, rejoining the path, he noticed again the unplanted borders. On the other side a line of bushes were draped with webs and torn plastic bags. There were pigeons strutting, dogs with owners and cyclists in Lycra. Here he thought, beating out a rhythm, was a slice of life. Leaving by a gate, he crossed a narrow road. Lengthening his stride, he headed for the river. His route led past shops, along by the estate (taking in flower tubs and bunting behind fences), over concrete and tarmac, cutting between walls and down steps, returning through the tunnel to the upstream offices and footbridge back.

By the river was quiet. The light was still, the bridge was empty and the water below was rippling slowly. Approaching the steps, Richard took the railing. He thought of Vanessa's cousin. Again he heard the words *a slice of life*. When he'd climbed to the walkway he stopped and looked out. Before him now were the river sights and buildings, the rooftops, skyline, and water with reflections – a bird's eye view. As he stood he felt the air, the brightness, the big drop below. He heard the sounds of traffic, engines, music, bells in the distance. And behind that, part-heard, advancing, drumming through metal (spreading and expanding with a surf-like weight, a shiver, an impact and loose percussive beat), the gathering thunder of the first departing train.

CHAPTER TWO

In the week that followed Vanessa was surprised by how much she felt. At first, immediately after he left, she kept herself busy, touching, examining, putting things in place. She heated up the kettle, glanced at magazines, sampled bits of toast. As she ate, she saw him as he'd entered, looking from the hallway, taking in the flat. It was, of course, a mess. But then he hadn't seemed bothered. *Interesting*, he'd said, and looked straight through it. Or perhaps he'd thought it lived-in. He'd even said he liked it, though to her mind too quickly, with too much expression, as if he'd an agenda. Either it didn't register or, out of sympathy, he'd chosen to ignore. One way or another, he'd have to have a view.

Turning in her chair, she gazed at the artworks. Clip-framed reproductions which she'd chosen for effect. Impressionist, mainly. Early and stylish, with parasols and cypresses and rowboats on water. Thinking of Richard, she wondered how he'd seen them. She supposed he'd not much liked. Or perhaps he'd thought them what he called *limited*. Something to kick against – or point to – a lesson held up.

For a while she sat back reviewing what had happened. The handbag, rail bridge, walk back home. She could still hear him talking – firm-voiced but tentative, with a slight northern accent – could see, as in a film, his face in close-up, his long appraising looks; could feel his hand-touch, body-clench – and the soft-hard pressure of his inward searching tongue.

Rising, she crossed to the lounge where she occupied herself placing cushions, then stood looking out. Seen from above, the back-to-back gardens were ragged and unkempt. They were bare and narrow, bordered by breeze blocks and half-rotted fences. Last night they'd seemed deeper, wider; grey-black and shadowy, concealed within the dark. Now they were exposed. And she saw herself with Richard, hand-close and vulnerable, standing at the window gazing into night. It was as if they were preparing, like her cousin, to step into air, kick away the chocks, take a leap of faith.

All that morning, as she slobbed around the flat, she wondered at her state. Up till then she'd known men in passing, tried them for a while, comparing as she went (with quirks and styles and types to watch out for). She'd chosen and sampled, kept them close to hand. They were her *lads*, observed for what they offered. But now it seemed, as she imagined Richard – his touch and attentions and fine-tuned smiles – that she barely knew herself. Because she'd had this persuasion (she told herself while dressing, with a half-ironic smile) that she didn't mind the guys if they knew their place. So she'd learned how to play them, how to have and aim and arrange things to advantage. In truth, in fact, she'd thought of men as other. As youths or boys or strangers to themselves. The ones who played it down, who went with what happened. The one-nights, the casuals and those not bothered.

But now, with Richard, she'd a whole new perspective. For or against, he'd said and he'd engaged. Showed himself willing, pushed to keep it real. And his face... level-eyed, passionate, a northern Giovanni. The highbrow kid. And behind that the attention, the fine line, the walkabout. They'd talked and they'd set out. A space had opened, a viewpoint and drift, a stretch across water. They were up there, first-foot, dream-led, as they climbed the metal walkway, looked out into sunlight and crossed the bridge together.

On the first day she kept a score. A mental timeline. An account, she called it, of when and where she met him and what they said in public – how far, how much and what remained hidden. On the second day he came round, stayed over, then left after lunch. The third and the fourth (she'd begun to make a rhyme, a variant on Solomon Grundy mixed in with mnemonics and snatches from skipping chants) they were already quite couply, declared at college and parading hand in hand. Five was busy with both on first placements and Vanessa seeing parents, so they saw each other late – on overnight again, talking and touching and waking early morning. Six was for study, an initial proposal with theory expected and updating journals (which meant for Vanessa long consultations with two other students). So it wasn't till the seventh that they put aside everything, Richard stayed over, and they spent the whole day on a trip out together.

"It all depends on feel," she'd told him from the start. By that she meant not only venue (outdoor for preference) but also process, how they got there, the act of deciding. Because since day one there'd been ideas floating, fancies, a range of possibilities. Richard had talked of walks or boats upstream, she'd thought shopping, they'd both named parks with outdoor cafés (one with a theatre) he'd suggested pedalos while she mentioned views (or maybe sculpture, or even writers' houses). For a while they'd talked of markets or districts or nightlife or touring the main sights. And each time they'd decided (or cut down to a shortlist) a new thought popped up or an old one returned or somehow they got sidetracked – resulting in a pause, a fall-back, and an evasive kind of smile. They'd too much to choose from, with nothing that definite. Decisions, it seemed, were that much easier if taken without forethought, arrived at quickly, agreed to on the day.

And since they'd a whole day, had time and leisure plus a promise of good weather, they decided, rather than talking further, to adopt a new suggestion (made by Richard and endorsed by Vanessa) to go with cameras and spend the time watching, taking in the habits and names they'd still to learn, as they joined the crowds of sightseers who filled the city zoo.

They journeyed there by bus, talking of first times, of packing as a family and wet summer holidays. Richard map read, transferring between stops and guiding from the terminus, then led through a park with ornamental gardens and a stream with bridges. On the way he kept up a commentary, observing the route, the flowerbeds, and the groups headed zoo-wards. He noticed as he talked how his role today was to lead on words, on gesture, while

Vanessa it seemed was content to play audience. In fact he felt the pull, an undertow of thought, almost as if he'd not made contact or there was something in the way. She was, it seemed, doubtful. Or maybe, he thought, she was just getting used and simply needed time. Though he couldn't help noticing a lag now between them, a clear space feeling, a gap beneath the real. So he kept up the talk, the one-line observations, quick thoughts and noticings and oddities in passing. Everything had its tics, its instants and surprises, its own specifics. It was as if they were provisional, first time, caught on camera. And his job was delivery, to talk and present and move the action on.

It wasn't till they got there that Vanessa, who was wearing moon-shaped earrings, declared one was missing. "It must have dropped," she said, checking both sides and scanning tarmac. "Might be anywhere... just anywhere," she added, tailing off. Suddenly there was edge. Her colour was up and her breath came slowly. This was a case, it seemed, for rescue.

Richard offered, Vanessa accepted and they quartered the entrance, peering into corners, prodding around walls and checking into bushes. When nothing turned up he suggested they walk back.

"Not now," Vanessa said, pointing to a developing queue. She was struggling to hold down. "Don't worry, it's nothing," she called, and waved him to her. She fixed her gaze forward, Richard joined her, and they shuffled to the window.

He offered coins, which Vanessa supplemented, and an attendant issued tickets.

"Well, now we're here – we have to see everything," said Richard, once in, examining the signposts and the times of feeding chalked up on a board.

"You mean that?"

He nodded. "We're on safari," he said, leading forward past a line of abandoned cages.

Vanessa smiled. Now they'd arrived and passed in through the gate, she wanted to indulge. Before, on the journey, she'd needed him to prove, to show himself willing, make things happen. She didn't want him casual. Or taking advantage. Or doing what people called 'the distance thing'. Because already she could see him (absurdly), pictured with family – all those briefings, meetings, stages up ahead – and *she'd* have to satisfy, play both sides, act as intermediary.

But now she felt different. A day, an outing, almost like a holiday – well, wasn't that enough? A first act and gesture, a kind of sizing up. Because now she saw him clear (out there, leading, angled slightly forward, advancing on the green), he'd his own fine line, his choices and personals. It was as if, she thought, he was on countdown (with her in close attendance) moving with purpose, about to start the show.

The green led down to a long curving lake. Set off to one side, it looked almost ornamental. It was grey-blue and vague, like a sketch for a painting. Intrigued, they approached behind a fence, glimpsing reflections in a still sheet of water. It ended in concrete at one end, with banks both sides, and an overflow beyond. Here it bulged out with stone-dammed pools, winding mud flats and intersecting basins. As they came nearer, they could see, gathered at the end in a loosely formed arc, something that resembled black-and-pink clouds, or a corps de ballet.

"Flamingos," he said, advancing slowly, camera in hand.

The birds were standing, half-asleep and sculptural, in ankle-high water. With their long thin legs, pod-like bodies and tubular necks they looked like they'd just landed.

"God, it's thick," said Vanessa, pointing to the water at their feet. "Reminds me of lentil soup. Only this smells more like those ghastly concoctions we used to make in chemistry."

Richard examined the grey-yellow liquid. It was solid-looking and cloudy. "It seems to quite suit them," he said, lightly.

Vanessa stared. The birds now were striking poses: some seemed to sprout, others jack-knifed, there were ones coiled like pipes and others standing tall. A group in the corner were head down, ruminative, poking in mud; a few were chain-linked; there were hook-shaped beaks and pseudo-plants, and a number whose dream-like positions resembled half-finished artworks.

"They look so strange," she said, thoughtfully.

"Surreal?"

"Gothic, I think."

"I suppose it works for them."

They circled the lake end, arriving at a viewing spot that overlooked the pools: a curved concrete space with bench and signboard, divided from the birds by a clear mesh fence. They joined a small group of photo-smiley visitors. A tall man with a map was finger-tracing a route, while the woman beside him was reading from the signboard. A family on the bench were listening to a radio as they filled up on drink squares, crisp bags and chocolate-coated bars.

Ignoring, Vanessa raised her camera and waved Richard towards an unoccupied corner. "Best spot," she called as she chivvied and pointed, checked in the viewfinder, then snapped. Exchanging places, he took her twice, clicking quickly, then motioned to move on.

Vanessa showed surprise.

"Lots to do," he said brightly, waving to the slope.

"Well, yes…"

He glanced at his watch. "It's a big place. Have to get round."

Vanessa pulled a face: "How far would that be?"

"I dunno. A mile, maybe more."

"You mean that?"

He nodded.

"Sounds like a route march."

Ignoring, he looked out: "Sights to see."

For a moment she was thrown. There was nothing more she could say.

"The big five," he added. "That's what we came for."

She shrugged, "Well, if it's really that important—"

Richard confirmed, nodding vigorously as he named them.

"Are you sure they've got them all here?"

"They certainly used to have. When I was a boy, visiting."

She smiled, superior now: "Ah, but supposing things have changed…"

"What makes you say that?"

"Chances are. On average…"

"Chances? Averages? Sounds like a lecture to me."

Vanessa stared past him, expressionless. "It's what I think, that's all."

He looked at her oddly, still grinning. There was challenge in the air. "OK. We'll go then… Find out."

Before she could reply he'd moved off uphill, climbing a path that curved through bushes. He moved inside a space, a direction separate, with Vanessa following, saying nothing.

She caught up in a dip where the path opened out. He'd descended to a double line of walls and was standing beside concrete, observing carefully through reinforced glass. The window looked out on a trench full of water and beyond that some protective netting, a few scattered rocks and a broad savannah-like compound.

"One," he said, pointing to a large brown-and-grey lion laid out on a platform.

Vanessa pursed her lips. "Four to go," she reminded, eyeing the animal as if it couldn't be trusted.

"I bet two's close," he said, wandering forward down a mall-like avenue with walls both sides and vistas through double-thickness glass.

"You think you'll find a leopard?" she said with an upward inflection, warming to their task.

"Voilà," he replied, moving to a window that had misted slightly. Behind it a long, muscular, brown-white cat was slumped on grass.

Vanessa took a breath: "Well I have to say—"

Richard nodded. He knew what she meant.

"I'm not sure I like it," she continued, touching his shoulder, "doesn't look too friendly." She shivered: "You can see it in the face. It's all about power. Blind, unquestioning power. And if it comes for you, you'd better get going."

"If looks could kill."

She squinted forward, then shifted in front. "Do you think it sees us?"

"Hmm. Don't think it's interested."

"Too busy contemplating the next meal."

He laughed and joined her, hand-shading glass and moving side to side to get a better look.

"I used to think big cats were boring," he said, "when I was young."

"And now?"

He smiled, enigmatically: "Two down."

Beside them two small girls were talking loudly, quizzing their mother. It really wasn't fair, she'd made them a promise. And they couldn't go much further. How long, they asked, before they'd see monkeys? She stalled for a while trying to interest them in big-cat stories, then, when they persisted, warned about distance and steered them off.

"So, lunch break?" Vanessa asked, smiling. Richard nodded and they walked. They turned uphill following a winding path which led past a rockery and a fenced-in paddock, emerging at the top at a soft grassy lookout with wooden benches and a stone orientation table.

The sky had cleared and the crowds were building. Families mainly, but also busloads: organised outings and tourists in groups. A few distinctly old, some middle-aged, others twentyish. But mostly children. A tide-flow of children, all over, everywhere; wave on wave filling up the zoo. So much so that the place was sounding and looking like a break-time playground. There were groups of children in lines and gaggles, some linked with parents, some eating and drinking sitting on grass, others it seemed on breakaway missions, still others gathered by cages and compounds. There were very small children with toys or sweets, slightly older children asking questions, older still wriggling or dodging or pushing to the front, notebook children carrying rainbow-striped pens, costumed children, red-faced children, moon-eyed children and yah boo sucks kids wearing oversize T-shirts and mud-splattered trainers.

"The human zoo," said Vanessa, gazing out.

"You don't like them?"

She laughed. "*Adore* them. Children are wonderful."

Richard, surprised by her vehemence, chose to say nothing.

They ate. Vanessa had packed two foil-wrapped pasties, each with a napkin and fork. Richard reached deeper into his backpack to add in apples, bottled drinks and a bag of peanuts. They spread them on a mac and lay out on grass, talking over what they'd seen and where to go next. As they ate and drank and chatted between mouthfuls they kept a kind of focus, a doubleness of view. Suddenly, it seemed, they'd moved on from spotting or collecting or ticking off the five. Richard wasn't bothered (floating options, different possibilities, while propped on an elbow, gazing into space) and Vanessa too was low-key and agreeable, quite without design.

When they'd finished and cleared, Richard moved closer, fitting to her mood. They smiled and kissed, then stretched out side by side, fingering flesh. Together they were involved, touching each other, while talking intermittently and dozing in the sun.

Vanessa was curious. She wanted to know his thoughts.

"Maybe you can guess."

She considered. "Well, I suppose I could try. But only if they're nice."

He laughed: "Oh, they're nice all right."

"Ah, but *how* nice?"

He smiled. "Triple tick I'd say."

"That much?"

He nodded.

"Well, let's see," she said, sitting up. "Your thoughts – are they about *now*: the zoo, the sun, where we're sitting?"

"Hmm. Could be."

"Could be?"

He turned and levered up. "That's part of it. They're definitely warm."

"Yes, I appreciate that. They're warm… Anything else?"

"Oh lots." He paused, then laughed. "I'm full of ideas: crazy things, projects, what might never happen."

Vanessa nodded. Gazing round slowly, she drew one hand lightly over grass. "That's good," she said, leaning forward. The grass was tufty, yellow-green at centre, edged with blue. Reaching sideways, she touched and tested, selecting stems. Choosing the tallest, she pinched out from the bottom then straightened to a bunch. "Very good," she confirmed, adding in some vetch and a sprig of clover.

Seeing her absorbed Richard cast round, selecting his own bunch. He pulled up a plantain, some pineapple weed and a twist of ivy. "Mine's rough," he said, waving them for show.

She looked up, surprised, then laughed: "Don't tell me that's my bouquet."

"You like it?" he asked, adding in sorrel and shepherd's purse. In response to her nod he offered.

Vanessa eyed it carefully. "You take them both," she said, counter-offering hers.

Richard blinked.

"Go on," she urged, "take."

"You sure?"

"They're all yours," she smiled. "And the task," she added, passing over her bunch, "is to arrange them – well."

Richard laughed, putting down his collection. After sorting, he doffed an imaginary cap: "England expects."

"Today's good deed," she continued, half-ignoring.

"At your service, ma'am."

"Well, if you don't want—"

"No problem," he cut in. "In any case," he smiled thinly, "we can use them as feed."

Vanessa looked puzzled: "Feed?"

Richard confirmed. He twisted to one side and, fishing in his backpack, tugged out some string which he knotted and doubled, securing the stems. "Some animal will be glad of this lot," he said, grinning.

"But you can't—"

He stood and stretched. "Hmm, you don't think so?"

Vanessa shook her head.

"Well I do remember…"

"I don't think they allow it."

He hesitated, weighing up: "I suppose you're right."

Before she could reply he shrugged, picked up his backpack and moved to the orientation table.

"I know what you've been thinking," he said when Vanessa joined him.

"You do?"

"What you said – about the route march."

Vanessa dismissed it as nothing. Really. She'd moved on since.

"But there is a point," he returned, placing the flowers at the centre of the table. "I mean you must have thought: why does this guy have to rush so."

Vanessa nodded slightly.

"After all," he continued, "it's a whole day free."

Again she showed agreement.

"But I'd thought, you see, if we came here, that I'd do it like before." He smiled to himself: "I mean like those kids," here he nodded out towards the crowds. "But now I see..." he laughed, "it's not that simple."

As Vanessa expressed doubt he raised his camera and, positioning carefully, sighted the flowers. Leaning forward, he clicked several times from all round the table. "And now," he announced, waving her to him, "both of us – for the album."

"Both of us?"

"It's on time release," he said, explaining the mechanism while balancing the camera on the bench head.

"You think it'll work?"

"Believe me," he said, pressing the button and drawing her close. "And smile."

The shutter clicked as they embraced.

"But how do we know if we're in the picture?"

"We don't," he said, "so we'll try again."

Vanessa laughed.

"And we'll keep on trying," he added as he button-pressed, moving position. "And again," he insisted, pressing and positioning, "And again," he repeated, "till we'll bloody well make it work."

For the rest of the day they worked the zoo. They went with their feelings, taking pictures and sharing observations. Following the signs they ticked off the five, visited the reptiles, went bear-watching, saw the seals feeding and ended late afternoon surrounded by children, viewing monkeys.

Vanessa enjoyed the babies, cooing at their eyes, their size and how they rode their mothers. "Perfectly formed," she exclaimed, fascinated.

"Great circus," said Richard, following their parents' tricks.

"Gymnastics," called Vanessa, watching as they tail-swung and danced across ropes.

And they went with the crowd, hand in hand, seeing what they could, peering into cages and taking pictures.

Richard liked the chimps. "There's my Big Sis," he said as a heavy-jawed female slid along a beam and dropped to a crouch.

"Hi there Old Man," he waved when a male climbed down to join her.

And it was when they reached the gorillas, Vanessa's favourite, with their long slow nods, rocking movements and penetrating stares, that they agreed they'd seen enough and were ready as a couple to finish for the day.

On the bus back, recovering, they named on recall, checked their impressions and totalled what they'd seen.

"Seems like we did it all," Richard said as they walked towards her flat.

Vanessa smiled. Had he found it different, she wanted to know.

He shrugged: "Some things have changed."

But in *himself*, she insisted, was it any different?

"Older and wiser, you mean?"

She demurred, then nodded.

"I think," he said quietly, "it's better now…"

His voice dipped and rose as they turned into her street. They stopped at the corner, touching.

"Much, much better," he added and kissed her on the cheek, the forehead, and finally with hot-tongued passion, deep into her mouth.

CHAPTER THREE

For the first few months it seemed to Richard that what they'd found together – their outings and overnights, their long talks, socials and ideas as teachers; their smiles, acknowledgements and understandings shared – but also their romance with its bright turns, its dramas and all-night sessions – was as good as it gets. In Vanessa he saw an equal, someone of importance, a woman who drew notice. She, of course, mattered. It seemed he'd landed a partner he could stand to – someone special other people regarded.

At college people liked them. With everyone on practice their friends (mainly Vanessa's, but now Richard's as well) called out greetings, shared what had happened, then wished them well. Being in school was a shock to the system, far more difficult than they'd ever expected (and in at least one case, it was said, had split a relationship). Also there was surprise – widespread, with questions – of all those training, and especially with their history – that *they* should get together.

But together they were good and effective and willing to stand up. They were at the front, talking and asking questions, making themselves felt. For and against, in gesture and delivery, they showed the others how.

When teaching ended they went out as a foursome with Ruth and Doug, Vanessa's closest. Meeting at college they popped round to the market where students often gathered to browse and choose bargains. Records for the men, jewellery for Ruth, and what Vanessa called collectables – mainly posters but also small art objects and tourist mementos. It felt like something shared, but also individual.

When they'd walked the side aisles trying on rings, examining prints and listening to bands, they moved into the concourse, a steel-framed hall with red-tiled avenues, strings of fairy lights and low-ceilinged shops. In one corner a metal flight of stairs rose to a gallery supported by pillars. It led to a café with tables both sides, on one side in groups stretching to the counter and on the other, where they settled, overlooking the market and the heads of passing shoppers.

They ordered coffee and Doug pulled out a newspaper. He held it up, blocking out the company, as if for protection.

Ruth, who'd sat herself opposite, was staring over, shaking her head. "Bit antisocial, isn't it?" she said loudly.

Doug looked up, apparently surprised. Brown and round-faced, showing hirsute legs and prominent forearms, he was wedged into the railing. His eyes strayed vaguely out across the hall. "What do you mean?" he asked quietly, colouring.

"Nose in paper. When we're supposed to be talking."

"Not really."

"It's what people call rude. Very, if you ask me."

Doug returned to reading his paper. A ball-shaped stud showed in one ear.

"There you go," Ruth continued, addressing her friends, "it's carry on regardless. Seen but not seen."

"Nobody's getting hurt," retorted Doug, peering round his print-screen. With his hair pushed back and shy, boxer-like grin, he appeared to be in training.

"Hey, no. I should have known. Don't bother me, it's fine. And I'm just a silly woman."

Doug continued reading. His hand on the paper was shaking slightly.

"Stupid. Like most women."

When Doug remained silent she poked at his broadsheet. "'Ello 'ello. Is anyone there?"

Twisting sideways, he pulled out of reach.

"Anyone at home?"

Smiling falsely, she screwed one finger to her head.

"OK. OK. Ignore us. Read your bloody paper. No one else counts."

Doug, still reading, raised his head slightly and made to reply. When Ruth cut in, calling him a boor – a me-only type, the

49

one who got away – he put aside the paper and fixed her with a stare. "Stop it woman," he grunted, then gazed off into space. Something indeterminate held him, a clear eye out: he'd better things to do.

Ruth grimaced. Turning to Vanessa she invited comment.

Her friend was noncommittal. "It's OK," she replied, avoiding Ruth's eye.

"A man's gotta do," put in Richard, grinning.

The coffees arrived and were passed round the table, cappuccino to Ruth, black for Vanessa, regulars for the men.

Turning to Ruth, Richard enquired about her time on practice.

"Oh that," she snorted, reaching for her cup. "Well, all I can say, if *that's* what teaching's about..." She shook her head savagely, staring round the hall. "I mean the staff were great, really helpful, but the kids..." She gulped down a mouthful then, putting on a voice, pushed up to the table with a calculating stare: "'ere miss, you one of 'em students? One of 'em weirdos. Cos if you is, then better be careful..." She pulled herself back with a shiver: "And that, by the way, was on a good day."

She cut to her coffee, draining quickly. She was observing Doug more gently now.

When Richard prompted, asking how she'd coped, she launched in again, putting on voices and adopting registers, then declared loudly that school was not for her.

She ended, white-faced, staring at the table. Her gaze returned to Doug and she ran one finger lightly across his arm. "*He* knows," she declared. "He's seen me afterwards."

Doug confirmed. The set of his face had lifted. He blinked and nodded as Ruth reached for his hand. In her eyes now there was gratitude and a hope of understanding.

"Because he's my Doug," she added, coyly.

When they left she was leaning, holding herself sideways, tucked in to his body with her eyes half-closed. Beside her Doug stepped out, narrowing his gaze and facing forward with a slightly child-like, self-absorbed smile.

Afterwards Vanessa asked Richard for his verdict.

"Surprising," he said, fingering her hair. They were occupying the corner of a long, sprawling, low-backed sofa positioned at the end of the student bar. In front, a table contained them, on one side was a window, while on the other a spotlight fell on a large-leafed cheese plant.

She pressed him again.

Richard eyed his glass. "Some people throw plates, or chequebooks – or even rocks." He continued, shrugging: "They use words."

She smiled: "You mean she does."

He nodded. "Lots of 'em." He paused, then flashed her an appraising look: "Whereas Doug understands the power of silence."

"Absolutely."

They continued drinking and chatting until Vanessa spotted Ruth, wandering solo on the far side of the bar. She rose to flag her down, warning Richard with a touch to his shoulder.

Ruth came over, greeted, and sat. When Vanessa asked for news, she shrugged. "Pissed off," she said flatly.

"Oh?"

Ruth pulled a face. Staring off, she swore repeatedly.

Suddenly she pushed forward: "You want to know something?"

Vanessa angled back. She was listening, she said.

Ruth, breathing hard, launched in. She'd had it with Doug bloody Jones. Enough was enough, she said, shaking her head. Her flesh showed white as she gripped onto wood. Frowning, she repeated. She'd had it with that man, really couldn't bear it, always putting off – and God knows she'd tried, made every effort...

Vanessa, attentive, acted as receiver.

Ruth continued, pushing herself forward, rocking. Doug, she insisted, was useless, hopeless – so much out of it, she couldn't gee him up. In fact, she declared herself really at *that* point...

Her words fell away. In the pause she blinked round as if in search of something – a handhold or keepsake – and picked up a coaster. It was head-and-shoulders shaped: sun face above, beer barrel below. Positioning her thumbs hard against the back she gripped and pushed, grunting slightly. A fault line appeared, running round the neck. Drawing breath, she held and flexed, twisting both ways. As the coaster doubled she bent to her task, worrying at one side until, with a final wrenching tear, the head pulled away.

Naming Doug, she held up both parts. Fitting them together, she looked and laughed. MR SILLY MAN, she called, waggling the head. He really was absurd, she muttered to herself. Just so childish. He had this knack – here she scowled – a way of *seeming* that putting her in the wrong.

She laughed again, rawly, and put down her coaster. Her face had contracted and her voice tone hurt. "It feels like a setup," she said, lowering her head. "Like one of those kitchen sink dramas where they fight over everything. Whatever I say, he has to go against."

Richard nodded. "Do you find that surprising?"

Ruth looked up: "How d'y' mean—?"

He shrugged; "What I said. Is it so unexpected?"

"Explain, explain. Don't understand."

"The point is," he said slowly, "do you *really* think Doug's that bad?"

Vanessa tut-tutted.

"I don't see—"

"I mean, how fair is it...?" Suddenly, before she could answer, he fired up: "Because if that's how you see him then I, for one, think you've got it all wrong – completely, absolutely wrong – and *you* need to back off."

"Richard!" cried Vanessa, as Ruth dropped silent.

He shrugged, rising from the sofa without saying anything.

"Richard! Apologise!"

He waved his refusal, moving to a distance.

"What gives you the right?" she demanded.

Still he ignored, gazing at a spot at the far end of the bar.

Vanessa looked left and right, from Richard to her friend. Both were saying nothing.

"Look, Richard…" She rose and stood between them, inviting retraction.

"Oh, don't bother," muttered Ruth as she, too, rose to take her leave.

"Richard—"

He looked round in silence. His gaze now was directed elsewhere. For a moment he hesitated, shook his head, then retreated slightly. It seemed he'd other business. One shoulder dropped as he backed off further and, maintaining silence, pushed towards the door. As he left Ruth reached for the coaster. Picking up the head she examined, blinked, then threw it to the floor. She watched it land then straightened, firmed her gaze and, holding her breath, heeled down into cardboard.

When they caught up the next day, sitting alone in the market café, Richard spoke quietly, stirring and sipping at his lightly-frothed coffee.

"I'm sorry," he said, "I can't always hold my tongue."

"I'd noticed."

"That's me. Just get that way sometimes."

"It's Ruth you need to speak to."

"I've written to her." He held up an envelope with papers inside. "It's an apology."

"In a letter?"

He nodded.

Vanessa held her gaze. "No, Richard, it's not that easy."

"You mean I have to go further?"

She confirmed.

"Public self-criticism, that sort of thing?"

Vanessa pursed her lips. She examined her cup edge, then ran one finger round the handle, saying nothing.

"OK, say what you think."

"You have to tell her. Face to face."

He passed her the envelope. "Go on. Read. It says I got it wrong."

Vanessa opened and studied the letter. As she read, she blinked. She was holding at a distance, fingers to the edge. When she'd finished she sat back, nodding: "Well, I can see it's an apology."

"Yes. And—"

"That's it. An apology."

"But you don't think it's enough?" Glancing up, he sipped at his cup.

She shook her head slowly, then paused. It seemed she was elsewhere.

"You think she'll want more?"

Vanessa remained silent.

He asked again and her expression hardened.

Richard caught her eye. "But I take your point," he said, "and I will speak to her."

"You will?"

"Definitely."

Vanessa nodded slowly, saying she was glad. She returned to her coffee then, staring out across the hall, mentioned Doug, inviting comment.

Richard considered. "That's what I don't understand. Why does he put up with it?"

She smiled into space, observing. Her eyes were round and brown and full of enquiry. Below, seen through the bars of the nearby railing, the shoppers moved in crowds.

"It's how things are," she said. She was leaning forward, sighting faces, as if Doug and Ruth might be visible amongst the stalls. "Some people throw words – remember? It's her way of saying, *show me your feelings*. She wants to break him down, force him to declare. You have to see it as a kind of play-fight. She's like the girl in the playground who slaps a boy and runs off. He's meant to give chase."

"You mean they *want* it this way?"

She shrugged, "I believe so."

"But like *this*, her in a rage, him obstructing?"

"It's how they are. They fill each other's gaps."

He laughed. "You sure about that?"

"Oh yes. Seen from their point of view, it's successful."

"But surely you don't really think it's good?"

"It works."

Richard turned impish: "OK. So what's the evidence? Can you back it up?"

Fingering her cup, Vanessa smiled. "You mustn't tell anyone."

"Go on."

"This is between us – promise?"

"Promise."

Taking a breath, she angled sideways to drain her cup then threw back her head, smiling.

"They're engaged."

At the term end party, held at Vanessa's, it occurred to Richard how many of their friends were, like Ruth and Doug, already committed. For them it was settled and assumed, they'd agreed the whole package – things were in place. What surprised him was how early they'd concluded, gone for what they knew: a life within limits, a quid pro quo. He saw too how they worked (or in Ruth's case with Doug went through with actions that kept them together – up and dancing as rivals in a ring). He saw, too, all the differences: how one couple were physical, others shared smiles or sat talking quietly, still others were all hype, while some kept their distance, barely seeming to notice when the partner grew restive or took off in silence to seek other company.

There was Lisa and Gary who talked health-and-lifestyle with friends Kate and Tony, comparing conditions and most-used treatments. There was Bess with her man, jiggling in a corner with a small group of dancers. James with Penny who struck up with anyone, playing out school scenes and telling off kids. Their friends, the JJ sisters sampling wine, a couple shouting jokes, another pair snogging, several eating, and even those who came separate were busy making out: smiling often and finding points of contact as they listened and shared and put themselves about.

Richard, while he hosted, played fly on the wall. The music and drink upped the volume. Stories were passed round, and things were said. They carried out their roles, exchanged in snatches, kept up the talk.

"Funny people," Richard murmured, alone in the kitchen with an all-smiles Vanessa.

"Sorry?"

"I've been watching," he continued, deadpan. "Good cabaret."

"Richard, do you really have to —"

"Quirky. Know their parts well."

Vanessa shushed him and they returned to the lounge.

A group had arrived who occupied the hallway, smoking and drinking and greeting other visitors. Male and thin, they were sharp-eyed, angular and excitable. For a minute or two they acted as unofficial doormen, directing to the drink, the toilet and the coat-pile. While they quick-talked and pointed, they passed round cans, dug out from a backpack. The cans, plus a few handy-sized bottles, were scanned for date and checked by label before being swigged. The group continued swigging and greeting until, when refills were needed, they searched the sack – to find it empty. A mood-change set in. Suddenly they were off, couldn't believe it; they needed their brew. Search parties were sent out: one to the kitchen, another to the lounge, while a third checked tables. They peered into corners and inside the fridge. Their return led to questions followed by an argument. There were shouts of *bloody Norah* and *what-the-fuck-d-y-mean*, an exchange of catcalls, jokey exclamations, and exit.

As they crashed downstairs the group could be heard joshing. They were debating parentage and the whereabouts of the nearest 'offie'. The last sounds were of whoops and yells and footsteps running off.

"Do you think they'll be back?" Vanessa asked Richard, shuddering.

"Unlikely. Didn't get their brew."

"Is that all they think about? Drink?"

He shrugged: "It's what's important to them."

She rolled her eyes, saying nothing.

"So you're not impressed?"

"Who would be?"

He laughed, "I suppose it's a choice. Makes *them* happy."

She snorted. "Hmm, it's carry on lads, regardless. What I don't understand is why anyone would want to behave that way. You'd think they were zombies. It's as if they've got some of their senses permanently switched off, so other people don't count."

"And not in front of the guests, eh?"

"I don't think," she said, looking round the room, "*anyone* here is interested—"

Richard, in reply, smiled. He could, of course, see that. They were, he imagined (allowing his thoughts to register unsaid) too much settled. Much, much too settled.

Over the next few hours they stepped up the hosting. He offered food and filled up glasses while she did the rounds: greeting, circulating, asking after health and news of absent friends. For her it was social (and somehow positional, a balance that she struck), for him a job. A stage for one, a window for the other. And for Richard – partly as a balance, but also by design (and out of interest, to name and examine, fit things into place) – his role was undercover.

Watching, eye-out, spotting, he listened and tried to reckon up (acting as reporter on ground rules and agreements – what made them tick). His interest, made evident, lowered their guard. They were happy and they trusted. And he noticed, as he watched and listened and encouraged them to say more, how simple it all seemed – almost artificial – how they really knew their stuff. They had the right turns, the you-me specifics, the ways of getting by.

But also he noticed how deliberate they were, how they looked off towards windows or hung around corners glancing at the doorways, filling up time with one-line exchanges and joke-book remarks. Poised and careful, *they* made the effort, or at least they knew their place. And their lives, it seemed to him, were full of disappointment.

During the evening he returned to Vanessa on regular report back, taking her aside to update on relationships and how people felt. Someone was 'off', a partner was 'loose-ended', there were people fitted and those who stood apart, talkers with supporters, and a number of oddballs who relied on entertainment, taking off themselves with self-mocking anecdotes and all-smiles remarks.

He'd just begun an item on James and Penny when the voice of a woman, cutting through the flat, stopped him midsentence.

"Sounds familiar," he said carefully, avoiding further comment.

Vanessa nodded, suggested they viewed, and they moved to the living room where a crowd had gathered.

Joining the watchers they could see, at centre, a red-faced Ruth with a drinks tray, raising a toast to the crowd she'd summoned.

"Trouble is," she declared, her voice tone lifting, "men."

She paused for effect then, pointing round the room, began asking questions, probing and challenging, inviting response. "OK, OK, OK – so give me something, anything, a-n-y-t-h-i-n-g a-t a-l-l about men that's even half-decent. No, not even that. A quarter'll do – less, if you like, one point above zero."

The faces around her showed nothing. At the back they were grinning. Stood to one side, Vanessa was watching, blankly. Her mouth hung open like a child behind glass.

"See. You can't bloody do it," Ruth called, glaring round, "because that's how they are. They're all 007 and my bloody dad. All so bloody blokey. Bloody, bloody men." She snorted, tipped back her glass and reached for another. "And another thing." Here she spun round, swaying forward. "Have you ever listened in? Heard what they call us? 'Birds and bits and hits and fucks and hey man what you're getting' – it's like we're just *there*, objects, pick-ups, throwaways, like so much stuff."

Putting down her glass, she seized a half-full bottle and began to wave it, walking the floor, pausing every so often to toss down a mouthful. Her audience now were shoulder to shoulder, giving way slightly wherever she walked. "And you know, they feel so sorry for themselves, so damned sorry – I mean can you believe it – they got it made and all they do is moan about women, call us naggers or slags – my bitch, my teaser or some such stuff... Because I tell you – and I mean it – if it comes to men take my advice just forget 'em, drop 'em, throw 'em all away."

A man by the door joked that he knew what *she* wanted. Challenging, she swore and pointed. When the man called back she invited him forward. Calmly now, Ruth offered a debate. One-on-one. A war of words. He shrugged, went silent, and moved off to the kitchen.

Ruth laughed, swigged from a bottle, then continued giving out. White-faced now, she was gazing into vacancy. It seemed she'd an angle, a private intention. She was speaking in asides, with pauses, reworking what she'd said.

She ended beckoning to her listeners. They had to come closer. Closer, she said, so they could talk. At her insistence they reached or touched, watching carefully. Wide-eyed now, she passed round the bottle, followed by glasses, then two more bottles with some extra plastic cups. She moved down the line, filling and replenishing until everyone had a cupful. Then, stepping to the centre, stood to attention, proposing a toast: "You ready?" she called and her audience nodded. "OK, folks, don't look now, it's raining men." Suddenly, raising both arms – one glass each – to a point above her head she let out a cry. "Because it's such a bloody mess," she shouted and, turning her wrists, upended quickly.

All round the room people began to laugh.

The wine splashed out, soaking through her hair and staining flesh. It ran all over, spreading and expanding, filling out her clothes. It ran and overflowed, dribbling sideways, spotting the carpet and puddling round her shoes. There were soak-away patches, streak-marks, and layered-in damp spreading all over.

As realisation came, she picked up another glass and sluiced again. The wine trickled down and she threw back her head, spluttering. There was a pain in her face and a floaty kind of smile. Her eyes filled up and her head dropped sideways. Calling and shaking, she pushed through the crowd to reach Vanessa. "It's a mess," she repeated, breathing hard, and stood there, crying quietly. Then, turning on her heel, she hunched herself forward and, depositing her glasses, turned in silence to walk out through the door.

CHAPTER FOUR

For most of the winter it was Richard who visited, crossing the city and walking to Vanessa's with backpack and umbrella, returning the next day to stand looking out from the walkway on the bridge. Rain or shine, the streets were quiet and he enjoyed the journey. It allowed him to think. To go with the flow. It also kept him levelled, buoyed up by exercise, by light and shade and movement. And while he was walking there were so many possibles – her words, his, their smiles and kisses and bed games together – so much that could happen, so much to enjoy. Or at least to keep him smiling, rehearsing how he'd greet her, their actions and the consequences. It was, he soon realised, a kind of living switch, a route back and measure – how far he'd come and how much he enjoyed it.

Of course it was a trek. It did take time, and sometimes he was tired. There and back was an hour from college, further from his flat. And where it was exposed the wind blew hard. He walked it at pace, ignoring the rain. But there was warmth one end and fondness looking back, and both ways a feeling that what they had was a line, a track between them.

There were practicals, too. Sometimes he stayed a second night or longer, which was when he found himself travelling back home and bagging up books and items of clothing or even, if he'd room, returning with his journal and cased-up Olivetti.

"My second home," he called as he arrived at the door with a rucksack full of worksheets.

"The man in two places," he quipped, living from the suitcase he'd stowed beneath the bed.

"Holiday's over," he said when leaving for his flat.

Vanessa thought him fun, enjoying his entrances, his exits, his street-scene observations and talk of living life. She called him her reporter.

"Exclusive?" he asked, laughing.

"Sensational," she replied, accepting his kiss.

At times he talked of style – the graffiti he'd passed, T-shirt slogans, the latest music, teen talk from the classroom – which he offered dryly, in sketch form, with carefully coded emphasis and a narrow-eyed smile.

"Of course," he added slyly, "it's kiss 'n' tell."

She smiled. "You mean you're undercover?"

"If you like," he nodded, "Notes from the Underground, that sort of thing."

At other times he did issues: things overheard, quotes from textbooks or incidents in staffrooms; buzz words, theories, self-fulfilling prophecies. He was in there talking, questioning everything. He smiled, he ridiculed and he passed comment. And when he left he was warm: expressing regret, saying he'd phone on arrival, then ring again next morning, for cheer up, wake up and next day return.

From the start he'd liked her place. He'd said so with emphasis – a bright-eyed tease of intention and proposal. He called it *The Bird's Nest*, admiring its views, the odd ends and collections, the freedom it offered. Up here they were on top, unscheduled, no longer deadlined by essays or obsessing over lessons. 'The' in *Bird's Nest* soon became 'Our', as his periods of occupation lengthened and he brought in more possessions. He began, at Vanessa's suggestion, to double on essentials – toiletries, socks and the odd patterned shirt – building up a 'nest set', starting with books and his own brand of coffee (Venezuelan, dark) then adding in sundries: a notepad, a biro collection, photos in albums, old certificates and a selection from his tapes.

The fact of his presence, established with friends and increasingly obvious to visitors (together with the need to simplify their story), pushed them to go public. To give out and acknowledge, make their declarations – and tell-all to her parents. Hers, not his – because they were nearer, and wanted information. And the politics of telling included, as sweetener, an offer of a visit together, an attendance at lunch (suggested at once by her mother on the phone) and transport to their house in a paid-for taxi.

"Why the cab?" asked Richard, when boarding.

"Appearances," answered Vanessa. "And because they're helpful."

"So. It's an act of charity – and meant to be seen…?"

"Well, they *are* my parents."

"And the cost?"

Vanessa sighed: "You'll see. It's a different lifestyle."

On the route there Richard was little-boy-defiant, dropping his h's and flattening his a's, while insisting that the visit didn't imply anything. He came, he said, to show willing – and nothing more.

"I don't know if you'll get on," said Vanessa as they arrived at the street, "but you have to try. I'd like you to see them as they are. Rich, yes: but decent people."

"Don't worry," he answered, narrowing his eyes, "I'll play the game."

They cruised down a double terraced row of Edwardian houses with wrought-iron gates, wide bay windows and panelled front doors. Stone-built at the bottom they were pillared round the doorways, rising to ornamental balconies, patterned brickwork and banded fascias. Vanessa named and pointed, and the driver drew up. They climbed out together, exchanging glances and finger-smoothing clothes. Entering the gate, they crossed a square-paved forecourt to climb a flight of steps. As they arrived at the top, the front door opened and a well-turned-out woman greeted with a smile. She was tall like her daughter, brown-eyed and poised, wearing a silk-sheen dress with matching accessories – and was all of one piece, shawl down to shoes, full-length in blue.

Vanessa stepped forward, kissing her mother. "And this is Richard," she said, moving to one side.

"So pleased you could come," said Felicity, appraisingly.

A handshake followed and an invite to enter. Richard noticed how she kept herself braced and spoke into vacancy, with a chin up manner and an element of delay. She knew how to welcome; had that air, the impression, the will to carry off.

Behind her in the hallway stood a red-faced man with a flashbulb expression. Introduced as Derek, he nodded acknowledgement. Sounding slightly nasal, he enquired about their journey while taking coats. Vanessa thanked him, praising the driver and shivering slightly when mentioning the weather. She and Richard moved to one side while Derek shut the door.

Felicity conducted to the high-ceilinged lounge and invited them to sit, indicating the sofa. When they'd made themselves comfortable, Derek wheeled forward a rosewood trolley with glasses on top and bottles under. Orders were taken, poured, mixed and passed round. Everything was levelled, measured and made up to taste. It all felt prearranged, almost like a reception. This was how they lived.

Felicity asked about plans, the course, its duration, and where they'd been to teach. "Not in this district, I imagine," she added, with slow-spoken emphasis.

Richard nodded: "Closed doors. All private. Not surprising really."

Derek, who had repositioned the trolley alongside his chair, inhaled noisily. His face had darkened.

Felicity raised one eyebrow. "You have views?"

"Don't worry about it, Mother," Vanessa put in, "it's just an opinion."

"But I am interested. It's always valuable to hear about ideas. We're all in need of a wider perspective."

Richard smiled: "Yes, I suppose it all depends on one's experience."

Derek nodded emphatically: "True."

Felicity ran one finger round the lip of her glass. "So I take it your teaching experience has been in the state system?"

Richard, watching carefully, formulated his reply. The father, he could see, was gearing up. With his small-jawed face and slightly shaky hands he was staring hard, holding to his glass. His ears, which were prominent, had coloured slightly. The mother was different. Wide-eyed, attentive, stately, she held herself in readiness. Something suggestive – doubt or admiration – played about her mouth. It seemed she wanted more. Vanessa, sat upright on the sofa, was staring at the carpet.

"I went to grammar," he offered. "Mind, you see the change when you go into comprehensives."

Felicity, nodding slightly, invited further comment. It seemed she was at centre, judging the case.

Richard explained, speaking with care, rerunning incidents, his schooling and its problems.

"It's a choice," he said finally. "And a matter of conviction – though that's always personal. For me, there's an element of giving back."

His answer seemed to satisfy. Resuming direction, the conversation moved on and out, steered by Felicity into viewpoints shared.

After news and leisure talk, then observations on weather and growths in the garden, she proposed a move. The lunch required checking, she said, if they'd like to bring their glasses. Raising her voice, she conducted downstairs to a tiled basement with a kitchen to one side, connected by a hatch to a wood-panelled diner. "Lunch," she called. "Please make yourselves comfortable."

The meal was served with the aid of Derek, who carved and carried and topped up the glasses, while Vanessa and Richard (after offering to be helpful) took their places at the polished wooden table. It was long and grainy, with a centrepiece display of white and red roses and a French window out to a courtyard garden.

During lunch they kept up the talk. Light talk and connections, people they'd known, observations on life. Names were offered, histories sketched, rumours repeated, stories told. There was buzz and there was inside. They were in the loop. And it seemed, as they gossiped or sounded on family, that they'd passed over Richard; or perhaps, now he'd said his piece, they'd accepted his presence and made due allowance. It was almost, he thought, as if he wasn't there.

When Felicity brought him in (asking deliberately about outside interests) he found himself briefly, talking about travel – a subject that Derek warmed to, volunteering some lines about friendship, footslog and overcoming barriers. Behind the blah his voice was concessionary. Richard felt an offer was being made.

The meal went slowly. Partly it was helpings – large, repeated, with sauce and salad and a variety of meats – partly out of habit: they were used to being leisurely – but also because they could. To linger was more special, impressive, gave them advantage; they ate and they *expected*. But also (thought Richard) they'd prepared and they'd spread. They'd put out for him.

It was when they came to coffee, upstairs, with chocolates and Amaretti (and Vanessa now in action, talking women's history) that Richard became aware of Derek leaning forward, speaking slowly with an open-faced expression and a slightly breathy smile. When asked to repeat, he reiterated slowly, emphasising content. There was something, he said, which he'd like Richard to see. His voice now was louder and weightier. This was man-to-man.

Richard accepted, wondering what might follow.

Derek made noises, mentioning the top room, and guided hall-wards. Turning at the door, he announced they'd be back. "A climb," he said and led upstairs, touching the banisters and puffing slightly. "Three flights," he added, without looking back.

They ascended past Manets and Monets, up across a landing with photos of chateaus and castles then higher, and steeper, by brass-plate cathedrals and prints of vintage cars. From behind Richard noticed how, when Derek arrived at a landing, his hand danced patterns over wood, before turning and gripping to continue upstairs. At the top, red-faced, he paused for breath then pulled out a key. Finding a hole in a metal-handled door, he inserted and turned. It opened slowly and he ducked in first, clicking on the lights. His voiced sounded hollow as he warned about the sill.

Richard followed. The space he entered was high and sloping, with crossbeams visible and a view at centre, rising to a ridge. The walls were bare plaster, the atmosphere still, and the light bulbs unshaded. Though large and dusty, the room felt lived-in.

On both sides and in front there were flat wooden tables, gangway-ed in between. Each tabletop was large, box-room-size, with pit prop legs and a surrounding ledge. Displayed on each were contoured landscapes – some flat, some rolling, overlaid by roads and intersecting track-routes. The tracks were zoned, beginning at the middle with bridges and cuttings and branch lines off. They filled up the tables: diverged over fields, split wide where they ran between hills, looped around lakes, were thread-like at the edge, and forked together sharply as they returned to where they began. Each line or link or network included engineering – tunnels and viaducts and spans across rivers – and in-town sections where they cut between offices; each had its signs – posts or boards or distance markers – and each (where it reached open land) struck out past garages and houses, to circle into papier maché fields and watercolour shorelines.

"Did you put this together?" asked Richard.

Derek nodded. He was plugging in a circuit and adjusting switches. As he moved round the tables the streetlamps lit up, the windows glowed and the trains began to run. Suddenly it seemed the room was like a fairground.

Richard followed, looking round the models. He noticed how they varied. The landscapes ranged from alpine through farmland to desert; there were small towns and villages built on the flat, farms between hills, buildings from all periods, and scaled down versions of palaces and churches – many of them reminiscent of famous landmarks. Around and between there were figures lined up in plastic. There were people walking dogs, mock-ups of weddings, commuters on platforms, tourists with cameras, cowboys on horses and even, on one table, an open-air theatre with audience and performers dressed as Romans citizens.

"It's a film set," observed Richard, admiringly. He moved between tables, studying the detail, then turned to his host. "Must've taken years."

Again Derek nodded.

At the far end, in one corner, Richard noticed there was a small gate-leg table covered with a dustsheet. The material stood chest-high, squared at centre to a tent-like block. It looked like a boxed-up wedding present.

"Is that of interest?" he asked, pointing.

The older man smiled: "Ah, that's the most recent," he said, weighing his words. "It's actually rather specialised. But you'd like to look?"

Richard showed willing and was pressed into service to lift off the sheet. They stood both ends, raised it to head-height, then walked themselves clear, using the gangway to fold and deposit. While removing and folding Richard was aware, but only tangentially, of what was underneath. There was an edge of brickwork, painted wood, something architectural. It was only when he turned to examine in detail (with Derek to one side, peering closely, murmuring to himself) that he realised he was looking at a perfectly produced miniature version of a late Edwardian, three-storey, mid-terrace house.

Derek leaned forward. He reached and grasped, then, lifting from the corners, removed the facade. As he pulled it away he glanced at his guest. "You recognise, perhaps?" he asked.

Richard nodded, surprised by what he saw. This wasn't what he'd thought. And yet it was familiar, well-worked, constructed for effect. What had seemed general and vaguely architectural was, in fact, a mock-up. A one-off, and an example. Because when he looked closer he realised now that what he had before him was a meticulously constructed, room-by-room copy of the house they were standing in.

His eye searched the floors. "So we're here," he said finally, pointing to the attic.

"Yes. Present and correct," said Derek, following his gaze.

"I'm impressed. Very."

"You'd care to look closer?"

When Richard nodded, his host reached in, using a wedge to lever up the floor. He drew it out carefully and placed it on the table, inviting comparison: model and original.

The correspondence was exact.

An analogue, a dead ringer, a replica.

Richard crouched down, level to the table. "It must feel good," he said eventually, gazing round the room. "Seeing this, knowing it's yours... Something to be proud of."

Derek grinned, staring at the model. "Well, yes," he muttered, "something like... it is indeed..." He blushed, adding his thanks. As his words tailed off his hands took over, raising and positioning the floor he'd extracted. He checked for fit, added the house-front, then switched off the circuits. Noticing the dustsheet, he suggested quietly that they lift and cover, then head downstairs.

As they emerged through the door, Richard heard the voice of Felicity rising from below. She was inviting return. Their time was up. Her long level calls, projecting up the stairwell, filled up space. Derek called down, then stepped back to the door. Searching for the key, he glanced inside. The covers were drawn; the models were still; the dust was settling. Joined by Richard, he paused at the doorway, checked all round, then snapped off the lights. Felicity called again and he retreated from darkness, gripped the metal handle and shut the door behind him.

On the drive back to the flat Vanessa wanted details. "What *did* you two do up there?" she asked, teasingly.

"What d'you think?"

"No idea. Major bonding, judging by the grins."

"Boys will be boys."

"True. It's the locker room effect. DIY and how's your father."

The vehicle turned a corner and halted at lights.

"But seriously," she continued, "you seemed to have scored a hit."

"I did? Was something said?"

"No, but I could tell. Mother has this way of *giving off*. You were approved."

Richard waited till the taxi pulled away. "Have you actually been in the top room?"

She stared out vaguely through glass. A fine haze of mist, gathered on the window, softened what she saw. "Not really. It was one of those places I just didn't go. A separate space, like a Masonic hall. Somewhere upstairs where my father did things. Even now I feel it's important, but all rather abstract. I know there are models."

"A gallery full. I think you'd be surprised."

Vanessa smiled. "You liked them?"

"Admired them, yes. In their own way they're perfect."

"With a capital P?"

"Lifelike I'd say."

"And do they do things? I mean move, light up."

Richard considered: "Yes. Lots of that. But it's not all fairground – or if it is, that's not what really matters."

"You mean there's something else…"

"I believe so. It's important – to him."

Vanessa nodded. She raised one hand, rubbing in circles against steamed-up glass. The hole that appeared was clear at centre, grey round the edges, and drip-run at the bottom.

"And for you?" she asked, gazing out. "You found it interesting?"

"Oh God, yes. He's done so much. Just half that and *I'd* be proud." He lapsed back into silence, facing forward. They were queued in traffic, moving slowly between shops and offices with other vehicles joining from side roads and a bus stopped ahead with people disembarking. As the blockage eased they advanced through lights, dipping into orange beneath a neon-lit bridge. They cut across lanes to emerge into brightness on an illuminated carriageway.

"So perhaps," she said quietly, "you, being a man, can tell me why he does it."

Richard sat back. Her question filled the air. It seemed she'd looked over, pointed to something and asked him what it was.

"I think," he answered, fingering the upholstery, "it's something about scale and ownership – putting things in context."

Vanessa sighed. "Well he's certainly been working at it – for years now. It's La Grande Obsession." Their eyes met. "Maybe, Richard, if I'd been there. Actually *seen* it—"

Sensing her doubts he paused and held back, considering angles. Her words, his, the street scene passing, her outline in darkness. There were signboards and directions, headlights, overhead reflectors. The interior of the taxi was cross-barred and lined by small spots of light.

"It's good. You'd be amazed."

She smiled. "It's always been his *project*. One of those this-is-me tasks that men go in for. His own way of being Derek. All his own, till you came along."

"Ah, so I've joined the Quintins. Honorary member, hitched to daughter, and well in with dad."

"But don't talk school."

He laughed, "True."

"Or if you do, old school."

Again he laughed, gazing out.

She offered him her hand. "Well, you did very well if you ask me."

For the rest of the journey Richard sat in silence, taking in the route, their closeness, the lights in darkness and the prospect (now glimpsed up ahead, seen in outline, eyes peering forward in windscreen view) of becoming – like their friends – committed, spoken-for, partnered for life.

The next day, at college, though they'd a seminar and a paper to discuss, they went without files or notebooks. They'd not checked the brief and hadn't read around. For once it didn't count who said what, how much was honest, and whether their tutor expected. It all seemed off the point. Nothing was quite that clear, or easy to predict. Because things had changed. In one sense they'd moved on (the parental acceptance, and where it might be leading), and in another sense they were aware that between them there were still issues and matters unsettled.

At the end of the seminar they spent a few minutes chatting in the bar with a serious-looking Ruth. She was wearing glasses (which, she admitted, she ought to – more often), had tied back her hair, and announced, speaking quietly, that she'd really got to change. She'd made her promises. Written it all down. A number of resolutions, mainly about Doug, but also a schedule to get through her studies. When Vanessa mentioned school she talked about weighing up, choosing best options, and scraping a pass. Ruth added that she planned to gain credits through retakes and rewrites while searching (she said, glancing quickly round) for non-school jobs – anything with people, outside the classroom.

She rose to leave soon afterwards, breathing hard, and hovered by the table. She was feeling pressured, with so much to do.

"It's a no pain no gain situation," she added, grimacing. "And I'm feeling pain."

Vanessa, colouring slightly, quickly shook her head. "Nonsense, you're fine, Ruth Draper. Just fine. You're you, and can cope. You always have."

Richard narrowed his eyes: "You're going to the library?"

Ruth nodded.

"You can afford, you know, to give yourself a break."

"Not for me. Not so."

"Really? Well, don't overdo it."

"Not likely," she persisted, grimly: "Not in the here and now…" She shrugged and stepped away. As she walked she shook her head, frowning. "No way. Not now," she repeated, dropping one shoulder. As she neared the door she took off her glasses and, muttering quickly, repeated her formula. It was as if she was an actor who'd finally learned her lines.

Vanessa sighed, watching her friend clear the room before suggesting that they go. Crossing the lobby they stood beside the exit, waiting, while a crowd pushed in. The group were all male, long-limbed and noisy. They teased and joshed and piled in behind each other. Their conversation was full of little-boy challenges and flat-voiced laughter.

When the doors finally cleared, Richard and Vanessa passed out into daylight, en route to the market.

Outside was grey and slightly damp. They walked along a row of blackened buildings with dirt-streaked woodwork and windows encased by bent wire mesh. The pavement was uneven and the road they followed was full of potholes and patched-up surfaces.

As they walked, Richard did the talking, replaying the seminar and their tutor's comments (her smooth-voiced invitations and leading questions). He also mentioned Ruth, speaking of patterns, her capacity for reversals, what might happen next – then switched back into critical (their tutor again, her way of twisting words) as he led off down a side street.

Vanessa, now quiet, went where he went – while remaining outside and beyond, involved in things apart.

It seemed, with the departure of Ruth, that they'd lost way somehow, slipped off into doubt. They were moving side by side, walking slowly. A step change had occurred.

At the market hall entrance, Richard paused. "Shall we look at books?" he asked, waving forward to a corner full of trestle tables and stacked-up boxes.

"That's what you want?" Vanessa countered.

"I thought, in a way, it might be—"

"Might be?"

He shrugged. "I dunno. A change, I suppose. Because all of a sudden I seem to have to deal with problems…"

"Problems?"

"Tutors, friends, whatever."

"And you'd rather look at books?"

Richard smiled. "I can read *them*."

Vanessa frowned: "Hmm. What are you suggesting?"

He laughed. "That we talk more. About what matters."

Before she could answer he led off to the tables. Behind one stood a man with beard and glasses who greeted with a nod. He was short and round with pastry-thick fingers and hair to the collar. His light blue eyes were small, attentive and slightly otherworldly.

When Vanessa approached he nodded once again. His presence was a reminder, and a caution. It was as if he knew, and could see right through her.

She leafed through a few volumes, skimming for content. Richard, meanwhile, was peering at some verse.

Vanessa frowned. "I can't seem to read properly," she said, looking slightly baffled. The man behind the table nodded and Richard followed suit. "I need to know," she continued, "what *is* it we've got to talk about?"

Richard shrugged, putting down his book. "Well, for one thing, my parents."

"Ah, back to that—"

He confirmed, narrowing his eyes.

"You're worried what they might say?"

"I don't think they're bothered," he replied quickly, returning to the tables and lighting on a hardback copy of her cousin's book. "As far as they're concerned, we live in a foreign country."

"Because they come from *up north*?" she said, imitating his voice, flattened at the end.

He laughed. "Well, it keeps them at a respectable distance."

He turned a few pages, reading out a sentence in lugubrious, mock singsong.

"Pretty bad, isn't it," he said, closing the book. He was addressing his words to the man behind the table, stalling for time.

Vanessa narrowed her eyes. "Not everyone in the family has my father's level of talent."

"Sorry?"

She shrugged: "It's nothing. Just a remark."

Richard frowned. "You're not happy with something?"

She shook her head and moved off down the aisle.

He nodded to the bookseller, then followed her to a corner and in beneath the awning of a flower stall. It was seaside-bright and pollinate, smelling of damp and soapsuds. There were step-levelled displays with trailing baskets, made-up window boxes, and mixed bouquets in see-through wrappers. Here he found her taking in the colours, with her face pressed close to a red-brown bunch of chrysanthemums. The stems stood tall in a large glass jar.

"Not much to smell," he said, as if to warn her off.

"These are my colours," she said, ignoring. "They suit."

She hadn't brought her purse so Richard stood by while she picked out stems, mixing for effect: red-brown, ochre, off-white and yellow. When she'd tried and compared, matching different lengths, she pronounced herself satisfied. He paid, then helped with the carrying.

On the way back he reverted to the question of moving in. It had come up this morning in relation to his parents. He'd begun with a remark that his stay had, for the first time, extended to four nights. He'd used words like *habit* and *belonging* – jokily of course, but also in appeal. In the talk that followed Vanessa (he felt) had sidestepped or minimised, she'd begged the question. She'd like it of course but wondered about timing, because he'd put things in a way, she said, that felt quite closed. She needed to consider. But later, when they walked to the market, she'd kept her distance, offering only platitudes in return to anything said.

Now, as they walked back, he returned to the subject. He was using what she called his 'cornering' technique (wanting words, a position to hold on to, something he could measure) and asking supplementaries – then putting in sweeteners, sudden declarations that he'd go along with anything, fit where necessary, in order to settle it.

"Maybe," he said quietly, "it's better – even if we both said *move in* tomorrow – if we wait."

Vanessa showed surprise. She was carrying her chrysanths, held out at an angle, almost touching his. "But I thought that was what you wanted?"

"Not if it upsets things."

They continued in silence, crossing the river and walking south.

"There could be a case," he said slowly as they entered the park, "for a trial period."

Vanessa looked down at her collection of flowers. She was smiling vaguely with her head to one side, as if for a picture. A distance had opened up. A gap between steps. The flowers, or her thoughts, were absorbing her. "How would that work?" she asked suddenly.

Richard frowned, then adjusted. Though the walk was familiar, it felt quite strange. It was a push, an effort, something undertaken. If he was honest, when they talked like this, he made the running.

"If I hung on to my place," he said, gazing round, "but moved everything in. Then we could try – but there'd still be a route back."

She continued walking, looking from the flowers to the path they were taking. There were grey-brown patches where the borders had died back. The path at the end turned past a boarded-up kiosk and a bare, fenced-in patch with swings and a sandpit.

"Richard," she said quietly as they passed out through the gate, "do you think we could manage?"

Her doubt became his. "Perhaps…" he began, then cut off to consider. They were turning into her road, walking slowly, connected now by a need to settle something. Their talk, which had begun as routine, had developed its own weight and pressure and now had narrowed to a choice between opposites, a jump either way.

"I think," he said finally, as they arrived at the door, "we should make a decision – now."

"What, right here?"

"Here and now."

Vanessa pulled a face. She held up her chrysanths, as if they might protect her. "Can't it wait?" she asked, sotto voce. "These things are difficult."

Richard reached out, shaking his head. "I need to know," he replied, taking her bunch as if she'd offered. With the blooms in one hand he stood beside the step, half-smiling. "What do you say: move in or not?"

"Yes would be good," he added, laughing.

Vanessa remained silent.

"Please say something," he continued.

"I think…"

"What?"

She returned to silence.

"If it's easier," he said, "you can just nod your head."

Vanessa showed surprise.

"You don't have to *say* anything."

Their eyes connected.

Richard looked long and deep; his gaze was encouraging. Her large round eyes were (he felt) already saying it. It seemed she was with him.

Suddenly he straightened.

"While I, being a man," he announced, holding out the bunch of red-brown chrysanths, "will say it with flowers."

In reply Vanessa smiled, stretched out her hand to accept the bunch and, slowly, with deliberate emphasis, nodded her head.

CHAPTER FIVE

Richard moved in during early spring. The timing and the season seemed just right – he called it a statement, she spoke of beginnings – and once they'd agreed, it seemed no longer necessary to plan for contingencies or have some sort of fallback. Suddenly it became definite, fixed and intended, yet subject to adjustment. It was, and was so – or it happened – and took shape as predicted, according to schedule, just as it turned out.

So he and Vanessa decided, having talked and thought and weighed up all the choices, that he'd best give notice. That way seemed simpler. Fairer on everyone, and more cut and dried. It also seemed more practical. Living with a couple and their friend, the owner, in a three bedroom basement, Richard didn't have much furniture, and since meeting Vanessa he'd not found time to build up extras; so his move seemed more like a room-change, a step across a corridor, carried off quietly, with a minimum of effort.

And once he'd decided, it went off as planned. He boxed and bagged up, taped round breakables, then arranged things in piles. And to achieve it quickly he fitted his journeys into morning and evening, walking the essentials, sorting both ends, and ferrying by car.

The transfer took a week, completed on Sunday with the help of Doug – who arrived after breakfast in shorts and sweatshirt, bracing his shoulders and declaring himself set.

"Let's see what goes," he said, while manoeuvring boxes and a flat-pack wardrobe to fit in his estate.

After packing and testing (with Richard helping, adding in extras and securing the back doors), they cruised to Vanessa's, taking a detour to avoid the city centre. On the journey Doug asked about plans, made the odd joke, queried arrangements. At the door he directed, unloading together and positioning carefully, checking before lifting. To him it seemed as if thought was needed, that they'd best tread carefully and that the move might be pushing it, rather.

"You happy?" he asked as they pulled out a pair of speakers, wrapped in plastic and conjoined by wires. Richard grunted as they shuffled to the stairs.

"It's a big step," Doug said when they reached the top, glancing backwards down the stairwell.

When the last few items had been turned round the doorframe and placed against the wall Vanessa thanked him, offering food.

"That's kind," he replied, looking to Richard for guidance.

"Well, there you are – please be seated. Guest of honour."

Doug stood quietly, looking doubtful.

"Go on, it's on the table," Richard beamed. "Open house."

"I'm not sure... Just don't want you put out."

The other man laughed. "Doug Jones, you're so bloody unassuming."

"You think—"

"I wondered," Vanessa cut in, "*if* you'd prefer... maybe we could do something. As a foursome."

The men dropped quiet, awaiting developments. "Perhaps..." said Doug slowly. "What would it be?"

"I've an idea."

Her words remained hanging as if she'd lost the thread. Whatever she'd intended, it seemed it could wait.

Richard smiled. By now he knew her habits. This was Vanessa.

"And your idea...?" he asked.

"Just something," she replied, as if it didn't matter.

"Yes?"

"A thought."

"Which is?"

"I wondered about visiting a garden."

Richard remembered the horticultural monthlies seen at her parents. They'd leafed through photos of flower shows, colour-themed borders and woodland walks.

"You've one in mind?" he asked.

"Yes, if you like. We'd have to check if it's open." She turned to Doug: "It's quite some distance, and you'd have to drive. But *we'd* do the honours."

"Yes, the lot," added Richard, catching on. "Our treat."

Doug stood smiling, shifting his gaze from one to the other. His round, boyish face had filled to a glow.

"Is that all right?" Vanessa asked him.

Doug took a breath. "Accepted," he said. "I shall await instructions." Before they could reply he added, dryly: "Whatever Ruth says."

They drove to Manor Gardens the next weekend. With Doug behind the wheel and Vanessa directing, they took the scenic route, climbing through fields, crossing bare hills and descending sharply into leafless valleys. As they journeyed south, a grey-yellow sun appeared between clouds. When Doug grew tired Ruth took over, revving on straights and braking into corners. As she drove she swore, quietly. Beside her, Vanessa cleared her throat and offered directions. Her task was to calm things.

They turned west at a castle and ran past farms in an undulating district, cruising by fields and tree-topped outcrops to arrive at a final line of hills. Here they did a loop to descend beneath a scarp and enter the beginnings of a flat coastal plain.

"Soon be there," said Vanessa, aligning her map.

At a sign for Manor Gardens, Ruth slowed, swinging right into a winding country lane. The lane was narrow, single-track, with passing places.

"Well, it's an interesting place to find," said Richard, gazing forward.

Close in to the hills, facing south, they entered a bowl-shaped valley laid out in terraces with steps down and up, dividing hedges, and early spring borders. Here they turned right through a gate. "Mind your bums," called Ruth as they bumped across a cattle grid.

"Drrrrrrr," cried Richard.

They parked on grass and followed a track which led to a lodge where Richard paid, then passed in through an arch.

"It's south facing," said Vanessa leading along a pea gravel drive with banks both sides dotted with celandine and white and purple crocuses.

The path led forward, past a birdbath lawn with a pool and stepping stones. Their route curved, passing through a wall and along by shrubs to a high-roofed house. They stopped by climbers, yellow, bell-shaped and scentless; then moved on to a terrace with steps down to a low-walled square. Here Ruth took Doug's arm. "Oh yes," she said gazing quietly at a large-bloomed camellia. "Don't you just *feel* it," she said, tucking in closer.

For a while they walked the square, taking in the sunlight, the stone, the first shows on wood.

The square led to a drop, a zigzag path with log steps and railings and a descent through trees. Here the grounds were wilder. They filed downhill past overspreading bushes, mostly just in bud, admiring the landscape. Vanessa led with an all-knowing air, shadowed by Ruth who kept asking questions; the two men followed, saying nothing.

At the bottom, set beneath trees, they came across a hideaway. It was bare to the front and bushy round the edges. In the centre was a thick green awning with a swing bench beneath. "Rest spot," said Vanessa, rather grandly. They approached, exchanging glances.

"Come on. All aboard. Room for everyone," cried Ruth, who was first to climb in. They packed the seat: Ruth and Doug at centre, Richard at one end, Vanessa at the other. The view forward was panoramic.

For a while they admired, talking gardens and childhood holidays until Ruth, losing interest, began pushing out. She was bracing, one leg to the floor, using her body as a counterweight.

"It sags," she laughed, foot-rocking harder. The seat began to sway, creaking quietly and scraping at the sides. She pushed again, using both feet. Vanessa joined in, and the seat began to lurch.

"Careful," called Doug as the frame began to shudder. Ruth lifted her legs, leaning with the movement, and the seat became a gondola.

"Flying," she called, then threw herself back, breaking into song.

Vanessa laughed. The seat was in motion, dipping and chopping like a rowboat. "Flying!" she echoed pushing at the frame. The motion shifted sideways. She pushed again and the seat began to tack, corner to corner. It rose up, sidelong and back, describing a parabola, hitting on metal and jerking forward.

Doug called again.

At one end a wing nut flew off, clattering to the ground.

The women chorused "Flying!" and kicked out together.

"This is silly," said Richard, gripping on a bar.

"Very!" Ruth called, laughing.

"Bloody silly," he insisted, forcing the seat downwards. He continued, gripping heavily and swearing intermittently, until the seat came to rest.

Silence followed. In the bushes there were birds, rustling and calling. An elderly couple appeared, descending the hillside, holding the railing. Their voices sounded muffled, absorbed by wood.

Richard, who was first to stand up, began searching for the nut. His eyes were directed and purposeful. Frowning slightly, he peered into bushes and poked around the frame. Head down, attentive, he was on task. "Should be here," he told Vanessa, nodding his acceptance when she offered to help. Ruth joined in, ducking and stretching to peer beneath stones. Doug remained in place, feeling into corners and hand-checking where they'd sat.

In the course of the search Ruth moved up to Richard and, gazing ground-wards, offered an apology.

"No problem," he said. "Bit of a laugh," he added, smiling.

They continued checking round. Apart from a spider-touch surprise (with Ruth in shivers dancing round) and a few muddy coins found by Doug, nothing turned up.

"Best leave it," said Richard in the end. "Vanish. Pretend we weren't here."

Ruth laughed. "You mean the Indian rope-trick?"

He grinned and licked his lips.

Vanessa glanced up the slope: "Shall we go then?"

"One more look," called Doug, reaching sideways. As he moved the seat began to drop. It shook and slipped, keeling sideways. "Wha—" he called, reaching into air. The bench went down, tipping still further. Doug cried out, one end collapsed, and the canvas imploded like a badly-made tent. As it fell it rebounded, tipping him forward. He grabbed for the frame, missed, yelled and landed in a heap, rolling his eyes like a punch-drunk boxer.

"Oh my God!" squealed Ruth, hand to mouth.

"You all right?" asked Richard, crouching down.

Doug lay hunched, back to the questioner, shivering.

"Is he injured?"

Richard peered closer, frowning. "Not sure. You OK?"

Doug continued shaking.

"Are you all right?"

No reply.

"Doug—"

Ruth pushed forward. She sighted and peered, invoking Richard's words, seeking a reply. "Hey there—"

Almost as she spoke (craning to one side, breathing hard) Doug turned suddenly, bared his teeth and levered up. For a second he appeared hurt. Then, with a quickly-taken gasp, he stood, pointed to the seat and doubled forward. "What a— What a—" he whooped, spluttering and shaking and dancing round. Arms out, he was windmilling both ways, as if he'd been stung.

Ruth stepped back: "You're OK then?"

Doug turned to face her, struggling for air. Before he could reply the others joined in, giggling and snorting. Even Ruth, after expressing surprise, was drawn in to hilarity.

They continued, high-stepping round and eyeballing each other. They'd entered, it seemed, a kind of charmed circle.

It was Vanessa who, moving to the path, recalled them to purpose. "Uphill?" she asked, pointing. Her face was flushed, her body set forward.

When Doug, having calmed, began another dance, she pointed harder.

"We need to go," she insisted. "Need to climb."

The others ignored.

"Now."

Richard responded first, nodding. "Come on you lot," he said, pointing upwards. His eyes were alive, and restless.

Ruth reacted next, closing to Doug and gripping his arm. "Uphill," she repeated. He in turn nodded, pushed back his hair, then led off smartly, climbing through trees.

The path back was steep and they moved in a line, throwing out comments and laughing, wildly. It rose in a curve, doubling sharply. At each turn they grabbed the railing and tackled the reverse slope. As they neared the top Ruth stretched up, one-finger-shushing and cautioning them to silence. Suddenly they were children with a secret between them.

On the upper level they looked around for staff. The air was still, the paths were clear and the flower heads were motionless. It seemed they were alone.

They walked and explored, circling round borders and passing through a wall. By remaining deadpan and moving slowly, they managed to stay low. To background into casual and play their part as visitors.

After forking right past rose beds they returned to the house, entering a conservatory through a half-glassed door. Inside, the air felt thick. A fine layer of mist had collected on the windows and the pipes. A tap in the corner was dripping onto tiles.

"Feel this. It's like stepping into a sauna," said Doug, squaring his shoulders.

An attendant stood close by. She was half-concealed behind a large glazed pot containing a butterfly palm. Beyond her was a glass and metal gallery with climbers to one side and a café at the end.

After agreeing they were hot they asked the attendant about serving drinks; then walked the full length to pull up chairs around a patterned metal table. Richard offered, established preferences, and went to collect. During his absence, the others gazed round. The corner they had occupied was tall and bare and painted white. Greened round the edges, it was damp and warm and echoed like a warehouse.

They were linked now by the occasional word: a reference, a tag phrase, a hand-rocking gesture and a slowly spreading grin. After bringing the coffees, Richard made an effort to switch to plant talk, but when Ruth mentioned flying and Vanessa began to splutter, their laughter took over, coming in waves. Small waves at first, then overlapping – ending in hand-gripping snorts as they rose and straightened and gazed out to the terrace, smiling.

"Silly," said Richard, keeping it low.

"Bloody silly," whispered Ruth.

"Bloody, bloody, silly."

"Bloody, bloody, bloody—"

They continued pacing, repeating in chorus. Behind and beside them Vanessa and Doug were watching every movement, grinning.

Seeing the attendant advancing from the doorway, Ruth pulled back. "I think," she said, steadying herself, "we may need to go."

Richard laughed. "And when you gotta—"

"Shhh," warned Vanessa, following Ruth's gaze.

"Careful," added Doug.

The attendant stepped round and back, staring at a point just to one side. She was tall and severe, wearing tweeds and a hat. Her movements were bird-like and edgy. When she'd finished her beat, returning to the doorway, Richard broke the silence.

"Right," he said, "best leave."

Ruth smiled, thinly: "Pretend we weren't here?"

"Whatever it takes."

He nodded, Vanessa smiled, and the other two joined them as they moved back along the gallery. They walked without looking left or right, ducking through the door to the garden.

As they emerged a bell rang. A voice called out, echoing slightly. "I think it's closing," said Vanessa looking round. Her expression had blanked. In the open air she was distanced and calm; studied for effect. Richard, beside her, drew one hand across his brow. Ruth and Doug, brought up the rear, arms linked together.

They advanced along the terrace in silence. The sun now was low, striking their faces, and the air was still. To one side, in the square, the shadows were lengthening. The walls of the house, on the other side, were bathed in brightness. Between them was the terrace leading to the steps, then the lawn, the pool, the path back to the lodge.

The bell rang, once, twice, and the voice called again.

"Time," said Ruth.

They descended the steps and crunched across gravel. When they reached the main drive the light had weakened. A drift of clouds had thinned out the sun. A breeze was moving gently, shifting over grass. Suddenly it was twilight and chilly. The bell rang again, followed by the voice – a single syllable. On the banks both sides the crocuses were closing.

As they passed out through the lodge Richard took Vanessa by the hand. "The voice in the garden," he said quietly, glancing round.

She nodded, he turned, and together saying nothing they walked back to the car.

CHAPTER SIX

The trip to Manor Gardens became one of their stories. Told in company or shared on the phone, it joined the other anecdotes: their cross words in the café, the handbag, the rail bridge and the zoo trip with bouquets. Delivered brightly, it was given out at parties as evidence of life (because the joys of youth had sobered into dull days in the classroom and late night preparation). It stood out as madcap, and linked in with their move. And it shaded, in telling, into something documentary, a straight-talk record that gave them definition. Then shifted, when questioned, into head-shaking grins and would-you-believe-it smiles. Often it was *there*, somewhere in the background, held in reserve as a conversational filler, or offered as a cameo: a step, a scene change, a chapter in their history.

Perhaps it also balanced, kept them on track, made for reassurance. They had that behind them. As a set-piece it fitted, and showed them as they were. They'd been that crazy. Or had been once.

Because school, in the first few years, came above everything. They worked and they delivered. Nothing else mattered. For them, each new lesson was a drama, a performance, a struggle. And each time they taught added to the pressure. It filled up their lives with what Richard called *fiddle*: detail, plans and long lists of equipment (what he sometimes called *crap*, remembering as he said it, their battle in the restaurant, and how she'd walked away). School, full-time, main-scale, completely took over.

On teaching days they'd a pattern first thing – a breath held or sigh, followed by a turn and an adjustment quickly offered. Or they volunteered remarks, chatted into air, filled up the spaces. Sometimes they signalled – a look, a shrug, a hand-spread gesture – or they went for finality: words of pressure, a block-phrase or token, a formula in passing. But mostly they just got ready, checking off items as they geared up for work, practising their one-liners and talking themselves up.

"We don't need no education," he sang, or hummed, as he rose in darkness then washed and dressed long before school time.

"Starting's always hard," mused Vanessa over breakfast, and again on the journey.

"Think free periods," he told her at the gate.

"Not sure I'm up to it," she said quietly, as she rested over lunch.

"One lesson to go," was his mantra, called across the staffroom during afternoon break.

Because his job was to register. If a lesson went badly he picked it over afterwards, reckoned pros and cons, then stayed up late to work on improvements. If Vanessa had problems he nodded and advised. And when management observed them, he made the running, speaking of dynamics, of what made for interest and how kids learned.

Also there were stories: joke scenes from classrooms, blunders, confusions and off-the-wall incidents which outdid Manor Gardens. Teaching, it seemed, was full of them. Lines said by kids, failures of equipment, parental interference, senior-staff cockups and a whole raft of anecdotes – apocryphal, mainly – about life and death experiences and nightmare classrooms where kids ran riot and teachers practised moves in unarmed combat.

But when it came to stories, one, a dream, returned so often that it displaced all others, taking on a quality of quiet actuality. And though Richard tried ignoring (or riding it sometimes, joking afterwards in staffrooms or bars), he couldn't seem to shake it. It crept into his life, had its own presence, figured often in thought and imagination, was always there in versions both hidden and felt. Its persistence (and its camera-like detail) made it seem, like a story heard in childhood, both all-too-familiar and *arrived* by magic from a world where things just happened, at random, without apparent reason.

The dream usually began – and repeated in a round – with kids in the classroom. Third-form, oversized, pushing to the front.

All on their feet, pulling faces. Bunchy and punchy, arguing behind glass. With a group at the back throwing paper darts and climbing on chairs. But like all dreams it also included views from the corridor, footage of football matches and birds pecking fat, quick snaps of wrestlers and puppets dancing. Largely silent, the dream continued with a time jump to the stockroom where Richard saw himself double-checking shelves. He was looking for a collection of red-spined paperbacks: an examination set. Fumbling at first, with a panicky awareness of the wall clock above. But also (in secret) relieved to find excuse. Slowing gradually, poking into corners, hearing (or imagining) the sounds of teachers calling, and time ticking by. Continuing the search, peering under desks and deep into cupboards. But now as diversion, wondering at developments, playing for time. Tidying and arranging, keeping himself occupied. Looking into space, a face at the window. Finally – ten minutes left, and the class in turmoil – leaving the stockroom, pacing the corridor, then returning for the register. A delay here too, hunting all over. Then out past classrooms, arriving at the doorway. Pip pip pip pip. Saved by the Tannoy, surrounded by bodies, and a time shift down the corridor...

> In the really-real world he managed.
> He negotiated challenges, set deadlines
> and batted back their comments.
> "You do this," he said, keeping it simple.
> "I'll have a page," he told them,
> when they wanted targets.
> "Here's a start," he added, pointing
> to a sentence written on the board.

...But the dream was different. It went its own way. Followed its own laws. Had false trails and sequels and many different versions. A series of sketches, set in classrooms, where kids took over and teachers lost their bearings. Incidents that merged – all involving muddle and mishap and errors of judgement. And a number of cameos, farce-like and crazy, where he held himself separate, observing from above. As if each story, with its twists and shifts and arbitrary developments, was a runaway ride with no discernable outcome.

In the first, the Sunday evening one, he was standing looking out at a dead-silent classroom. His mind had blanked, halted midsentence, the lesson forgotten. He was gaping, fish-like, at puzzled eyes and faces. The audience were fidgety. They'd lost all interest and now were gearing up. A group in the centre were exchanging whispers, preparing to call out. He was humming and hawing, gazing round the room. The joke was on him. Searching for papers, he tried to head them off. Still his voice was silent as the class began to heckle. Their comments turned nasty. Shouting now, they were glaring, waving, challenging to a fight. Something inside him was about to break inward or do something violent when quite without warning the storyline changed…

> And between each dream, sandwiched
> like an ad break, the do-words and imperatives,
> the repeats and insistences, the steadyings, cautions
> and say-so expressions:
> "That's enough!" called without warning.
> "Volume down!" sung, with authority.
> "Try this," quietly, smiling.

…The second situation, which sometimes followed on (and sometimes lay dormant, appearing unexpectedly in a turn, a jokey remark or occasional piece of writing) was the 'perfect classroom'. In this, punishment was electric, with students strapped down to wired-up chairs and the teacher at the front, with one finger raised, firing questions. The finger was the threat: poised over buttons it administered a jab, sometimes repeated, resulting in shocks at various levels. A moment's inattention could earn a small half-jab, an answer off the point might lead to a jolt, while rudeness or rebellion was several-times-blasted, leaving the pupil (and the desk) charred and incinerated…

> "Good," with dignity.
> "Well done," with feeling.
> "Your best yet," enthusing.

…Then there were the dreams which cut back and forth, took turns or passed, dealt round endings. In one – or one version – he wiped out the class, in another he issued orders which they jumped to, smiling. In some he bargained, exchanging work for no more shocks. In a few he ignored them, and in one – the most common – the class became hardened, sparking and buzzing and glowing till their skin shone like angels. (And in that one became addicts, laughing wildly, insisting on shocks with ever-greater voltage.)

The other dreams were vaguer. As mood-thoughts, coded, they existed for themselves. Set after school they were odd or quirky or last-man-left-standing. Often post-party-ish. But then rather drifty, moving at whim through zoo scenes and boxed-in episodes with attackers jumping out and well-known troublemakers confined behind bars. These too varied, including runaway moments, dives into caves and footslogs through jungle – all of them desperate, but also inconsequential.

So he dreamed. Or he dreamed he dreamed, because after the beginning (the start of term, when the thoughts took over, and each successive term, each more pressing) he found himself surprised by the thought, the way it just happened. There were events all around, lined up, in preparation, and then there were the *truths* – moments of intermission, the hollowness within. He'd his own sense of lack. Of time ticking down and things still to do. Of aim gone off and chances overlooked. Of a spot he hadn't reached, where he'd not have to fight or hang in there to register. A life uncornered, at leisure, set back from the rush, the need to be on top.

Because teaching, and its dreams, was (he'd soon realised) a world in a box. An all-out, tasked-up dance without meaning. A rough ride and a fiddle; a never-ending round. A battle to make out, to keep himself alive and not go under. And it led him and forced him and kept him chivvied up. He'd set off, it seemed, across unknown territory, without drawing breath, on a one-way journey…

For Vanessa, school left her frazzled. It was all too much. Outwardly calm (and still talking pedagogy, the university of life), she coped and she managed. But inwardly she distanced. At school she marked time, got through as she could, made do, functioned, ignored all problems. When kids played up (which they did most lessons), she looked straight through them, took things as read, carried on regardless. She talked and she appealed, while they pushed harder. And, as the noise level rose, she dished out worksheets, wrote up instructions and tutored the front row. 'Working independently' she called it when they played cards at the back – then told on the boys when they spent the whole lesson doodling desktops or chewing down rulers and dismantling pens.

But the act of reporting simply made them worse. Next lesson they sulked, and threatened to shop her.

"But you know how to behave," she replied, when they claimed she'd got it wrong.

"It's up to you," she countered, when they contested what she'd said. "You can discipline yourselves."

"Because I know," she continued, ignoring their objections, "you can behave like adults."

But her words didn't wash. The more she appealed the more they obstructed. In reply to her questions they shrugged, played innocent, complained she didn't help. Whatever tasks she set, the work was too easy. They'd done it all before, she'd not told them anything. In any case, school was pointless. It didn't lead anywhere – and as nobody paid them, why bother?

Then there were the girls. For them, what was called learning wasn't worth the effort. School, they announced between glancing at mirrors and leafing magazines, was a bore. It wasn't for them. There were teachers not listening, rules and restrictions (which no one took seriously), boys being stupid, other girls chatting, and a problem with Vanessa who spoke too much like a lady, complained about manners and wore the wrong clothes. They didn't like her voice, thought her fussy, rated her low on strictness, fairness, experience, and how she did her hair.

And for Vanessa – marking late at night or searching early morning for material that would please them – it seemed so unequal, so all-out and forcing, so much a matter of us against them. Which didn't seem right. Because she'd only ever wanted, as she said to Richard, to offer what she could. To coach and encourage, give what they needed – a hand up, an opening, a broader understanding.

"Does it ever get easier?" she asked at dinner parties attended by colleagues who had all been through it. Her guests (hand-picked individuals, super-teacher types who really knew their stuff) were usually forthcoming. They drew a line at this, said it and meant it, took no prisoners. Survival, it seemed, was what mattered.

"The thing to do," said Frank, their senior staff friend who visited most weekends, "is keep 'em guessing."

Slim and dynamic, Frank was what Vanessa called 'very Robert Redford'. He spoke with finality, paused for effect, emphasising his thoughts with a slightly stagey grin.

"Because if they're kept in the dark," he added, sipping his wine, "they stay frightened."

"You really think so?" asked Vanessa, maintaining her gaze.

Frank confirmed. Beside him, his wife Jackie nodded her agreement. Tall and gaunt, she sat hunched forward, inclining her head to get a better look. Side to side and umpire-like, she followed what was said.

Vanessa leaned forward, indicating glasses and offering top-ups. "Isn't what you're describing all rather mediaeval?" she asked between pouring wine. "After all, why not parade them in the town square, or put the leaders in the stocks and pelt them with rubbish?"

"But it works. Scares 'em rigid," Frank called, with relish.

Pursing his lips, he quickly looked away. It seemed he'd said his piece.

They were talking by candlelight, grouped in the lounge with the windows open. It was late, and quiet. The night air was hot and the sky, which was cloudless, was lake-like and still. Through the open window a grey-white moon was clearly visible, and higher, sharper, a small group of stars.

Richard called through from the kitchen. He was nearly finished.

Vanessa called back: she'd do the rest. "Just soak the pans," she added, airily, relighting a candle. When Frank cracked a joke she offered an anecdote, a bike shed story leading to thoughts – college words mainly, taken from her essays – about learning from experience and the hidden curriculum.

Jackie took her turn, speaking with edge about her time in secondary and the relief she'd experienced, moving to college. "More civilised," she said wryly, fingering her drink. Her face by candlelight looked careworn and painterly.

While she was talking, Frank had stretched out. He was informal tonight, in jeans and T-shirt, with his hair slicked back and eyes all over. His gaze was stern – tight-eyed and challenging – his mouth line ironic, while his voice tone was expansive.

As Jackie finished off he blinked and wiped one hand across his face, offering his support.

Richard entered, announcing he'd done. After topping up glasses, he took up position squatted on the carpet.

Vanessa, addressing Frank, asked a supplementary about controlling kids.

"You want the formula?"

She nodded.

"Start off tough," he said with a foxy grin, "get tougher."

"Really?"

He shrugged: "It's who's on top. You or them."

"But isn't that bullying?"

He paused, looking down into his glass. It was as if it was a pool, and somewhere at the bottom he'd find an answer.

"Well, you know me…" He smiled, directing his attention to a burnt-down candle. Leaning forward, he fixed his eyes on its soft yellow glow: "Insecure. Need to impress."

Richard laughed, "So it's an act?"

Frank confirmed, backed by Jackie.

"But, Frank… isn't that difficult?" asked Vanessa, frowning. "Why?"

"To keep it up. Isn't it hard work? Don't you wish sometimes you could just be yourself, let down the barriers and *talk* to the kids? Isn't your method all rather stressful?"

He reached for his glass: "Once you get used, it's fine. Pure practice... and body language."

"Sounds awfully strenuous to me."

He shrugged, looking off.

They returned to drinking and exchanging stories. Frank told one about his old school. It involved words like 'taming' and 'training', was quietly spoken, with pauses for effect, shifts between viewpoints, and invited the audience to laugh more at the teller than what he had to say. During the story he finger-wiped his face, sometimes backwards, sometimes chin-dabbing, and often all over, kneading into flesh. Afterwards, as he listened, he continued fidgeting, eyeing the walls.

Prompted by Vanessa, he spoke of getting heavy and acts to choose from. There was, he said, *The Bastard* – who spoke low, with menace, said things only once (here he dropped quiet to an interrogative whisper) – *The Revenger* and *Grudge Pursuer* – both relentless, keeping notes of everything – and *The Madcap Clobberer*, who struck when least expected, joked as he punished, behaved as if possessed.

"So actually," said Vanessa, widening her eyes, "behind it all you're afraid – same as us?"

"Uh-uh. Terrified. In case they see through me."

Jackie confirmed, inspecting her partner.

"And I thought it was just me..." Vanessa said, holding her drink up towards a candle.

Richard knelt forward. Where the flame showed in glass it was blue, blue-yellow and softened to a glow. He noticed, lower, a faint spread of orange and, where her fingers held the stem, a near-white axis.

"The harder they come," he nodded, registering the clear-toned music, repeating on the stereo.

Frank smiled. "Now that's what they call real fighting—"

Vanessa shook her head. "Only if you're a macho and think it's about what you're *against*. A man is a man is a man. And that's it, end of story... There *are* other ways."

"Hmm, but do they always work?"

"Well, if everyone was willing—"

Richard grinned, "You mean if we had a be-nice-to-the-kids week?"

Jackie shuddered, "God forbid."

"You wouldn't fancy that?"

"Too many yucks. Rather not think about it."

Richard turned his gaze on Frank. "So what's the secret, boss? What goes through your head when you're hammering kids?"

The other man sat back, stroking his chin. "Not much, if I can help it."

"But behind that. What're you thinking about?"

"Misspent youth – and my father."

The room fell silent. Richard nodded, replenishing his glass. The song's last notes issued from the speaker.

"It's about what you can get away with," Frank added. He reached forward, cupping his palm and bringing it down slowly on a half-lit candle. Hissing quietly, the flame spluttered out. He removed his hand, and a wisp-line of smoke curled towards the window.

Outside, a plane passed over, droning quietly. Its navigation lights moved across the sky, winking on and off.

Frank sighed. "The trick is," he said quietly, "to keep 'em looking the other way." He reached again, facing his hosts and grinning, as he passed his hand through yellow spurts of flame. "Of course it'll get to you," he said, slowing one finger till the flame licked the skin. "But it's nothing. An illusion. All smoke and mirrors."

A faint sweet smell drifted in the room. Frank smiled, unflinching. His flesh had darkened.

"And however much it hurts," he added, withdrawing his finger and smiling even harder, "make 'em think you enjoy it."

The evening with Frank and Jackie was, as it turned out, both an end and a beginning. From that point on, the first shock of teaching, with its panics and exhaustions and its all-out demands, began to slacken off. They'd learned how to handle it – to get through whatever happened – to think on their feet, joke, give orders and build a reputation. Known by name, with a year group to tutor, they were listed by department and appeared now in the bulletins as established staff. Their presence was accepted. And with experience, they knew what to watch for, how to dodge, how to deliver and gap-fill as necessary. They were in the clear as qualified teachers, judging and presenting, looking back on where they'd come from, looking all over (sometimes) for worksheets and equipment, and forward to the holidays. And as they moved into the break they saw how they'd changed.

They developed their downtime, their quickly taken pleasures, living for the moment at off-times and weekends. They were on the A list for contact, pop-ins and late-night entertainment. And being always busy – awake and alive and pushed to the limits – although it raised the tempo (and left them feeling breathless), it also made for pressure, a singleness of aim, which blocked out the day job. To work exhausted overrode their feelings. It meant they didn't notice. Especially for Richard who felt he'd lost his bearings. He'd gone in, committed, and now he needed something – a true sense of purpose, a long-term view.

He'd no words for it. Whatever it was he'd sensed it all his life. A feeling that behind the actual, tricked in and hidden, concealed within the flow, was a pattern and a code. A hang-thread of meaning. Something understood. A signature and a pointer felt within life, a shadow line of being.

In the past he'd tried to ignore. Told himself, as a teenager, that it only ever happened when he went *looking* (usually on walks where he made himself feel it, lived through his senses, searched for what went deep) – and what he called uplift or presence was something which he'd generated, was all rather wished-for and only ever touched him because he'd made it so…

"Breathe deep," he told himself, walking.

"Too much chatter," he repeated, standing.

"Just be *quiet*," he hissed, choosing to move on.

… Because there was this element of will. An all-too-conscious purpose. He'd gone for the scenic, ignored what didn't suit, and closed his eyes to anything inconvenient.

In fact his walkouts were not that remarkable. The paths were quite narrow, fenced and overgrown, sandwiched between opencast and newly-built estates. And where he struck through fields or climbed through trees there was still the sound of cars, hammers striking metal and shouts from pitches. And even on his moor walks (longer and more remote, through gorse lands and heather with skylarks climbing over burnt-out patches and yellow-lichened rock) when he moved beyond habitation, there was a suspicion that he pumped himself up, his vision was contrived and that the transport he experienced was of his own making.

In any case, he'd things to control. A number of distractions. Internals, fragments, familiars. Aspects of self he'd tried to hide away.

The odd bod was there, the one he called 'the haggler', the clever-clever mouthpiece who put on different voices, whispered leery comments and said things brusquely, cutting in often to rerun his worst moments and point out where he'd failed. Odd bod and friends. The cartoon menagerie. He knew them well. The jostlers, the moaners, the never-satisfied watchers (with their crew of commentators, chatterers, speakers, message-givers) – the hey-theres and the bores. Flies in the bathroom, theme tunes, sirens, and engines running rough. Broadcasts, sound bites, radio static. Babel-like, his head was full of them.

And the meaning, it seemed, had slipped off into nothingness.

"Oh no oh no no no no no," he heard (or imagined).

"Ugg-ugg-ugg-ugg-ugg," his inner voice stuttered.

"Da da da da da," echoed in his head.

Later, in the sixth form, he'd found it again, this time in his jottings, song lines, wordplays, automatic writings. Suddenly the words made sense. Or at least he'd a beginning, pointers, clear terms of reference. What he understood was tone and register, the loose run of language. Feather-light phrases suggested by his studies which floated to the surface, appeared with the sun, popping in and out. They were the carriers, the expressives, the one tenth of consciousness that signalled off. Scraps and keepsakes. Slogans, reminders. What he called his 'lines'.

He wrote them down on envelopes and loose bits of paper which he added to the reminders stuffed into his pocket. When the collection built up he transferred to a bag, then archived to a drawer where they lay piled up like unread letters. Occasionally he sorted, chucking some, wincing over others, and attempting rewrites where a line or expression sounded promising.

But somehow that was all. Once he'd turned a phrase or juggled with a sentence he couldn't see beyond, a block set in and however hard he tried the words remained shy. Something dropped out. His writing lacked substance; it wasn't really there. The whole thing was diversionary. It was as if he'd run himself out, had reached the home straight, and anything further was more than he could do.

So when teaching started he put aside the words, forgot or ignored, and worked the here and now. And for a while his life was taken up by marking, instructing, looking round for extracts and rehearsing lessons. He'd no time it seemed for thoughts about life-choices, truths about self or what really mattered.

So he managed, or put aside his feelings. He kept himself busy and what he called aware – balanced, directed, always on the case. He'd always had presence and now he'd added knowhow and what passed for judgement.

He called it *doing Frank*.

With Vanessa he called it (in private) *reckoning* and (in public) *presenting*. Sometimes playing host, he called it (to himself) *juggling,* as he settled and passed round. Out drinking he was floorshow; late night, talking, he was up for it; and when it came to dinner parties or drop-ins he was on the case.

In fact he made it happen (as he sang, internally, when hosting Vanessa's birthday with guests arriving carrying plastic-wrapped bouquets and bottles for the fridge). He welcomed, and he led off.

"Eyes closed – everyone!" he called from the kitchen, bringing out a heart-shaped cake, topped by candles.

He placed it in the centre of a fold-out table which he'd fully extended and positioned in the living room, pushing back the sofa. Looking round the room he counted faces – seven in all –

arranged on four sides, bench-like, as if they were in session. Jackie sat at the head, one side was occupied by Ruth, then Frank, then his own empty chair, at the other end Vanessa had the window seat, while the fourth side was occupied by Doug and two friends of Vanessa's: Lorna, a smooth-faced narrow-lipped beauty, and Ginny, who was short, broad-mouthed and flushed around the brow.

With their tightly closed eyes and candle-lit faces they looked for a moment like a group-shot from a film.

"Open sesame!" he cried, taking his seat.

"Oh, look!" said Ruth, opening first.

The other guests opened, adding their comments. There were laughs and gasps and expressions of surprise.

Richard led the singing, the call for blowing out, and orchestrated the applause which followed. He also produced the knife, presented the cake, and helped Vanessa to pass round slices.

"Did you make this?" asked Ruth, as she licked and sampled.

Richard grinned, "Don't ask."

They ate, chatting and comparing. The room was busy and warm and full of shifting voices. There were people singing out, chairs drawn together, glasses raised. As the evening progressed the voices overlapped, merged, then took their separate ways. Though different and quite distinctive they shared a common purpose. They were allies in the struggle.

Richard found himself sparring at first with Frank and others. Then acting as link-man, passing on messages, dotting here and there. Later in the evening he played the role of interviewer: listening, probing, inviting comment. Still later, he picked up on threads and summarised back. In the end he returned to sparring, putting down markers with a narrow-eyed Frank, fishing for 'inside' on policy and plans.

"Sworn to secrecy," the other replied.

"And when you're Head—"

"He'll sack the lot of you," Jackie put in, expressionless.

The two men engaged in banter about hard-man tactics and taming classes. When they moved on to politics Richard, who had his eyes elsewhere, leaned towards Lorna inviting her views.

"We need a different agenda," she said, flicking back her lightly-frizzed hair. It was red, red-ginger and fell to her shoulders.

"Different – how?"

Lorna glanced towards Vanessa, who was listening in. "Women in the lead. Supported by men."

"Fat chance," Ginny snorted.

"You never know," said Frank, "it could be popular."

"I'd like it," Vanessa said brightly. "We could be the trainers. Operant conditioning. The Skinner approach."

"You like rats in cages?" Richard countered.

Ginny cut in. "I object," she declared. "Rats are super-intelligent animals. It's the experimenters who should be caged."

"And throw away the key," added Frank, grinning.

"I'm serious. How would you like it: being locked up and given shocks?"

"Sounds like my childhood," he replied, wiping one hand across his face.

"I heard," interposed Richard, "that rats are cleaner than humans."

Ginny nodded. "That's a fact."

"And so much more cuddly," added Frank.

"Unlike men."

"That's true," echoed Vanessa.

"Indeed," put in Jackie.

"Exactly," said Lorna.

"Absolutely," concluded Ginny.

Next morning Richard called in sick. As he told himself quietly, before Vanessa left, he really wasn't well. Whatever it was – something he'd eaten, a bug, or simply lack of sleep – the effects were unpleasant. His answerphone message, giving name and timetable and describing the work, was carefully worded. Though precise it came out, even to himself, as hollow-voiced and strained. He sounded rough but was trying not to show it. What he didn't give was background, or any kind of reason, mainly because if he said 'migraine' it might invite suspicion. And in any case what he was experiencing was far more uncertain, more off-centre, and far less specific.

Five hours earlier at the end of the party, he'd been on a high. After seeing people off and pinching out candles, he'd drifted bed-wards. Undressing slowly, he'd slipped beneath the sheets, where he lay thinking back. Hearing Vanessa washing in the bathroom he'd rerun the evening, replaying voices, seeing expressions, matching words with faces. When she'd flicked out the light and joined him, he'd squeezed and kissed, then returned to his thoughts. The dark was his screen. It brought things closer.

As her breathing slowed he'd pictured her surprise, the jokey encouragements, passing round the cake. He knew from things said how much she'd enjoyed it. The evening had gone well. He'd given what she wanted. In the dark he touched flesh, shifted on his side, matched to her breathing. Despite the thickness – the wine-soft glow, the blur around the edges – he saw it all happening, was awake and in the picture.

The clock tick, magnified, seemed to fill the room. Voices and footsteps echoed on pavement. Somewhere in the distance a siren circled.

Knowing it was late made him restless. He'd only a few hours. Although it was dark, a brightness held him, a backlit feeling, as if the room's outline was a curtain, a veil across the actual, soon to be lifted. He could sense already the bodies moving, the radio-alarms, could feel in himself the sense of things stirring, the shift between modes. Soon they'd be yawning, calling out questions and collecting their things. Then last words in hallways, and doors clicking shut.

For what seemed hours he traced back and counted, moved positions, tried different angles. Unable to settle, he felt there was a grip, a pressure-lock and tightness building in his head. For a while he lay still, hoping it would pass. But the ache had its way. The more he ignored, the stronger it became. Head pains like this, he remembered from childhood, came on strong, usually without warning, and could remain for days.

Rising, he passed out quietly, feeling into dark. In the hall he was cornered. Mixed in with the outlines was an unseen brightness; a glare, and an avenue back. Shifting round the flat, he placed himself outside and beyond, standing by a window, somewhere without feeling. The pain, and the quiet, absorbed him in whiteness; his life till now, the things locked under, the backlog and the loss.

For a while he sat, then stood. He visited the kitchen, boiled up a kettle, sipped at coffee, returning after dawn to lie beside Vanessa.

When she woke he smiled, touched her lightly, limiting his expression. He wondered about school, gauged his own fitness, then told her quietly that he wasn't that grand...

"You feeling ill?"

He nodded.

"Hangover?"

"No, not that. Just not good."

Vanessa sat up, switched on the side lamp and examined him.

"Really. I'm not..."

She raised one eyebrow.

"I mean, not well."

She asked about symptoms and he repeated.

"Oh dear, are you staying at home?"

He nodded.

"I'll get ready then," she said, "hope you get better."

Feeling slightly awkward he nodded again.

"You'll manage?" she called when ready, standing by the bed. "I mean by yourself?"

Richard sat up and squared his expression. "I'll be fine," he said, waving her off. She asked again and he shrugged. "Unwell," he added, sliding down.

He repeated his watchword, once as she left, twice on paper, then often (during the day) as fallback or secret reminder as he lay out on the sofa, imagining the school buzz and what people might say. He could see himself nodding, sitting in the staffroom drinking coffee, greeting people, chin up and jokey. He was with them and separate, careful with his answers, and alert to what they said. Somehow he'd become subject, stepped back, turned towards image, and had put himself out of it.

That day made it clear. While he picked at biscuits or lay out on the bed listening to the radio (turned down to a whisper, imagining Vanessa – her chalk-face efforts, and how she might feel), he came to see himself as someone at a distance, a stranger or oddball who didn't really fit. The illness (what was it?) had turned him back. Of course, he *could* have taught, wasn't that poorly, but had chosen the dodge. And in faking or simply ducking out he'd entered (it seemed) a shadowland feeling, something unexpected, an area in reverse. He'd touched on meaning.

When Vanessa returned – late and tired, pushing through the door with a bag full of books – he'd framed and reported, sketched his condition. He'd listened then, asked about work. What sort of day... and had anything happened? Not much, she said, mentioning an incident, an event, one name, two. People, she added, had wished him well.

In reply he'd nodded. They'd not discussed feelings or gone below the surface.

During their meal, which consisted of leftovers, they'd talked about domestics. Later it was next day's school and whether he'd get there. Still later, after clearing and watching television, she'd asked for the time then suggested, yawning, that they move off to bed.

It seemed all over. Whatever had touched him had passed without remark.

It was when Richard found himself lying awake (reworking experience: the day off and what it might lead to) that he saw – or glimpsed – his life in replay. A build up of images, accumulated incidents, stories running back. Yes, they were all there. Tricks played by memory, anecdotes, spin-offs, items in the flow. Counting, he registered. Frank's finger in flame. Nights by the window with plane lights and stars. Car drives and talk. The accident in the garden. Train sets and covers, pictures on the stairs. Ruth at the party. Walks in the park. Bookshops, stations, florists, music shops and markets. And – reaching back further – his search for Vanessa, the handbag, the river-bridge and the slow-moving thunder of the first departing train.

CHAPTER SEVEN

When she first heard him say it, Vanessa wasn't pleased.

Enough. ENOUGH, with emphasis (then muttered, as an aside). Or *Enough is enough*.

The phrase or word pronounced as given, then repeated with edge. A word of dismissal, a quick word with a frown. A voice on the up with force and control and direction and teacher-like intonation. A phrase or expletive which he gave out as pointer, lecturing almost (with self-forced assurance, an act of definition) and then left it.

Enough, or too much.

Because when he'd first said it (huffing and puffing as he decorated the lounge) she'd repeated to Ruth – told her with a grin and a throwaway gesture. She'd echoed how he'd spoken, narrowing and hardening and setting her expression. The man at a distance. The one who pronounced. Who thought and weighed and reckoned, expecting silence. For him it was definite. He'd got that straight. And from then on she took note, kept up a count, a mark each time, so that soon it was established – voice tone, incidence, minor variations, overall total and positions taken.

He'd used it on the children, only too often, turning their marriage – until then an up and down business – into something close to war. A small war in bits, unsettled and niggly, a struggle not to say things – shifting into blow-ups with cross-shots and appeals and claims of obstruction. He'd implied it daily in the way he took offence, making out she'd said things or alleging intention, and he'd kept it in reserve, hidden behind jargon, when they took things to counsellors, speaking about listening and investing time.

He'd said it most recently that very morning when the children had been arguing (one of those blow ups, with Charlotte in the bathroom and a red-faced Stephan rattling the handle). He'd said it again when asked at the table to exercise patience, and had – typically – repeated at the door. It was, after all – as she said to him quickly as he questioned timings – *her* turn with the children and *his* to go to work.

During the day she ticked off other mentions. The second on an outing – seaside, blowy, with Charlotte as a baby – the third after school, several in the car, others at random and various interruptions cutting through her thoughts, calling or frowning or speaking at volume, either bossing children or loud in the hallway while she chatted on the phone.

"Richard's got problems," was what she gave out – at least to those politicos, women like Lorna who wanted explanation.

"He has this *agenda*," she added, speaking slowly, when round on visits.

"It's textbook really: the XY factor," she concluded, with an eye to effect.

And part of her believed it. Held it as established, a fact of life. He needed control. Ever since marriage he'd adopted *positions*: theories about work and the treatment of children – arbitrary mainly, but some so determined that she felt the need to counter, to pose a different view. Though she also recognised the pleasures of obstruction, the need to level up.

Of course she understood. Knew what to expect. Or she understood the patterns, the pull-backs and the twists, the line they had to tread. And Richard wasn't that easy or relaxed or obvious – or at all like other people thought. He'd his own fads, his traits, his ways of fitting *everything*. Whatever was the latest – well, that was it. And when he'd pronounced or named or fitted, then suddenly without warning he lost all interest. It was as if nothing mattered, or things just existed as objects recognised, given shape and format by what he had to say.

So she was prepared when she returned to the house. Watchful and set. Ready for off. The kids led in, occupying the lounge and arguing over channels as they squatted on the carpet. For a while she watched and smiled (still hearing Ruth: her quick one-liners and jokes about men) – while holding to delay. Here she felt safe. Surrounded by her brood. She appealed on volume, once, twice, asked them to be sensible then, after idling on the sofa and listening vaguely, retreated to the kitchen. On reaching the door, she paused and checked down the room.

She knew he'd be marking (sat out in the garden with a drink, holding to his patch). By now he'd be on concrete, moving with the sun, retreated to the fence. A watcher in the garden, notebook in hand. Perhaps he'd be relaxed, maybe even Friday-ish, but also he'd have *thoughts* – on supper for a start, but most likely on the children – with his own expected timings, his whims and theories. He'd have his own angle, a laid-out plan. Something dogmatic, a portion of himself. And because she knew him well (and judged it best to ease things into place), she made herself busy, brewing up and nodding, looking when he called, and greeting on-the-level when he entered.

"You're home then?" he said quietly, glancing round the kitchen.

Vanessa confirmed.

"How've they been?"

She answered off the point, and offered tea.

"Uh huh," he continued, blinking.

While pouring, she talked – vaguely, in abstract, posing questions. The cups filled slowly. Every so often the pot in her hand, which was dark brown and chipped, had to be shaken.

"Don't mind," he replied when she asked about milk.

"Same old, same old," he said, shrugging, when school came up.

"Done for today," he added, pointing down the garden.

Following his gaze, Vanessa gave a nod.

Outside and at a distance the air had thickened. Close-to, there were patches of grey and green, shading into purple. Cross-hatched shadows had spread across the lawn.

Richard drained his cup, then asked about her day.

"Not much to report," she said.

When asked again she offered more tea, half-filled carefully, then went through in detail, missing out Ruth. She'd delivered to school, mailed out to contacts, cleaned and shopped – then picked up and taken to the park.

"And now…" she said vaguely, looking round the kitchen.

Richard shook his head. "I'll do it," he said, meaning supper.

She started to offer, then thought better. "OK. I'll be upstairs, in my room," she said, setting her mouth.

In fact, when she arrived at her office – after pausing mid-landing and listening to the children laughing – she sat by the table considering what to do. She could still hear him talking. In her mind he was the presenter. The sound of his voice, magnified back, echoed like a jingle running round her head. Underneath the casual was a charge. Words inside words. Sounding correction.

But up here it was quiet. A space for doing tasks. Her hideout, workshop and camera obscura. Tucked into the eaves, with a cast-iron fireplace and two shallow alcoves – she'd made it her own. Filled it and used it and put up her pics. Stored her film, tied back the curtains and lined the shelves with plants and cards. Because this was where she was at home. But also where she worked – with its date-lists, post-its and invites to shows – and place of refuge.

Yes, a room of her own.

She sat in silence, examining the desktop. Something about it connected backwards. It touched on Ruth and their talk about the photos. Like them it was so. An everyday reminder.

Carefully she considered. It was wooden and split-level, with a wide central area, surrounded on three sides by a low containing edge. At the back it thickened, where a row of handles gave access to pull-out drawers.

They'd found it in the market. Bought it for a song and humped it back, for Richard to work on. He'd stripped and sanded and stained as required. Putting it in place had been after decorating – a week or so of scraping and banging and up and down stairs with paint pots and rags and large mugs of tea. He'd occupied the room as if it was his studio. Filled it with dust sheets and radio voices and muddled guitars. Getting up early, he'd worked all weekend, DIY-obsessed. She remembered as she sat there: his hair pushed back, body-line, angle and bright-eyed abstraction. He'd that very-special-look. The look of awareness, of doing his own thing.

She drew her fingers lightly along the top. She remembered how they'd carried it. Lifted and turned, resting on the landing. Forward and back: she could still feel the balance, the push-pull and the hump. And Richard, calling out. Do this, do that. Whatever he said.

She rose to look out. The light had extended: bright and watery but solid as well, in places it had pooled, filling into outline. In the gardens it had spread; on the walls it shaped blocks – while above that, and advancing, it planed off into grey.

She pulled down the sash, and cool air entered. There were sounds of preparation: of taps running water – door slams and choppings and plates that clashed. She could hear, further down, voices in the garden and party-ish music. The other way a dog. TV theme tunes and a baby crying. An argument beginning. And beyond that and off – shifting and extending and filling in the gaps – the sounds of traffic.

It seemed as she listened that her thoughts had expanded. She could see it all, laid out and magnified, a bird's eye view. They'd come here, renovated, made this place their own. Set up as expected and given their vows – with mortgage and children – seen things through. They'd played the perfect couple, done what people did, made their moves.

And now, after talking and trying and so much effort, they'd arrived at this.

Downstairs, something registered. It was Richard in the kitchen, on supper-call. His voice came in snatches that held around a note. They were required.

Suddenly she shivered. Pulled back and away. Felt the distance. The highs, the lows, the need to stay separate. She was above that now. From here she could see it: a contract, an exchange, a textbook case. A matter of economics. Or security. What they used to call settling. A norm-referenced thing. Mainly, of course, for purposes practical. Arrangements, dispositions, a question of timings. And soon – here she scanned the gardens – she'd be down there at table, back within the narrowness, the insistence, whatever had to be. She could hear him now calling harder, pitching into air. Hand-cupped (probably), heavy and determined. His voice on the up, the TV at volume, the meal sounds and directives (with stops and starts and demands they eat up) and after-supper battles when he cut through their protests and forced the kids to bed...

While outside, in the garden...

For Richard, Vanessa's retreat made it easier to regulate the kids. It allowed him to be. It also avoided issues that rankled. Power-led splits and matters of dispute. Intention and opinion: how things were decided. The rules, and how to bend them.

So part of him hoped, when he called her down, that she'd delay her appearance or regard it as optional – because when in fact she showed (without, he noticed, any recognition of what he'd done for supper) he had to admit, in all honesty, that he didn't really like it. Her presence was obstructive. She put in, cross-called, encouraged opposition. The more he did, the more she stirred up. It was her and the kids matched against him.

During the evening there were several up-and-downers: firstly at table when the kids (before even tasting) appealed against the food, a quiet period when they picked and complained, a go-slow stretch leading to gloom, then later (cheering up) when Vanessa agreed to a fridge-raid before they'd finished.

"Just wait. I want you to eat a portion each," Richard said, taking a knife to each plate. He divided both down the middle and presented back. "You choose – which half."

"But Dad!" protested Charlotte.

"Which one?"

"I'm full," complained Stephan.

"Choose."

The children dropped silent.

Vanessa took their part.

"One or the other," said Richard, grimly.

Vanessa, frowning, pleaded their case.

"Oh, Dad..." Charlotte added.

"What I said. Choose," he insisted, scowling.

Vanessa tried again, more reasonable now.

"It's necessary," he shot back.

"But is it working?"

Richard grimaced. He wanted to insist. To make her see what was happening. How she set it all up. But also he wanted to take himself off, shrug and walk away. It seemed so predictable. All rivalry and shoot-outs. It needed to end.

And yet, he wondered. The kids, it seemed, were out there in the middle. Caught between camps.

"You tell me," he said, glaring.

"I don't want them… to have… problems."

"Problems?"

Vanessa gestured behind Charlotte's back. She was refusing food.

Richard frowned: "They have to get used to eating – and without a fuss. You know what Ruth's boys are like."

"But this is a fuss."

He shrugged. "Maybe it's fuss that works."

Later in the evening, when the kids had been bedded and she'd cleaned the front room, Vanessa took her turn to watch TV. Switching channels, she settled on a film. Although not exactly chosen, it fitted to her mood – could be watched vaguely, as a filler, without close attention. Set in the 50s, it was clipped and rather upper, with the kind of mannered style that Richard – speaking offhand with his *I'm-in-charge* expression – called 'ha-ha stuff'. As she lay back and viewed, she could hear his dismissals. 'Lightweight' or 'clichéd' or 'of no real interest'. He'd have no time, didn't know why she bothered, it really wouldn't do. His opinions were on record.

In any case, with him in the background – writing his notebooks or playing the piano – she was happy. It gave her space. There was no need to battle or present a point of view.

When the film finally ended – after meetings by chance on harbours and yachts, leading to fly-aways and beach-walks with drinks – she flicked between channels, sampling different shows. She knew, or hoped, that by now he'd be in bed. That way, when she joined him, he might stay asleep. As she lingered at a sitcom which seemed half-familiar, her attention wandered. A smoothness entered, a feeling of immersion, as the screen began to blur. There were voices and movements, sometimes colour-blocks, occasional scene-changes and faces in studios, talking or listening, but mostly looking bland.

Divided now, she was drawn to bed; but an edge – or indifference – kept her on the sofa. She was on duty, and didn't want to stop. It was as if she was on night watch and had to see it through. Of course there had been movements – door shifts, sighs, footsteps overhead – but she still preferred to wait. Watch and wait and plan her next move. Not till she was ready…

Finally, after sampling soaps, holiday tasters and sports she'd never heard of, she turned off at the socket and climbed to the bedroom.

As expected, it was dark and quiet. The door handle creaked and a corner scraped across carpet. Once in, she adjusted. She could see his outline, pushing up the covers. His breathing had stilled, and for a moment she wondered. There were words she'd like to say, abstracts, reckonings, matters of importance. As she moved to the bedside she talked herself through. She supposed he might be listening – imagined how he'd counter – questioned and adjusted, calmed her expression. Perhaps, she thought, observing a light-streak falling on his hair, he wasn't that bad. She sat on the bed edge, peering at his face. Though worn and slightly sunken, sleep had smoothed it. Caught in the light, like a reprint from an album, his boy-face had returned.

Undressing, she rolled in. Lying full-length and touching against flesh, his name came up. Not flat-voiced and hostile but warmer, more rounded, spoken into thought. As the syllables repeated she noticed him stirring. Awareness returned, his eyes flickered slightly, then opened.

"Time?" he asked sleepily.

"Late," she returned quietly.

His hand touched her waist.

"Did I wake you?"

"I'm not sure. Maybe."

Vanessa weighed his mood. In the half-dark he had softened.

"It's weekend," she said.

He grunted. His hand found her breasts.

"You OK?" he asked.

She allowed, not saying anything.

He continued feeling and touching lightly. There were kisses exchanged, turns and attentions, a work of hands. While her thoughts went on running (hearing the children, recapping incidents, recalling TV) Vanessa felt her body, her otherness taking over. She was at centre, given into feeling.

His hand found her hers and guided downwards. "Nice," he said as she stroked and cupped back under. She was playing with him now, smoothing and grooming as if he was an animal. "Hmm, that's it," he said and began to shiver. Suddenly he hauled up and mounted. A force took over, a quickness and insistence, and he was pushing into dark, driving his way in. A rhythm set up, jerky at first but gradually lengthening and deepening. She could feel him in her, going forward: short-breathed and urgent, making it happen.

The rhythm gathered pace. Vanessa felt inward and cupped, filled with softness. The thoughts kept interrupting – random and scattered — but her body was in action, rising and expanding – firming itself up. She had that feeling: a shooting, running, in-out pressure. It held and fitted, pushed and took up, then gripped all over. She wanted and had to, and yet she was deliberate – deliberate or forced – and then, with a wriggle and jump, it really didn't matter. All ran together, the dark took over and she clenched. And when she came it was short, involuntary and repeated.

Richard followed on. He stiffened, heaved and pitched himself forward. His body came down, for a second he sprawled, then side-rolled, panting.

They lay there side by side. Vanessa was breathing deeply, like a swimmer on her back. Richard had one arm crooked up, with his elbow dug in, planted on the pillow. His face had smoothed and his hair was matted.

"Enough?" he asked quietly.

In the dark Vanessa nodded.

That weekend they made a fresh start. A new way of doing things. At first by implication, between eating breakfast, supervising children and opening letters. For once they shared a space, a moment of arrest and quiet between them, a settlement. While the kids watched television, they occupied the kitchen, with Richard sampling poetry while Vanessa scanned the paper. Between reading and clearing and one-off observations (on weather, on friends, on weekend outings) and a walk-out by Richard reporting on the garden, they kept themselves together, in touch, almost (it seemed) returned to how it was.

Later they'd a meeting, an invite from Lorna to what she called the group (a collective set up, she said, to talk about the struggle and support women's feelings) – which sounded, they thought, of interest – though mainly for Vanessa, who didn't want to miss out. Lorna, she felt, was on the same wavelength. First time round she'd recognised their kinship – an eye for what mattered. They put women first.

So when Lorna phoned, confirming timings and who might be there, Vanessa took the call (talking of 'warmth' and 'shared experience') while Richard bowed out. Adopting the role of observer he sat on the stairs, two steps up. Leaning against plaster he followed, nodding, as she hmm-ed and aah-ed. For now it seemed he didn't have to sort things, and for that he was thankful. He'd rather sit back, play the role of follower. In any case he could tell (catching Lorna's drift from Vanessa's manner) that the process of decision was seen by the women as important.

Richard continuing listening as he moved into action. It seemed, from asides and confirmatory statements, that there was lunch provided, a large attendance likely – friends and their supporters – and some kids' entertainment, planned for later, involving an actor and physical theatre.

When the call finally ended, Richard was smiling. The television was silent and the kids were upstairs, dressing.

Vanessa looked around. "How on earth did you manage that?"

"Just told them."

"Told them… that's it?"

"That's right."

"So what did you say?"

"Oh, a few suggestions."

"But you actually *told* them?"

"Uh huh. I made them an offer…"

"You mean—"

"Followed by a clip round the ear."

"I hope not…"

"Shouted and yelled."

"Richard—"

"Then threatened them with death."

Vanessa set her mouth. She knew of course, but wasn't backing down.

"I gave them ten to dress," he added, glancing at his watch.

"Seconds?"

Richard sighed. "Hours, of course."

Vanessa ignored, switching to the weather and what Charlotte would wear.

"The red skirt, I suppose," he said. "But I don't think it matters," he added, "as long as she wears something."

"Yes, provided it's clean and sensible," Vanessa said, glancing up the stairs.

"Ah well," he laughed, "best if I pass on this one."

She nodded. "As you wish," she said slowly, gazing into space.

"Not my thing," he added, ducking to a drawer and pulling out bags.

Richard left the children to Vanessa, saying he'd some items to pick up, and popped out to the shops. His absence, which was deliberate, was a kind of intermission. A breather for them both. It allowed her to function. To calm and settle and think without pressure. And for Vanessa, his walkout – which turned out to be

116

lengthy – offered opportunity. Her own clear space. It meant she could be there to help and give what was needed.

Stephan that morning wasn't doing well. It seemed he'd been picked on. Bad things had happened. In fact the word *unfair* was written all over him. There'd been a dispute, a battle over programmes, then a wait for the bathroom, so that by the time it came to dressing he'd lost all interest. Vanessa encouraged, then left him. He had to learn, she said as she left, to do things by himself. But when she checked back later he was still in his night things, sat on the bed end fingering the buttons of a hand-held game.

"Come on, lovey," she said, "dressing time."

Eyeing the screen as if it might be dangerous, he continued playing. Strange bleeps and whizzes issued from the consol.

His mother repeated, examining the display.

Stephan twitched, pressing buttons. Something popped, followed by repeated explosions.

"We're going out," she added patiently.

"Just finish this game."

Vanessa nodded, then asked how long that would be.

"One minute."

She smiled, and air-gazed quietly.

Charlotte entered, brandishing a hair band. It was red and shell-shaped, with a curled-over top and elasticated grips.

"Mum!"

Vanessa turned, widening her eyes.

"Can you do this... the way you do..." Reversing and tossing back her hair, the girl held out her band.

Vanessa examined, then gathered and shaped to a hair-knot, which she crisscrossed with elastic. "How's that?" she asked, manoeuvring to the mirror.

Charlotte looked and approved, then noticing Stephan, pulled a face. "What's he doing?" she demanded. "Why's he not dressed?"

"In a minute," said Vanessa evenly. She turned to the boy: "That's what you promised, isn't it Stephan?"

The reply was a crunch and a series of metallic hits.

"Then why's he got that game?"

Her mother, smiling, referred the question on.

"Take it off him," Charlotte cut in. "Take it, or he'll never get ready." She hovered her hand forward, threatening to grab.

Stephan rocked back, shielding his game. Battlefield noises filled the room.

"See! You must stop him!"

Vanessa flushed. "Don't, lovey," she said, glancing back and forth.

"Turn it off!" Charlotte demanded, covering the screen.

Stephan squealed and pushed her away. As they struggled for possession the game slipped sideways and dropped to the floor.

The boy swung down, attempting a save. Before he could reach it the screen gave a clatter and a high-pitched whistle, then cut off into silence.

He gathered it up. "Look!" he cried. *"First time ever.* I was winning!"

He turned his attention to his mother, brandishing the game and demanding reparation.

Vanessa listened, expressionless.

"It's just a stupid game," his sister cut in, speaking flatly.

Stephan scowled. "Not yours," he muttered.

Returning to the bed end he sat, switched on his screen and began jabbing buttons.

Charlotte shrugged, "Leave him to his *game.*" She turned to the mirror, twisting sideways to view her hair. "We can go without him. *He'll* be happy anyway."

Stephan flared, "You'd like that!"

The girl stepped behind her mother, poking out her tongue.
"Don't!"

She pushed it out further, rolling her eyes
"No!"

Curling her tongue, she flicked it in and out.

Stephan pointed. "See her! See her!" he cried screwing up his face.

Charlotte ducked forward. "See her!" she echoed, grinning.

Vanessa, looking baffled, appealed again.

"Not nice," he said, more quietly, putting down his game.

"Not—" his sister began, then cut off, looking thoughtful.

Richard appeared. Expressing his displeasure, he asked about the noise. His enquiry, which was delivered without emphasis (yet sounded rather threatening) had a calming effect. There was menace there, hidden. When no one answered, he checked on his watch.

"I don't know what you think you're doing. We should have left already."

His gaze swept the room as if in inspection. He'd set his expression to a warning smile (a school trick he'd adopted, modelled on Frank). Seeing Stephan he paused, took measure, then finger-stroked his chin. "So what're you up to?" he asked. When the boy remained silent he asked again, more sharply.

"Best just leave it," interposed Vanessa. "Things will sort out."

"No, no. He's not happy," Charlotte sang out. Her voice tone faltered. "It's 'cos of me."

Peering at his son, Richard raised one eyebrow. "That right?" he asked.

Stephan nodded. His face was white.

"So what will make it better?"

The boy shrugged vaguely. He was close to tears.

"I know," said Charlotte, "I can do it." She sat down on the bed and turned to face her brother. "Sorry Stephan," she said.

"That's good – very kind," chorused Vanessa.

Stephan looked doubtful.

Charlotte smiled warmth. "I mean it," she added. "Sorry Stephan."

Her brother nodded.

"Well," concluded Richard, "when you're ready—"

"Shall we leave?" asked Vanessa.

Stephan confirmed. Standing, he picked up his game and placed it to one side on the bedside cabinet. After pressing several buttons he peeked at the screen then offered to be ready. He'd do it in five. As his family left the room, the game gave out a series of whacks and crunches, followed by a bang, a high-pitched whistle and a bell-tone, ringing.

On the drive to Lorna's, Stephan played his game, Charlotte divided her time between colouring in and staring out the window, while Vanessa guided. Richard, driving, took direction.

They passed through the city, quiet and empty with plate glass offices, constructions in steel, neo-classical buildings and boarded-up plots. There were pubs with bunting, billboards, paper stands and the odd small café selling drinks and snacks. Richard named the churches – often only towers, or walls with plaques – while Vanessa looked for road names. At a station concourse there were couples with suitcases and men hailing taxis. As they moved beyond the centre they drove past a market, a cinema, a large municipal building, then turned left at a pub to follow a one-way road between tall Victorian houses. The buildings hemmed them in. They were terraced without gardens, mostly residential but occasionally with signboards and shops beneath. Near the end Vanessa called a street name for the kids to spot.

"Combination Row. Should be last on the right," she said, smiling.

Charlotte saw it first, naming at a distance, and again as they turned in. "We've been before," she reminded.

Stephan, when they arrived and parked, was first out to the gate. He marched up the path, leading his mother, and banged on the knocker. Charlotte joined him and the two stood waiting, pressed against wood. Stephan banged again then peered through the letterbox. He rattled the flap and his mother shushed him. When Lorna appeared, embracing Vanessa, the boy slipped through. Calling to his sister, he led to the back room where two pink-faced girls were squatted on the floor surrounded by rubbish. Behind them a half-open French window led to an overgrown garden.

"Hi," said Xena, the older, who was leaning forward, eyeing the television as if it had offended.

Charlotte entered, and the younger girl looked up. Echoing her sister, Melissa greeted. They were spread across the floor with picture books and comics and see-through plastic wallets. The wallets, which were large, were filled with ribbons, heart-shaped stickers and name-strips on cardboard. On the couch behind there were collected soft toys, a games compendium, theatrical bits and pieces and a scattering of tapes.

Xena, who had picked up the remote, started channel hopping, while Melissa, reaching for a wallet, fished out some pairs of tinted glasses.

"You're all in red," she said, laughing, holding up a lens and covering one eye. She switched between glasses, calling out colours, then spread them on the floor. "Try them," she urged, scooping up pairs and offering them as overlays. "More than one," she said to Stephan, fitting them together.

The boy was admiring. He squinted, tried out different combinations, studied his own hand (close-up, distant, palm-side and reverse), then passed them to his sister.

Charlotte looked briefly, sucking in her cheeks. Taking the glasses she waved towards the door. "I'm going out," she called.

The other two girls glanced at each other.

"The garden?" asked Xena, addressing herself. She looked round and considered. Her breathing had lifted and her face had coloured up. Suddenly she was alert and interested. "OK, could do... why not..." she continued, smiling with surprise at her newfound awareness.

Her sister laughed, rehearsing the phrase back; she was pitching up slightly, like an actor trying lines.

"Yes, the garden," Xena cried, standing and moving to the French window. "Garden with glasses."

For a moment her words hung, unrealised, filling up the room. She scooped up some glasses, gestured to the others and they all moved out, pushing through the doorway and standing, smiling, wearing multicoloured lenses, before advancing in a line on the overgrown garden.

In the front room, where the adults had gathered, it was talk time. Seated in a circle, they were taking turns, saying things that mattered – their thoughts or feelings or concerns since last meeting – speaking by arrangement, with pauses to look around. The circle was informal, spread round the room – some seated, some squatted – ten along the walls and two more in the bay. Tea had been poured, passed round with biscuits, sipped while talking, and the cups with dregs had been deposited on a tray. Beside them, positioned on a low-level table, was a collection of pamphlets, some stacked-up newspapers, a bust of Rosa Luxembourg and a vase of red-orange tulips.

This was their time. A pause for reflection. United as comrades for catch-up and exchange.

They'd begun with introductions, giving name and domicile and something about their views. At this stage, though they were in session, the remarks were glancing, offered ad hoc, with an element of intention. It was almost as if they were trying out an act, a pitch for interest, with a few connective phrases, before walking off.

When deep-talk had begun it was led from the corner by a thin-faced man in a frayed denim jacket. His hair was spiky and his expression rather fixed. There were lines around his eyes and mouth. He introduced himself as Justin Peters, father to Xena and Melissa, and Lorna's partner. Working his hands and gazing at the floor, he set out his position. There were, he said, reasons – complications – difficulties – but truth in what they experienced. He knew and he'd learned. As a man he'd resisted, defended his advantages, set himself up – so he'd needed to be broken (here he glanced at Lorna on the sofa). But now he was clear – clear-eyed and attentive, focused on women, on giving space and backup.

"We're *all* political," he added, "especially where it hurts."

The others reacted by nodding to themselves. It seemed he'd struck a nerve.

For an hour they'd talked, revolving their problems, thoughts about relationships, the wider network, their ideas on change. The commitment was to sharing, and to what Lorna called (glancing quickly at the friend sat by her) *absolute recognition*. She continued by urging what she called 'total awareness'. Staying on top. Seeing the problem, acknowledging how it happened, not backing down.

"It's all about correctives," she added. "Matching theory and practice: getting it right."

Her friend, Caroline, a large-framed woman with close-cropped hair, murmured her agreement. "Right theory, right practice," she mused, shifting closer. The two were arm in arm, squeezed to the front of the soft-backed sofa. Positioned slightly forward and facing the doorway, they appeared to be hosting: introducing topics which they offered round for comment.

One, which Lorna led on, her friend endorsed and Justin elaborated, was 'coupling'. It went with 'divisions' and 'emotional weakening'. 'Coupling' was exclusive and not good for women. It involved being owned, kept from each other, bossed by men. The opposite was 'open' – a state of empowerment and mutual support – and two-way solidarity, which centred on involvement, and a number of relationships where people shared partners.

As Justin explained, fixing his eyes on a quietly receptive Vanessa, "It's all about the women. They have the choice."

She smiled: "Of course. Mother knows best."

Richard asked a question, a bland one-off, requesting information. He used it as cover. A reminder of presence. But he wondered as he spoke if he'd come here to be chosen.

As the meeting progressed, with people putting viewpoints, patterns being questioned and one or two reminders about principles ignored, the extent of choosing became apparent. Of the twelve there present eight had 'networks' – mostly triangular, but also linear – with a group around Lorna (which included Caroline, Justin sat opposite, and a small man called Ken who, it turned out, also partnered Ginny) and another, looser group, consisting of Lorna's half-brother and Justin's two girlfriends.

At the break – two hours in, with some people wandering, others still debating and Vanessa in the garden checking on the kids – Richard found himself standing in the hallway chatting to Ginny. Her hair was pressed back and her heavy-set face, which was stern and child-like, had calmed and straightened. She peered up and round, then offered him a smile. Realising she was interested, Richard shared a few observations, then, lowering his voice, asked what she thought.

"The usual," she said, colouring slightly. She continued, glancing round. "Some people here want it both ways," she said, shaking her head.

When asked what she meant she glowered. "History. And some women's egos."

"So there's a problem?"

Ginny snorted. "Could say."

"I did rather wonder…"

She looked him over carefully. "Hmm. So what do you *really* think?"

"Well, I suppose it all sounds rather perfect and wonderful…"

"Ah, so you're not that impressed."

"Still taking it in, I suppose."

She narrowed her eyes: "But really, you can see—"

He shrugged: "It's called taking stock. Vanessa would say I'm hypercritical."

She grinned. "I call it being straight. Reading the signs."

"Well, it's only first impressions. After all, they can be wrong."

Ginny shook her head. "If you feel it, then it's there." She appeared to be studying something which only she could see. "And the first twenty seconds," she added slowly, "that's when you know."

Justin approached them, greeting and showing his teeth. He was touring the rooms, speaking as host and checking on feelings. "You caucusing?" he asked, grinning slightly.

"Yes, against you," Ginny shot back.

Justin nodded, conceding nothing. "You're not happy?" he asked.

"Not so you'd notice. Better things to do."

He licked his lips and considered, "Well, it's in your hands. If that's how you feel…"

"You mean I'm excused?"

"Not necessarily. Only if that's what you want."

She snorted. "Translation: *we can do without you.*"

"No, no. It would be much better for everyone if you stayed."

"But don't rock the boat."

Justin shrugged. His eyes closed slightly as he began to walk away. "Think about it, Ginny, think about it. You know you're always welcome here."

As he moved along the hall and out towards the garden, Ginny grimaced. Turning to Richard, she crooked her thumb. "Justin the lech," she said quietly.

Shortly afterwards, at a call from Lorna, echoed by Caroline and relayed by Justin (who made himself busy, acting as marshal through house and garden), the second half started. It began with looks and half-veiled smiles. People were surprised. The front room had changed: the chairs and table had gone and a large coarse-grained rug, dotted with cushions, had been stretched across the carpet. The rug, which was patched, had double-thickness borders. At the centre it was spread with flower-patterned napkins, an assortment of dips in see-through containers, veg strips in mugs and a bowlful of fruit. It looked like an improvised picnic.

Invited by Lorna, people gathered and sat between cushions. Ken joked about time on the carpet, Ginny scowled, Caroline nodded, Justin ate, while Vanessa and Richard gazed round expectantly. After words from Lorna – reporting on the three who had, she said, been claimed by commitments – the meeting started.

Their talk in the second half was less ideological. They were watchful of each other, putting in asides, offering half-formed thoughts, ideas in reflection, words as they came up. Sometimes they sat motionless, considering. Then they seemed set, braced into silence. But easy-eyed as well, as if they were in transit, observing things passing. At other times they were warm, spoke with passion, took up and stood firm – then dropped back to silence. A few spoke in code, blinking slowly and peering into space – considering all sides, the factors, the wider issues. Some were quite vague – then changed tack and register, to level their expressions and set out what had happened. Some spoke often, others were receivers, a few seemed surprised. All showed interest (their attention shifting from one speech to another, nodding and gesturing and sometimes rocking forward to ask for information or offer their support).

"It's about *sharing*," said Lorna, passing round food.

For Richard it was strange. With the bodies cushioned or squatted on carpet, it all felt quite inward. A self-defining world, made up of thoughts and remarks and voices in succession. A discourse and a round. But also (he felt) a space they'd cleared, a measure and a limit. A commitment to each other. It was, he realised, a gesture of intent.

"And entitlement," added Caroline, catching Lorna's eye.

Later in the session Richard's doubts returned. He felt uneasy, wasn't quite sure, couldn't really settle. He'd a frontline feeling, a sense of exposure – and in a place where anything might happen. Because he saw, looking round, that things were disordered. The room wasn't cared-for. It was raw-edged and messy – more like a cell than a lounge. It made him think of *living rough*. The finger-food at centre had been tried and discarded, leaving crumbs and smears on screwed-up napkins. The rug was stained, the cushions showed marks, and the empty fruit bowl was full of peelings.

He noticed Vanessa. Already, it seemed, she was warming up. Her voice could be heard interjecting thoughts, giving, receiving, sharing observations. She seemed to know her script.

A phrase about *after the party* passed through his head, followed by music. He wondered why he'd come here. Perhaps, he thought, the meeting was a put-on – a one-off presentational designed to test their commitment – or some sort of contest.

Curbing his thoughts, he looked round carefully. Suddenly he was aware. A doubleness held him, a sense of something missing. Without showing anything, he was studying the group. There was Justin playing guru, Lorna making waves, Caroline agreeing,

Vanessa questioning, Ken speaking up, the girlfriends smiling and Ginny digging in. They had their positions – quoted, corrected, they worked their patch. It all felt rather stylised, something they'd arranged, a form of demonstration.

But then, of course, there was Ginny.

Tight-eyed and alert, she'd wedged herself in, sunk between cushions. It seemed, from her movements, she'd really had enough. At the start, when Justin spoke, her expression had hardened. Later, when Lorna took over, she'd thinned her lips and gazed out the window. When Ken said his piece (a breathless kind of pitch about balance and support and being torn both ways) she'd cut in more than once, stating her case. At one point, when discussion developed about *owning problems*, she'd offered comment – mainly barbed, with asides and queries and head-shaking warnings. Later she reacted – by grunting or sighing or fidgeting with the rug. Towards the end she merely looked, frowning occasionally and refusing to speak.

Discussion ended with Justin summing up. His remarks, which were delivered slowly, were couched in first person. They centred on feelings and theories of self. At the end, after quoting from a pamphlet he'd just co-written, he introduced Ken who would, he said, deal with matters practical.

"So, Vladimir llyich, what's to be done?" he added, grinning.

Ken took over. Speaking quickly, he pulled out a pen and a torn piece of paper. It was, he said, about keeping up. He emphasised his purpose by ticking off a list. His points concerned *Activist*, the group's newspaper which needed, he said, jobs done. His voice rose slightly as he ran down his list. There were production days, distribution runs, sellers needed, subscriptions to collect, circulation targets and articles to be written. Moving on to things in the movement he reminded them of scheduled meetings. In reply to Lorna asking about women, he counted up selections with female shortlists. When pressed by Caroline he named the seats, denounced the opposition, and sketched out their response.

When he'd finished there was an update from Justin on an issue, current in the party. It centred round some words he'd used in *Activist 29*. The leadership didn't like it. There'd been a spat, allegations, talk of expulsions.

"We must understand," Justin concluded, "it's a smokescreen. They want to turn the clock back. Our answer needs to be unequivocal. We have to hold the line."

In the debate that followed references were made to leaderships past. There were patterns to elucidate, historical parallels and lessons to be learned. Words like 'opportunists' and 'defeatists' circulated the room.

"Together we are strong," said Ken, holding up *Activist*, "that's this week's headline."

Justin wrapped up, speaking of priorities, of personal closeness and pointing the way.

The last words were Lorna's, backed up by Caroline. There was an outing to arrange – their holiday annual – with a date for diaries. Everyone was invited. Whatever the weather it would be, Lorna said, a shared experience.

Afterwards, as they took their leave, Richard held back. Vanessa, he supposed, would handle their goodbyes. He collected the kids and kept them amused while she worked the room. She did so with poise, like her mother. It seemed she knew how.

At the end of her round, when she'd talked and given out (oblivious, it seemed, to lateness reminders) Richard became aware of something new – she was talking to a man who'd appeared from the garden. He was solemnly attentive, with dark curly hair and metal-rimmed glasses. As she spoke he adjusted often, applying his forefinger carefully to the bridge. When she stopped he nodded, gazing floor-wards. He was absorbed, it seemed, in some sort of special awareness.

When Richard came over Vanessa introduced. Lance, she said, was a community activist; he ran the local crèche. They'd met through Lorna – here she laughed – who held him up as some sort of hero. A man approved of. Because *he* was the one, she added, who'd stepped in last minute to entertain the children, replacing the actor who hadn't turned up.

To Richard he seemed an unlikely stand-in. Back-foot and watchful, with blue-hazed eyes and prominent teeth, he took observations. He could have been an academic or a consultant doctor.

Vanessa, to finish, revisited the company. She introduced Lance to those he hadn't met, chatted about kids, laughed with Lorna, re-engaged with Justin, and didn't seem to notice Richard, or the kids' impatience. She was at centre, enjoying herself. Her voice was raised and she was in the flow. It was as if she was on tiptoe peering over a wall.

Lance himself said almost nothing. He followed her, smiling as if he was her minder. He was there for her.

It was Ginny who cut it short. Noticing Stephan in single combat with imaginary intruders she called to Vanessa. "Looks like we're front line," she laughed.

"Are you winning?" she added, addressing the boy.

Stephan glanced round, and switched to fly-swatting.

"Does this mean by any chance that you've nothing to do?" she asked.

The boy paused, looked towards Vanessa, and nodded.

"Been here long enough?"

Again he nodded.

"Well then—"

As Ginny spoke, Charlotte pushed forward. "We have to go," she said firmly, addressing her mother.

Vanessa delayed, smiling vaguely. "That's what you want?" she asked.

Charlotte confirmed.

"You mean now?"

Her daughter frowned. "Go home," she said.

Vanessa stared. "I think——" she began, then relapsed into silence.

"Go, Mum. Go now."

"You sure?"

"YES, Mum. Please."

"There's a TV programme—" put in Stephan.

Richard grinned; "And when there's something on the box…"

"OK. We'll go soon."

"*Mum!*"

"It's time – now," put in Ginny quickly. "You all have to go. I shall count you out…" And she stood in the hallway, pointing and waving, as she descended the scale, calling out numbers.

The last thing Richard saw, as the kids reached the car, was a red-faced Ginny standing in the doorway signalling encouragement. She seemed (he thought) placed there for effect. Her expression was set and attentive, as if for camera. She was grinning and gesticulating in a way that recalled him and Vanessa a few years back, in an earlier version, posing brightly and smiling into air as they stood with children, waving into sun for their first holiday photos.

Next morning was Sunday lie-in.

The Lawrence family, gathered upstairs for a once-weekly meeting. Comrades and supporters linking arms. Pyjama Party members exchanging feelings, with no set tasks. Holiday-ish.

In terms of place: main bedroom, early.

In terms of those present: Charlotte, Stephan, Vanessa – father, apologies.

In terms of women's power, this was giving audience.

In relationship terms: open-armed, accepting – and making a point.

Minuted as follows:

With the curtains half-closed, a sleepy-eyed Vanessa received both children, taking them in bed to play games and snuggle. The games went through stages: cards that didn't last – they slipped beneath sheets or fell beneath the bed – ROCK PAPER SCISSORS (which began three-way but soon petered out when Charlotte lost interest), under-sheet-hiding games with ghost calls and giggles, itzy witzy spider games, word games and joke games and pen and paper games which involved joining up the dots and colouring in pictures.

Vanessa made them welcome, smiled, asked questions, directed.

This was the good life.

Their own special time.

Close-up in touch.

Children with mother.

When their father returned from practising piano the games had ended and children and mother were enjoying one last, squeezing, slightly defiant, three-way hug.

In terms of parenting, this was happy families.

CHAPTER EIGHT

"A get together," Vanessa announced as she stood in the kitchen gazing down the garden, "that would be good."

Behind her Richard, who was cooking, had a matchbox in his hands.

"I think," she continued, "it could draw things together."

The thoughts were in the words, appearing slowly. She was musing, considering her own likings. Words, and where they went. "Invite round everyone. All the different groups."

She continued musing and staring. Even as she looked, the garden was darkening. She could see it in sections, divided like a map. A sun strip at the back, shadows in between, twilight closer. Long and bare and worn round the edges it had developed its own function, a space for living. A run for the kids, a corner shed, a patio at the end – grassed to the middle, with borders. This was the place, she thought. Their own, for recreation. She could imagine hosting it with fairy lights and chairs. Welcoming and arranging, introducing faces. A summer evening sit-out for drinks and a chat.

Richard showed interest. "All of them?" he echoed between slicing veg and warming pans.

Vanessa nodded. A guest list was forming: Ruth and Doug, *the group*, politicos, some teachers, a few students from college-days and others in the network – they'd mix and mingle, meet new faces, re-establish contact, find things in common.

Richard paused, examining a collection of herbs in see-through jars: "But what about the kids?"

She thought for a moment. "My parents will take them."

He returned to his pans, frying and stirring in flavouring. He arranged his mixture in a dish, then committed to the oven.

"Sounds good," he said. "When?"

Vanessa, going vague, said she'd ring and see.

"You mean they'll sleep over?"

She nodded, "The children like it."

Richard considered. Behind her words he sensed something more. A statement of intent.

"I think," he said quietly, "we should book them in, asap."

That evening, after Vanessa spoke to her parents, Richard did the ringing. He went through his address book, crosschecked with hers and dug around in drawers pulling out numbers he'd scribbled on paper. He continued the next day, listing acceptances, and using contacts to lead to other numbers. By the end of the week he'd talked and invited and left so many messages that he'd lost track of names and who might turn up. But he'd done what was asked, put the word around, covered all the groups. As Vanessa always said, when Richard took something on – then that was it.

"He has his uses," she told Ruth on the day of the party as they positioned cushions and bowlfuls of nibbles at carefully chosen spots. "Richard's a byword for action. You are what you do. I wonder sometimes if it's in the genes. That kind of single-minded one-track mindset, like a runner near the tape. It's all about getting things in place – and now."

"Ah, the male of the species…"

Vanessa grinned.

"But it keeps them busy." Ruth added: "Occupational therapy."

"Well, I suppose," said Vanessa, "they like being useful…"

"Yeah, like skivvies. They need to be given tasks."

Vanessa laughed, resisting the urge to answer in kind. With Richard and Doug out collecting drinks, it seemed somehow off. An act of disengagement. In any case she'd a view (now they'd talked together) that they might find things easier if they looked for something different, a change in how they functioned.

"The obsessive sex," added Ruth curling her lip, "that's them."

Vanessa smiled as she stood back and examined the cleared-out lounge. Her voice now was braced up and ironic, delivering her reply. "Well," she pronounced, narrowing her eyes, "whatever happens, we'll just have to see…" and she busied herself placing cushions and excavating cupboards in search of glasses.

By party time – with all rooms cleared, lights in the garden and music playing – Richard and Vanessa were united briefly in welcoming guests, taking phone calls and showing round the house.

First to arrive were Frank and Jackie. They entered with a bottle, greeting loudly and looking round the hallway. Frank cracked a joke and Richard led in, conducting to the kitchen. They picked up drinks en route to the garden. Outside, they stood talking, discussing Frank's promotion and his move, now imminent, to head up a school.

"It's a chance," said Jackie, dryly. "He's busy making ground – on the inside lane." She was eyeing her husband with a slightly edgy stare, as if he was a racehorse that might gallop off.

Frank grinned. "It's a big job. Super-heavy stuff. They want the place sorting."

Richard nodded: "Meet the new boss."

"More like bouncer," Jackie countered. "He's been given what they call special powers."

"You mean of the hey presto sort?"

Frank wiped one hand slowly across his chin. "I think that's what they're looking for."

Richard introduced them to James and Penny, friends from college. When it turned out they were teachers Frank checked where they worked, then invited their views. How much were *they* suffering, he asked, offering a grin. Soon all four were sounding off. Schools, they agreed, were pretty much in chaos. Messed up places falling apart – with too much expected, too much pressure, and not enough backup.

As they moved on to salaries Richard nodded. He'd taken in and registered, heard their talk and knew what followed. More complaints, of course. A catalogue of woes. A long list of gripes passed around staffrooms with eyebrows raised and feelings aired.

First this… then that… and would you believe it? On and on. Automatic stuff… And he wondered when they might call time – imagining teachers sitting on the toilet or talking in their sleep repeating their mantras about stress and tiredness.

Though of course they'd got a point. Everyone felt it. It was only, he thought, that he'd lost all interest—

By now the group had turned their attention to politics. They were complaining about cuts, identifying councils and those who'd sold out. It was, Frank said, a problem of will.

"It's about who you put there," added Jackie quietly.

Frank wiped his face. "And what sort of lead you've got 'em on," he said.

Waiting for an opening, Richard pursed his lips. To him it seemed almost like a game: they were playing with words, balancing, juggling, trying out effects. As a group they had their lines, an act they ran through. They knew what they were doing.

When a break point came he nodded to the house. "See you all later," he said, casually, "have to play host."

Moving indoors he greeted Justin who'd arrived with admirers. Squeezing through the crowd, Richard welcomed some college friends, then joined Doug who'd taken up position, covering for Vanessa halfway down the hall. He'd been asked to keep an eye out and to help with directions.

"On guard?" offered Richard, raising his voice above the wall of music issuing from the lounge.

Doug blinked. "Awaiting developments," he said dryly, glancing down the hall.

Richard followed his gaze. Seen through the doorway, the kitchen was busy. It was full of noise and movement and familiar faces. Looking to the middle he could see two women – Lorna and Caroline with their arms linked together, surrounded by drinkers. Both were giving forth, working their audience. Their faces were child-blank, and full of excitement. Behind them was Ruth, now in full flow: offering quirky comments while mixing drinks. Beside her, waiting for an opening, was Ken. Beyond that there were others, both known and less familiar, calling greetings and sharing one-liners. It was standing room only.

Richard nodded to his friend. "You mean the percentage proof," he said, glancing at Ruth.

"You think that's a problem?" Doug asked.

Richard considered. From where they were he could see her in profile. She was laughing and exclaiming, arguing both sides. This was Ruth as performer.

"I don't think so," Richard said. "She's doing well."

Doug said he hoped so. While they'd been looking he'd moved forward and sideways to occupy the stairs. He was sitting, peering through banisters, checking round the arc: front door to kitchen. "I suppose it's fingers crossed," he said finally. "After all, it might not happen…"

"True," said Richard. "Belief's the word. At least I think so." Here he laughed: "You know what they say: *I drink therefore I am* – it's a variation on the self-fulfilling prophecy… And if there's one thing likely to bring it on, it's too much thought."

"Hmm, I see. So that's what you *think*?"

Both men grinned.

"I mean," added Richard, "don't accept any kind of ideology. Question everything. Stay outside the box."

"I did it *my way*, eh?"

"Maybe. The Sid Vicious version."

Doug smiled. "Ah yes," he said quietly. "What *they'd* call revisionism." He waved one arm in the direction of Lorna and friends.

"Them?" Richard laughed, "I suppose they would say that. You could call it enlightened self-interest…"

Doug shrugged: "You agree, then."

"To be honest I'm not really sure. Mind you, they are pretty keen on slogans."

"Hmm, platform talk…"

"Well… yes. They're not exactly *listeners*."

"Of course. They're VIPs."

"I don't—"

"Otherwise known as head-bangers."

Richard supposed so. He added a few qualifiers and attempted softeners, then, after asking Doug not to get him wrong (the women, he said, saw things differently, had their own priorities) returned to playing concierge. Doug nodded and they worked together, meeting and greeting, with Richard leading. After several more arrivals – mainly allies but also old acquaintances and friends at one remove – he excused himself again.

By now the party was loud. The front room had filled up and a wall of music mixed in with shouts flowed and echoed through the house. There were queues for the toilet, people in corners, couples dancing. Passing through the kitchen Richard smiled and chatted, topped up his glass, then sought out Vanessa at the end of the garden. She was talking to Lance.

"Hi there," he said. "Party's going well."

"Oh yes," Vanessa responded vaguely.

"You enjoying it?" Richard asked, and Lance nodded.

"That's good," he added, conceding nothing.

They were joined by Ruth. Vanessa introduced Lance, and her friend acknowledged, nodding and smiling.

Ruth laughed. She was, she said, on best behaviour. Doing the necessary. Trying to please Doug. "It's FHB," she added – which Vanessa translated, speaking to one side, then at volume, with eye contact, for the benefit of Lance.

"I see," he said, adjusting his glasses. "Family hold back. Now I understand."

Richard noticed a catch in his throat and slightly mannered smile. Though young (and slightly child-like), he carried himself seriously, on stand-by. He wanted, it seemed, to be helpful.

Ruth was enjoying herself. She had to know the names, who was with who, and where they all came from. She also quizzed Lance about his job – and how he put up with it – drawing out his thoughts and sharing theories about raising kids. "You wouldn't care for mine," she said, laughing. "They're all over the place – just like their mother." Before he could reply she rolled her eyes and launched in again, imitating what she called their *baby-wants-niggle*. Of course, she said, the joke was on her. Food fads and moans, fusses, day-long battles. "It's what you get," she added with a shrug, "when you spoil 'em."

137

Lance nodded slowly. He asked after names and ages.

Ruth gave details. "As you know," she added, "boys are impossible."

"XY," quipped Richard. "We just can't help it."

"Otherwise known," put in Ruth, "as *not me guv.*"

For a moment no one spoke. They were standing, facing, awaiting the next move.

"So what do you think?" Vanessa asked, turning to Lance. "Do we accept that *boys will be boys* and that this is the planet of the apes – or is the future female?"

He eyed her intently, without saying anything.

"The male mindset," she reminded, "is it fixed?"

"She means: are we doomed," Richard interjected.

"Not in children," Lance responded, ignoring. He was speaking slowly like a diagnosing doctor. "Or just the first phase… and then only in some."

"But otherwise," said Richard, "it's terminal."

Vanessa looked away. Richard sensed something – an understated feeling, a held back formula which she offered up in general, a line and pitch which she put round for effect. It was (he realised) a kind of invitation.

"I think," she said, measuring her expression, "that boys, given a good example, with the proper upbringing—" Vanessa paused and considered. Her eyes were large and round and set towards a point. She was viewing Lance's outline. She wanted his endorsement.

"–Will turn out just like their dads," Richard said quietly.

Vanessa gazed off, moon-eyed and calm, still smiling to herself. "What we're debating is the big question," she said. "Temperament versus conditioning – and do we make a difference. We all believe in self-improvement, but when it comes to it, family *don't* hold back."

Ruth laughed: "Too true. It's always the way. You start off trying to be different, and end up willy-nilly like your folks. It's the law of life." Her voice tone hardened: "Take my dad: I used to call him the world's biggest bastard. A real Mr Nasty. That was until I met *his* bastard father, and he was a communist. You'd

138

really think, to look at 'em, they had nothing in common." She paused and shook her head: "But, like it or not, folks is folks. They make you who you are. Whichever way you go, it gets passed down."

Richard said nothing. His viewpoint had shifted. He was looking at Vanessa, remembering their first meeting. Her short purple jacket and glimpses of waistline. The garden walk, the river, the footbridge. Her theories and pronouncements on how it ought to be.

Both women nodded.

"Together with the genes," said Vanessa quietly.

"And the surname," Ruth added.

Richard shrugged. "Plus ça change," he offered, gazing at Lance.

The other man smiled. He seemed agreeable.

Ruth raised her glass: "What comes round—"

"Indeed. So it's party on," Richard concluded, bowing ironically. His gaze took in the lawn: "Because that, at least, seems to be going well."

The garden now was dark. Its area had softened. It was bright beside the house where the path and patio were streaked with white, shadowy further out with grey-edged lines and bars, and black towards the back where the last few yards had blurred and thickened. At the centre, gathered on the lawn, there were people in groups, some listening, some gesturing and others on crowd-watch: talking, eating or drinking in silence.

To Richard, who had moved towards the kitchen, the party had the feel of good times past. It was as if he was a guest, an unattached visitor taking in patterns and observing couples at a student party. He could see how they operated, understood their habits, had them in his view. It also offered focus, something immediate, a close-up on life.

He crossed to the counter and filled up his glass. A quick glance round confirmed his first impression. The kitchen was busy. It was full of wide-eyed people, talking brightly, with deliberate animation.

He moved towards the hall, thinking of Vanessa. He could picture her face, olive-dark and composed, her long smooth neck and Mucha figure, her attentions and invitations directed elsewhere. In the garden she was special. Offering and accepting, she was queen. Taking interest, with Lance as sidekick, she was round-eyed, animated and full of supplementary questions. What they'd talked about was happening.

As he reached the front room he saw himself reflected in the mirror. He realised, almost without looking, that his image had changed. Age had made him stronger – at least in appearance. He'd life-lines and experience and a mouth set firm. Seen from a distance he gave nothing away.

The room was hot and dark and filled with music. There were bodies moving slowly, some bopping, others clenched, and a number sprawled on XL cushions, holding their glasses and nodding to the beat. The volume held them in.

As Richard stood watching (peering through the doorway to make out faces, one hand tapping wood) he heard himself called. The voice was directed, half familiar, and repeated. It said his name briefly, then again, followed by a longer, supplementary shout. When the third call came Richard, realising, turned to the front door. There, by the gate, waving and smiling, with her hair tied back and a rucksack on her shoulder, was Ginny Hammond.

Putting down his drink, he stepped out.

"Hi," she said, blushing slightly. "Am I late?"

Richard laughed: "No, not especially. It's open house." He glanced at his watch: "And in any case – the night is young."

Ginny laughed. She asked him how it was going.

"The party?"

She nodded.

"Oh, it's great. Really gr—" He pulled up, frowning hard. "No. That's wrong." Suddenly he found himself changing tack. "It's nothing really, nothing at all." He waved towards the house: "So I wouldn't bother. The truth is the air's a whole lot better out here."

He paused, Ginny nodded, and they both dropped silent. The sounds of taped music filled up the space. It seemed they'd got in touch, without saying anything.

He studied her closely, using the dark as cover. He could see her in detail, outlined by the street lamp. She was wide-mouthed and cheery with a soft-edged expression and a slightly awkward stare. Her face was set, shoulders hunched and her body tucked in, as if she was a runner. She wasn't, he thought, what you might call beautiful – though the street light gave her presence. It added to her glow. It gave her something other, an element of wildness. With her quick green eyes, swept back hair and prominent features she looked like an expressionist portrait.

"Well, I've just come back from a walk," she said.

He asked what she meant.

Ginny laughed: "You'll think I'm crazy."

Richard shook his head. "Not as much as me," he said, examining her thoughtfully.

"Well you'd better watch out," she smiled. "It's infectious."

He returned her smile. "So, you say walking is catching?" he asked.

She shrugged. "Could be," she returned, blushing slightly.

Again, they both dropped silent.

Richard looked. He felt something developing, a line of connection. Suddenly he could *see* her, she was (he now realised), something of an oddball. He noticed her pendant: a carved wooden sun sign suspended on a chain. The sack she carried was double-thickness: strap-hung and buckled in black and green.

Returning to her walks, he pressed for details.

Ginny paused. "I can show you," she said, suddenly little-girlish.

"Show me? What would that involve?"

"Night walks," she said, "mainly in parks. If I can get into 'em."

Richard expressed surprise. "So you walk in the dark…"

Ginny nodded.

"By yourself?"

She nodded again.

"Isn't that rather dangerous?"

"Not if you're careful. And know where to go."

Richard considered. They were outside the gate, standing beside the overgrown hedge. Its leaves were lit up. Party noises were issuing from the doorway and the wide-open windows. Ginny, who was half in shadow, was staring into darkness. He could see she was shivering.

"So why do it?"

She shrugged. "To see. And because I can. In any case, once you've got the bug…"

"And the sack?" he asked, pointing.

"That's for food."

He laughed: "Ah. It's an expedition, then?"

"If you like—" She turned, inviting him to join her.

"Where to?"

"You'll see."

Ginny led off and Richard followed. As he walked, he was in doubt, yet excited. It seemed they were adventurers, stepping into shadow. This was unknown.

They crossed the road, turned left and right, then cut through an arch, emerging together on an unmade-up track. At the end, reaching some concrete blocks and a corrugated iron fence, she waved him close. "There's a hole," she said, pointing to a gap between an elderberry and a crumbled mass of brick. "I came this route an hour ago," she added, testing the blocks. She grunted, levering herself sideways and up. At the top she crouched cat-like, blinking. Outlined by the street light she checked both ways, then disappeared over, encouraging him to follow.

Surprised by her agility, Richard scrambled up. When he reached the top, she handed him over, warning it was dark. On the other side he dropped, guided by her hand. He landed against her, touching, and she laughed. "Richard," she cried and pulled him to her. Suddenly he was hot. Hot and breathless and held to her body. "Is it OK?" he asked, feeling the glow, and picturing Vanessa, positioned on the lawn angling her comments to take in Lance.

"It's nothing," she said quickly, and unhanded.

They were standing in shadow on the edge of a disused railway track. On their side it was overlooked by street lamps and backed by fences; on the other side it was bounded by brambles and a head-high bank. "Let's go. We'll toe the line," she said quietly, pointing forward to the levelled sleepers. They set off together, treading carefully. "Mind out," she said when they came to a section where the street light had failed. She reached out to steady him and they shuffled forward, hand in hand.

Richard, as he went, tried not to think. It was, he supposed, a childhood game. An episode in the dark, unseen, and possibly imagined. If it was happening, it wasn't that serious.

Ginny squeezed his hand and drew him to her.

"We're the railway children," he laughed.

They continued through shadow then round a bend to a lit-up patch at the back of a factory. At the end, where the track narrowed and dipped, Ginny led down and stopped. They were standing together with three walls facing: blocked to the sides by rocks and weeds, and sloping ahead through nettles to a bricked-up tunnel.

"What happens now?" Richard asked.

Ginny gestured. "It's up and over," she said.

Where she pointed a line of footholds, angled through weeds, offered a way up. "Follow me," she added and began to climb, digging each foot into mud. Halfway up they reached a ledge which curled and levelled, leading sideways across a drop. Ginny stopped. "Seems harder this way round," she said quietly.

Richard, peering forward over her head, suggested caution. Taking the drop-side, he squeezed into the lead.

"Hmm, need to be careful," she said.

They regrouped then, at his insistence. Positioning themselves side-on, facing outwards, they walked the ledge with one arm linked, acrobat-style, hands to wrists.

"You all right?" she said sharply when Richard stumbled.

"Fine," he replied, straightening. Below him, in the dark, the slope fell away to a grey-green mass of weeds and nettles.

"Keep going," he insisted as she, too, slipped. She pulled back and they moved rather slower, balanced. By now they were breath-short and sweaty. Their hand-grip had shifted. Palm to palm, they were squeezing hard.

At a point close to the top, where the path curled back, Ginny lost her footing. "Richard!" she cried, lurching sideways. The ground gave way and she began to slide. Richard, still holding, flattened to the bank. For a moment they hung, his weight against hers, then both went down. With a short yelpy shout they rolled and plunged and tumbled to the bottom, landing side by side, still holding hands.

"Ugh," she cried, struggling for breath. "Nettles."

At first he didn't notice. The fall had shocked him and the blood was up. He heaved against Ginny, grunting. Then suddenly he was wild. He was grabbing for her, squeezing and pressing, kissing cheek and mouth.

Ginny grabbed back and they rolled and clenched. As their mouths worked together, he felt the stings. Hot around his neck. Hotter and painful, on arms and sides. A peppering of stings, aching all over.

He was hot and bothered. Everywhere tingled. The backs of his legs, his thighs, his shoulders, his hair roots and scalp, even his tongue. It was as if they were kissing in a dust storm.

And yet he didn't care. All at once he was alive. He was wild and he was in touch. A red-raw, burning kind of wildness, an overflow of hurt.

And then, just as suddenly as they'd begun, they stopped and rolled apart.

Richard sat up. In the dark he was shaking. Part of him was amazed, another part was ashamed, while a third part wondered what would happen next.

"My God, my God," he said rubbing his flesh.

"What can I say?" he added, standing. Leaning forward, he helped her to her feet.

Even in the dark he could feel her redness.

Ginny took a breath: "You don't have to say anything."

"But it hurts – yes?"

"Only when I laugh."

He nodded.

"Or move," she added, wincing.

He looked back up the bank: "I think we'll both have some explaining—"

Ginny shook her head: "Don't worry. I've fixed it."

"Fixed it? How?"

"I've talked to Vanessa, on the phone. It's allowed."

He stared, taking in her words. What she'd said broke through everything – the stings now were nothing. He'd known of course, somewhere, subliminally.

"You mean it was a setup?"

"I thought you wanted it."

He laughed. "Nettles and all?"

She shrugged. "Ah well, when you're busy, things can happen…" The cat-green of her eyes was visible, reflected in the lights.

Richard nodded. "So it's been okayed – but where does that leave us?"

Ginny laughed: "Outside our comfort zone."

"True."

"With two red bodies."

"Indeed."

"Stung all over…"

"Absolutely."

"… But then, of course, some like it hot…"

CHAPTER NINE

After the party Richard and Vanessa told each other that their marriage had changed.

"It's like opening a window," said Vanessa, "and taking a deep breath."

Richard smiled. For him, he said, it was more open-ended.

Though when they used the word 'open' (which they did at first carefully, feeling their way in private) they meant a kind of turnaround, a surprise direction off.

The rules were now different. Whereas before they were held in by family and habit and established routine, now they were on the lookout. Their ideas had developed. It felt, they said, more upfront and flexible, a bigger kind of structure; it was lighter, fresher and freed up hidden feelings.

"Better out than in," was Vanessa's view – a remark which Richard echoed, quoting lines from Blake. But he wondered about their marriage. It seemed they'd reached an edge. A cusp or limit where things might end, or break open suddenly. They'd walked out, it seemed, into a life in the open, a bare bright spot where anything might happen. A point of no return, a step up and off – though what felt dangerous was also exciting.

They'd agreed a regime where risk was possible, where they could (at least in theory) look and ogle, put themselves around, could proposition even – and that made for challenge, a shift in patterns, a new flush of interest. It put them on the spot. Forced them to live it, to go with inclination, take the risk and look for other ways. It all felt more adult, and allowed them to be.

In reality, of course, they were constrained by life. By jobs and kids and what could be fitted. So they needed something practical. A deal they could live with. Something balanced. Which meant, when it came to it, they arranged their lives around a once-weekly swop, usually on a Friday, when Lance came over and Richard went to Ginny's.

They'd begun with a trial. A one-off for Vanessa; a first night, she said, before they really started. Richard was willing – he'd agreed, he said, to an open relationship – and Vanessa was careful. She spoke about parity and keeping things together. They ought, she said, to test how it felt, and whether they could handle it. In any case, she added, it wouldn't be overnight.

She left that evening, promising return. As she walked out she'd been warm – touched him on the shoulder and murmured reassurance – then told him not to worry. After her exit he could still see her smile, awkward and yet eager, looking forward. Her aim wasn't him.

While she was out he'd tried making tea, listening to music, reading poetry, but his heartbeat was up and his thoughts wouldn't settle. He saw her with Lance, talking in the garden. It seemed they shared a view.

In an effort not to think, he went to the back room, selected a score and practised on the piano. He nodded as he played, beating time. The notes came and went, like reflections in water. When he arrived at a key change, he broke off and moved towards the hall, where he stood, facing the doorway. A shadow came over him. He switched off the light and the street lamp shone through, yellow-barred over wood. Turning to the stairs he followed its glow, climbing to the landing. He gripped the banisters, pausing at the top to overview the hall. Its emptiness struck him. Though there were feelings, there was no one there. Suddenly he was wary. He felt as if this was a prelude, a first step in a process, a shift into otherness which would soon take over and might well be dangerous.

He checked on the children, preparing his lines – words of reassurance if they woke and wanted Vanessa. When he tried their doors, one was stiff, the other squeaky. He prised them open, lifting slightly to minimise friction. Inside felt warm. Peering into darkness he heard the sound of breathing.

Both were asleep.

Climbing again, he entered the bedroom and clicked on the side light. He directed its beam round and down, picking out a photo of Vanessa. She was standing by a lake, smiling, with flamingos just behind. He recognised her expression, the angle chosen, the slightly worn look. Already he could see it. Round-eyed and distant, she'd her own world view. A kind of special pleading.

That night he tracked her. Following in thought, he pictured her journey, observed her arrive, saw her with Lance – though when it came to detail a blur-spot took over and he only half-heard, missing out on content. In his mind they were both there, appearing in cameo. He supposed that they knew, could read from a distance, and had their own intentions. Between them, it was decided. At times he saw a look, at other times something signalled. He even imagined devices, recorders, quiet interceptions. They were lined up against him. Whatever he did he couldn't shake the feeling that he'd sleep and dream then wake next morning (though still, perhaps, dreaming) alone in the bed with a note on the cabinet signed by Vanessa saying that she'd gone.

In fact when she returned (just after three) she entered quietly, slipped into bed and pressed up close, asking how he'd been.

Richard remained still, murmuring in the dark.

She asked again, touching his arm.

He lay square, saying nothing, then levered up. "To be honest," he said, "I was worried."

"You don't need to be."

He considered. "You sure?"

"Absolutely."

"So it's OK?"

Vanessa confirmed. There was, she said, nothing to fret about.

"I get…" he began, then shifted down. "Well, it's all very new."

"But OK."

Richard paused. He pulled up the covers. "Yes, OK."

Suddenly quite boyish, he leaned into her side. Vanessa shifted round. "It's OK," she repeated, stroking his neck. They were together, and everything between them was calm and considered and full of sudden warmth.

Their sleep was short. When they woke it was half-dark and quiet. After talking and touching they rose as a couple, ate with the kids and moved into action. Suddenly they were in step (had found, it seemed, something more personal, more at ease and expressive) – and all that day Richard felt himself liked. There were words of approbation – with Vanessa sounding arch – and a sense of focus, of clear space and smiles and things come together. He'd regained his shine.

For Vanessa it was an opening.

"We've chosen," she told Ruth later, sitting in her neighbour's garden, "and we're going to try. It's a new way forward."

"Makes for interest," her friend replied, stretching on the bench. "But I'd go nuts."

Vanessa raised one eyebrow.

"Too jealous," Ruth added, pulling a face. "My insecurity levels would go sky high. Especially when it's all so open. I couldn't cope with being public property like that. I'd imagine everyone was watching, waiting for their chance."

"But don't you sometimes wish—"

"In any case, I'd be worried stiff Doug would clear off."

Vanessa gazed out across the unkempt borders. It was mild and they were seated, with the shed behind them, blinking into sun. The lawn in front was bare-patched and grey, the path to one side was uneven, and a tangle of rubbish had collected around the shed.

"Could be a way of forcing his hand," smiled Vanessa.

"Love me or leave me?"

"Well, it might at least gee him up."

"In your case, maybe…"

Vanessa laughed. For them, she answered, glancing through the gap-toothed fence, there was nothing definite. "It's all a bit up and down," she said. "A kind of adventure."

Afterwards, she wondered. Her words, she knew, had their own dynamic. *They* were what counted. Strong words that came, said with purpose. It was words that steadied her. She needed their delay, their power to make good.

Because what she'd called an adventure (and thought of as a challenge), soon became a slog. Suddenly there were pressures. It was partly, she thought, a matter of timing – how often and where, and when to disengage – and partly balance; but also there were spaces, things left hanging, and a number of disjunctions where the feelings didn't fit. It was as if she'd been dating and found herself cornered, caught between rivals with a case to answer. They, it seemed, didn't know their place. There were pressures on all fronts.

So her next time away was daytime and brief. Arranged while Richard took the children to a film, it was afternoon-only. In fact he thought he detected an element of delay, a slight hesitation once they'd eaten. It was as if it was a duty, a task to carry out, something to get through. He estimated her absence as two or three hours, and when she returned it seemed, once again, that her interest was up. Her focus was on talk and exchange and living together – and even with the children things were that much easier – a space left clear, an allowance.

From then on they were paired, with Ginny included (phoning often, going through Vanessa to square all arrangements). They fixed on Fridays and worked out timings, aiming at balance and stability, especially for the kids.

So it was Richard, this time, who went overnight. He set off for Ginny's, leaving quietly after marking books and practising the piano. On the drive there he was up. Suddenly he was excited and both ways connected. Aware of himself and what he had with Vanessa. It seemed they'd found a route, a new way forward. Though for him it was positional, he'd accepted her wishes, gone with the theory, and now it was his turn. This was what he wanted.

It was dark when he arrived. Ginny appeared quickly and welcomed him in. "Good journey?" she asked.

Richard confirmed. He stood for a moment, looking. When Ginny met his eyes, he smiled. "You all right?" he said moving forward and they embraced. Her mouth came up, and his closed over. Something automatic began beating up. He was hot and warm and breathless. They were kissing (he realised) as if it was a party.

Ginny broke first. She eased herself back and down, breathing like a singer. "Let's get comfortable," she said, leading to the front room.

He followed, saying nothing.

They settled on the sofa. It was worn into hollows and smelled of incense. There were tables both sides: one with flowers, the other displaying ointments and herbal remedies. The room in front was thickly-curtained and papered in green. It was crowded and private, with gilt-edged pictures, ornamental brasses and dark-stained furniture.

She asked about the children.

Richard smiled. "You know what they're like. Ultra-lively."

She nodded.

"I suppose it's in the genes," he continued. "But then again, I always *wanted* them to stand out."

Ginny stroked his hand: "They learn by example."

He drew her to him, kissing again. His tongue entered slowly, pushing and curling. He was beginning the journey.

"I think," she said afterwards, "I'd like to walk."

"Ah, the call of the wild," he said, laughing.

"*Without* nettles," she said quickly.

"But somewhere crazy?"

She nodded.

"In that case... ready when you are."

It was dark in her street as they passed out through the door. Ginny led, turning at the end beneath a broken street light, and following a path that led between fences. The path opened out to a tree-lined road with a garage on the corner. Ahead, beneath the trees, was a sweep of grey, visible through the bars of heavy iron gates.

"The park," she said, crossing the road and peering through metal. It looked like a film set.

Richard glanced round. "So, we're going in," he said, as if it was obvious.

Ginny confirmed. Taking his hand she led along the railings to a corner where a twisted tree trunk had thrust through the bars. It was as if they were searching, as explorers, for a long-lost route. She waited for a traffic gap then showed him where to grasp. "There. It's easy" she said, placing his feet. Richard grunted as he shinned up and over, followed by Ginny.

They were standing on grass, panting slightly. "Uphill," she said, pointing to a slope that rose into darkness.

Richard looked forward. As his eyes adjusted he made out a path, rising slowly, some shrubs by a wall and steps to a terrace. Above that a wide swathe of grass, greyed by darkness, spread towards a hilltop.

"Now for the night walk," he said, and they set off hand in hand.

The light changed as they ascended. They passed from silver, with spreading pools of whiteness, up through shadow – yellowed in part by the street light glow – and beyond, in darkness, to bare black space. Here they were unseen. No one could touch them. They looked across trees, then turned the whole arc, taking in the roofs, the street signs and office blocks, the lit-up city centre.

"Unreal," he said quietly.

Overhead, a plane passed over.

They clenched by a tree, mouths pressed together. They were high up and floaty, lost in darkness. Above, the sky was faintly luminescent. It showed like a pre-dawn flush.

Ginny drew back. She was breathing heavily. Her arm described a circle, taking in the city. "Belvedere Park," she said. "I come here to get away from it all. Best view in the city."

Richard looked. A line from Keats ran through his mind.

"It also has," Ginny continued, "its own walled garden."

Before he could answer she directed forward. "This way," she called, linking arms to lead towards a tennis court and a high brick wall. Keeping in its shadow, she turned a corner and paced downhill.

"The garden's inside," she said, steering to a gap with one side fallen. Where the pillar had been, a chest-high gate lay propped against brickwork.

Entering, they stood. Inside was shadowy. It was secret and warm and richly-scented. There were radiating paths at uneven angles, leading into darkness. To the sides, they were gravel, to the middle, crazy-paved and bordered by chicken wire. At a distance there were walls, outlined in blocks. Above them, the sky showed clear and dark and overarching.

Ginny moved forward, choosing the path down the centre. Her breath came quickly. She was holding her body close to Richard's.

At an arch with roses they paused to embrace, taking in the scents and the low-level echo of running water.

Something dark and scrawny wheeled above their heads.

"Bats," she said, as another zigzagged over.

Richard tipped his head back. "Strange animals," he said, watching them loop and turn.

"In a different world."

They were close by the pond. In the centre was a stone, lit from below by a blue-grey penumbra. A curve of water was issuing from a dark metal nozzle set into its side.

"AB see D fish," she said, pointing.

Three silver-and-brown carp were circling in the glow. Moving slowly, easily, they looped around each other. Their bodies were knotted like scarves.

"I've got something for them," she said, slipping off her backpack. She pulled out a plastic bag of food sticks and examined them by the light of a small torch. Each was brown and thin and pellet-like. "See. Feed," she said, picking out a small handful and scattering on the surface.

Her words echoed back. As the water stirred, Richard saw an image of a bunch of wild flowers. His mind flashed back to eating at the zoo.

The fish idled round, set themselves at angles, then shot to the top. Their mouths sucked in, swallowing. When they'd hoovered forward, they twisted sideways and gulped down more. Finally, when all the sticks had disappeared, they dived.

"Watch the large one," she said quietly.

The leader nosedived, ruffling its gills. As it descended it bubbled out food sticks. They drifted to the surface, chewed up and sodden.

"Fussy eater," said Richard.

"Knows what it likes."

"Like children, wanting pudding first."

Ginny laughed. "Pretty cool kids."

She looked up at the sky. A moon had appeared. It was half-sized, cut down the middle, as if it was a fold-out. One side was hard-edged, the other was hazy.

She began to hum. Suddenly her voice sounded strange. It was odd and low and rawly wavering.

"Blue moon," she said, breaking off to clear her throat.

Richard looked up. The moon seemed painted.

"Another country," Ginny continued, speaking slowly.

She looked away. A bareness had set in, a dream-bright defiance; she was absorbed in feeling. "There's a shelter," she said, pointing, "over there."

She led round the pond and they approached together. The building, outlined by the moon, was low, pillared both sides and open at the front. Inside was curved, with crumbling brickwork and a full-length bench.

Ginny entered, glancing round. She walked about examining the bench, peering into corners and fingering the slats. It seemed she was preparing. "Clothes off," she said, suddenly.

Richard searched her face. Her expression was serious. "You mean you want to—"

She shook her head. "Better without clothes. That's all."

Her everyday tone surprised him. It was as if she was an agent, showing him a property.

He shrugged, "If that's what you want."

"It's best."

She began stripping off. As her flesh became visible Richard joined her, laying his clothes out across the slats. He noticed her folds, her heavy-set breasts, the broadness of her body.

When they were naked, Ginny stepped out, alone, into moonlight. "Come on," she said, extending a hand.

Richard paused. He was aware of his slightness. Compared with her, he was stick-white and bony.

"There's no one watching."

She was beckoning him out. With her large round arms, she looked like a wrestler. "Think beach." Her voice was easy and relaxed. Suddenly it seemed simple. Drawn by her calm, he emerged and took her hand. It felt warm and comfortable.

"Have you ever done this before?" he asked, thinking of youth-talk he'd used in parties.

Ginny laughed, "Not with anybody else."

He grinned, imagining her alone, pink and naked, patrolling the night.

They followed the path which cut across the garden, skirting the pond and crossing the flowerbeds. They were pacing carefully, placing their feet as if the stones were hot. By a corner they stood looking, scenting sweetness. A jasmine was sprawled across a head-high trellis. Pausing at a bench they hugged; by a wall they kissed. In the end they slipped out through the gate, finding grass.

Ginny now was humming. Her voice, which was soft, had filled and deepened. There were long-held notes, pauses, and rhythmic repetitions. As they circled barefoot the sounds seemed to change. They shifted and ran together, blending with the air, the sky, and their bodies in the dark. She was moving in step, breathing and singing, contained in being.

"I'm tuning," she said, breaking off.

Richard nodded. "Tune on," he said, quietly.

Ginny returned to her hum. It was louder now, half-droning, half-scat. The notes wavered slightly, becoming raw and chant-like. She started to move round, circling and stepping, with her arms uplifted and her head crooked forward. With Richard at centre she skip-stepped sideways, calling quietly, then pulled up suddenly. "What we must do," she said taking his hand, "is celebrate."

The moon now was higher. Its glow had flattened and hardened. The light it gave out was blue-white and reflective.

Ginny led back into the garden, taking the path to the shelter. "I've just remembered," she said, picking up her sack, "something I brought along." She fumbled in canvas, pulling out a fist-sized pot. "Ointment," she said, unlidding and sniffing. The mixture inside was grey-green and gelatinous.

She pulled out two more, levered off the caps and placed them on a birdbath just outside the shelter. "Red, green, purple," she announced, counting on her fingers. She paced a few rounds, circling her collection. When she urged him to smell, Richard bent forward smiling. The aroma from the pots was richly herbal.

"Plant stuff," she added, "mixed with oils."

In the moonlight the pots glittered dully. Balanced on stone, they looked like melted candles.

"Good for special occasions," Richard said, allowing his eyes to stray from the birdbath. His gaze took in her flesh. She was broad and chunky and heavy all round. He could see her as a washerwoman in a Flemish painting.

Ginny glanced skyward. "Mrs Moon's watching," she said.

"And what does she see?"

"Oh, everything. A world. A city."

"Anything else?"

"A park and garden."

"And what else?"

"A man and a woman."

"Who are doing what?"

Ginny pursed her lips. "Enjoying themselves."

Richard nodded. "Like children…" he began, then paused.

While they'd been speaking Ginny had thrust two fingers into a pot. She stirred then extracted, sniffing the bouquet. Her fingers were coated with thick green blobs. Before they could drip, she blinked shut and rubbed all over, covering her face.

"Creamy," she said, opening her eyes as if she'd been asleep. Patches of green were smeared across her cheeks. There were stains around her mouth and chin. In the dark she looked like a cross-channel swimmer.

"Let's mix it," she said, finger-stirring red. She smeared her neck, coating down her shoulders, then smiled and stepped forward. "Your turn," she continued, dipping into purple.

Richard didn't question. His eyes met hers and he grinned. This was party.

"You can start on my back," he called, turning and squaring his shoulders.

Ginny rearranged the pots and began to smear. She oiled down his spine and circled to his sides. From there she transferred to his arms, rubbing in lightly, then shifted to his chest. Here she used both hands. As she moved up and down, exploring and stroking, his body took on a painterly texture.

"Nice," he murmured.

She descended to his legs, brushing them downwards. "Mud bath stuff," he added as she worked down to his knees. With the pots now close by, she was crouched, head forward, breathing hard. When she reached his ankles, he touched her on the head. "Enough," he said, "I'll do you."

"When I'm finished," she muttered, half-rising. Her face became set as she kneeled again to her task. She was scooping up handfuls, dipping back and forth, spreading round his thighs. She completed with a flourish and stood back, smiling. "That's you," she said, appraisingly, "in your own element."

Richard nodded. His body felt warm. The ointment had sunk in, leaving him smooth and solid and glowing. He was sheathed in colour.

"Now you," he said.

He reached for the pots, dipping, mixing and smearing slowly. It began as decoration: circling her flesh, rubbing down her spine, oiling her front and around her waist. With her breasts he was gentle. As he kneaded her sides he adjusted, skimming her lightly, butterfly-style. He spot-touched her arms, her wrist, her fingertips, then moved to her hips where he lingered, two-handed, thinking art. Returning, he filled up the gaps, particularly on the arms. He circled round, inspecting, then descended to her torso.

Here he slowed further, working and turning and cross-hatching flesh. He shaped her bum, palm-rubbed her thighs, stroked down her legs.

When he'd finished, he stepped back to admire.

"Painted lady," he said, gazing.

Ginny narrowed her lips. "You mean *that* sort of woman?"

"Not exactly. I was thinking…"

She faced him. Their eyes connected. Her stance was full-square and strong. It seemed, in the moonlight, that she could see right through him.

"It's a type of a butterfly," he said.

"Oh, I see. And you reckon the name fits?"

He smiled. "There are other types."

"Such as?"

"Peacock."

She laughed.

"Or fritillary…"

She laughed again.

"Or skipper."

Ginny looked him over, smiling archly.

"But I shall call you beauty," he continued, "because you're red, green, purple and," – here his voice dropped low as he closed up to her body – "very beautiful."

They embraced. Their mouths met again. Together in the garden they stood by the birdbath with their arms around each other. A cloud passed over and the moonlight paled. They continued in a clench, touching and kissing. When the sky cleared again, they half-stepped back, drawing breath. Suddenly they could see. The moon now shone out, sheet-white and clear. It outlined the walls, picked out the path and edge-lit the flowerbeds. They were there by the shelter, and everything was visible, open and exposed. Exchanging looks, they smiled. They were in their own world, with moon and sky and clear bare earth. And they knew they were naked.

When Richard returned home early next morning he entered quietly, in a state of readiness. His mood had darkened. The house felt different – things had changed or shifted on. It seemed he'd arrived at a place he'd once lived but now didn't recognise. Suddenly he could see it: a blank between spaces, a kind of drop-spot or repository where things seemed to lie – and remained there unnoticed. Not just the things, but also (and mainly) the undisclosed *feelings*, the discards and one-offs, the throwaway remarks.

It really was a mess.

Looking as he entered, he took it all in. There were edges showing – floorboards in corners and drips on woodwork – a paper-piled table and coats on the banisters. Narrowing his eyes, he checked his watch. The house was quiet. An air of suspense, of things-not-dealt-with hung around the hall – and though it wasn't that early the curtains were closed and television sounds were issuing from the darkened front room.

As he slipped along the passageway a half-dressed Vanessa became visible in the kitchen, sitting by herself drinking coffee. Her face, which showed nothing, was smooth-set and calm.

He greeted, adjusting. Her words, when they came, appeared from somewhere else.

"I thought I'd wait with the children, till you got back."

He wondered what she meant. There were questions bobbing up, thoughts and speculations, queries about Lance.

"That's fine," he said, pouring coffee.

"Things are OK," she offered.

Richard took a mouthful. It was dark and strong.

"You have plans?" he asked.

Vanessa said not.

"Play it by ear, eh?"

She nodded.

"So, it's all down to us…"

At that moment the phone rang.

"I'll go," said Vanessa, putting down her cup. She crossed to the hallway where she picked up quickly, paying out the wire. As she greeted she dropped her voice, then shuffled off sideways, entering the back room. Even as she spoke, Richard knew.

And he wondered as he listened (hearing Vanessa, low-voiced and whispering, trying to turn the talk) whether he should tell her – not about the night walk, not about the garden, not even the painting, but just about Ginny: about life-style and energy and feelings and being there together and how much easier—

When Vanessa finished talking and returned to the kitchen, the back door was open. There was sunlight showing and the air was dry. Looking down the garden she saw Richard at the end, sat out on the patio. He'd positioned himself side-on, head down, with his back to the fence. A small plastic table was balanced, front legs on earth, back legs on concrete. He was doubled to the table, pen in hand, covering the pages of a soft-backed notebook. Beside him, on the ground, was his coffee.

He looked like his weekday self, marking books. While he wrote, his expression remained narrow-eyed and fixed. He was on task.

Light-spots appeared. The sun grew stronger. Its white-yellow beams, crossing the table, picked out the notebook.

Richard continued writing. With his eyes on paper, he was concentrating hard. Leaning forward, he was formulating carefully, mouthing the words. It was as if he was addressing someone imagined, a figure in a book, a secret correspondent.

Even as she looked, Vanessa knew.

CHAPTER TEN

"It's a matter of consciousness," Justin pronounced.

He was addressing his audience – members of the collective – standing by a fence overlooking a hawthorn patch, a slope, a gully and a steep grassed hill.

"And this," he continued, waving to the hill, "is where they did their thinking."

"You mean their theoretic base?" asked Ken, blinking round.

"A seat of learning."

Richard pulled a face. "Where they stood around listening to lectures—"

Ginny, angling her head sideways, laughed. When Justin resumed she interrupted twice. He acknowledged her feelings – speaking softly and grinning – before repeating his quote. "My own words," he added, beaming round the group.

"So... this is – was – a temple, you believe?" asked a puzzled-looking Lance.

"More than that," put in Ken. "Base and superstructure."

Justin nodded, "And entirely person-made."

Lorna moved forward, heading for a path. A shout went up and someone started singing. Lorna, who was bare-limbed and brown, pointed forward. "The top's that way," she said, tossing back her hair. "Let's go."

With Caroline's help she coaxed her children downhill towards a gate. Vanessa joined, with Charlotte and Stephan. The others followed on, debating.

It was a clear, bright, late-August day. The fields were dry and powder-brown round the edges. Small spiked stems were showing by the path.

They'd left from Lorna's about four hours earlier. Squeezed into cars, recalling the weather and last year's outing, they'd arrived midmorning to walk through what Justin called *The*

Temple of Stones. This, he said, was Middle Earth. He'd led down an avenue of winding sarsens, expounding on snake-lines and computational patterns. At a rough-cut ring of jumbled stones he'd talked about the Goddess. Naming various rocks he'd guided past earthworks (calling them mandalas) and out along the ridgepath to visit the hill. After talking women's history, he'd moved to the observation point. It was here he'd mentioned dreams and university archives. "A hill of the unconscious," he'd called it, quoting his own writings. And when Lorna led off he'd followed on with Ken, discussing workers' power as they passed through the gate.

The hill was terraced, ascending in tiers. Rising abruptly, the ledges were connected by a series of steps. Sharp and angular but softened by grass, it looked like an overgrown pyramid.

Led by the children they followed the path: circling round the back then climbing steeply. At the bottom there were insects – butterflies and wasps – halfway up the drone of grasshoppers filled the air, at the top there was wind and brightness and skylarks on thermals.

They looked round from the summit. Crumbled at the edges, it dropped away suddenly: on three sides in terraces, on the fourth hollowed-out. The view was panoptic.

The children toured the edge, shouting, then descended to the hollow. Here they ran up and down, laughing, and waving their arms like spooks. Their voices were magnified by the cut of the hill.

Vanessa, who was looking over, called out a warning. When the children ignored, she turned towards Lance, pursing her lips. "I suppose they're safe," she said. He nodded.

She switched her gaze back across the top. "Now, that looks good," she said slowly, advancing towards Lorna who was laying out food on a large plastic sheet. Caroline was beside her. She was digging out boxes from a backpack, which she opened and examined, offering the contents like lucky dip prizes.

"Hmm. Looks good," echoed Lance.

Ken approached, waving his arms. He wanted to know when they could eat.

"When you're told," Lorna snapped.

"And not beforehand," added Caroline, grinning.

Richard, who was stood at the edge next to Ginny, cut in. "If it's OK," he said, speaking generally, "I'd – we'd – like to explore."

"Before food?" asked his wife, pulling a face. Her voice, though quiet, carried clearly on the wind.

Before he could answer Ginny intervened. "So what're our options?" she asked, looking round and blinking. "Because I'll do," she added quietly, "whatever people say."

In the debate that followed (a few bright phrases passed round by the women, plus offhand challenges aimed at the men) Lorna took a decision, backed by Caroline, that eating came first. But there was, she said, staring at Ken, one condition.

"Which is?" he asked, colouring slightly.

"The men clear up."

"Unsupervised?" asked Richard, grinning.

Vanessa tut-tutted. Her eyebrows had creased up.

"Don't worry," cut in Justin, speaking hurriedly, "it will be done."

"Terms agreed," added Ken.

After they'd eaten and the men had cleared, Richard and Ginny went off to explore. They climbed downhill, pausing to wave to the children. When they reached the observation point they stopped and waved again, then set off along the ridgepath. The sky was patchy as they followed the track, climbing out of sight. Ginny walked ahead, looking round calmly.

"It's hidden by trees," she called, pointing to where a side branch dipped down to turn behind the hill.

They forked past grasslands dotted with small pink and blue flowers. At the bottom of the slope they passed through a gate and entered an old oak wood. The light levels dropped as they followed a path that wound through groves, enclosed by leaves and branches. The forest floor was dark and mossy in places. Walking hand in hand, they passed by overgrown mounds and dried-out hollows. They moved steadily, taking care where they put their feet.

"It's a long time since I've been this way," said Ginny, peering round. "All I remember is that we follow the main path."

"You're sure it's here?"

She nodded, "Definitely."

The path now was rocky. They walked in the middle of the track, Ginny first, with Richard at her shoulder. The trees had twisted all over. Some were low and sprawly, others were grotesque.

When they came across a pool, she stopped.

"We're close now," she said.

The water made a break, a grey-white space where light could enter. It was still and calm and slightly otherworldly.

Richard nodded: "I think I can see it."

He was half-turned, facing uphill to a clearing. Through the trees a mound was visible. It was fat and long and bulged at odd angles.

"The passage grave," she said, pointing.

They approached, stepping quietly. The mound was grassed, with bare rock showing through. It was the size of a garage, but much longer. Rising sharply from the forest surface, it curved towards the top, which was ship-deck flat.

"And this must be the entrance," said Richard, as they walked up to three large stones set across one end. They were twisted sideways and gapped like teeth. Behind them was an uneven stone doorway that came up to their waists.

"I'm surprised they haven't blocked it off," said Ginny quietly, bending to look in. It smelt of quarried earth and rock.

Beyond the doorway the chamber opened out. It was stone-lined and shadowy, with niches both sides, light holes above and a hollowed-out floor. It looked like a rough-hewn crypt.

They ducked and entered, then stood to inspect. Inside was still. The air was dense and slightly charged – either with silence or something pitched beyond hearing.

"It's large," said Richard.

Ginny nodded. "Let me show you something," she said, taking his hand.

They advanced, moving sideways, along a tunnel which led to a stop. They were facing a wall. It was an undressed stone, all of one piece. In the grey they could make out, at either end, two shallow side-chambers. Turning right, Ginny led along the rock face, stopping at a corner where the wall fell away. "It's a second chamber," she said. "The big stone's a kind of screen."

They pushed through. On the other side it was dark. A solid, all-surrounding thickness which enclosed them. It was deep and still and closed-in on itself.

"It's all right," whispered Ginny. She was crouching down, fumbling in her backpack, tugging out an object that rattled.

Something scraped then crackled into life. The chamber came back as a match head flared.

"There's a candle in there," Ginny said, pointing to her backpack which had dropped to the floor.

Richard crouched down, groping into canvas. As Ginny chain-lit one match to another he drew out a burnt-down candle. "Good," she said as he handed it over.

Narrowing her eyes, she applied the flame. The wick curled, then spluttered into life. A waxy-yellow glow filled the air. As she lowered it floor-wards, the candle flickered.

Richard glanced round and up. The chamber was corbelled. He recognised the shape from one of Vanessa's photos. Compartment-like, it ran along the back of the large front stone. At the far end he noticed, where it widened to a square, the floor was higher, contoured round the edges, with some sort of raised-up covering. "What's that?" he asked, advancing carefully.

The square was padded with inch-thick bundles of dried vegetation. They were crossed and inter-woven like hair extensions. The air smelt dry and herbal.

"It's for ceremonies," said Ginny quietly. As she stepped out on the covering, it rustled like silk.

Richard stared. Ideas were pressing. It felt for a moment as if this was a setup.

"What kind of ceremonies?"

165

Ginny paused, then answered with a smile: "It's called the marriage bed."

He hesitated.

"Don't worry," she continued, "it's only *called* that. It isn't really for vows."

"What's it for, then?"

She shrugged: "People who get on."

"Ah," he nodded, "comrades."

Ginny reached out, offering her hand: "Soulmates."

Richard stepped forward. The vegetation sighed and crackled as she drew him to her. Whatever his doubts, they dissolved at touch. Their mouths came together, his tongue pushed in, and they stood there in candlelight, rocking slightly.

When they broke for air Ginny was blushing. Her lips were trembling and her breath was short.

"Undress me," she whispered.

Richard stooped forward, pulling at her clothes. She helped him, releasing her top then kicking off shoes. Undoing her belt, she allowed him to roll down her jeans. She leant against the wall, repeating his name. His expression softened as, fumbling slightly, he removed her underwear.

"Your turn," she said, unbuttoning his shirt.

When they were naked, they kissed. Ginny drew him down and they stretched out on the floor. At the centre, where they lay, the plants were thicker. They were overspread with petals and live green stems.

Richard touched her, delicately at first. A slow, searching insistence possessed his body. He kissed her breasts, stroked her thighs, then directed her hand down onto his penis. As she worked and teased, they both began to shiver. "Ready," he hissed, and rolled up to mount. He paused, suspended; then, fumbling and flexing, entered. Ginny shuddered. "Yes," she sang, and grabbed for his back. Richard kicked forward, beating time. He was holding his breath, pumping hard. Suddenly he was all-out, grunty and forcing. Something was rising, pushing and thickening and filling up the chamber. For a second he slowed, hung in air, then accelerated towards climax. When Ginny shouted, he felt himself leap, then shake and shake and shake.

In the silence that followed they lay out side by side.

Ginny stirred first. Sighing, she levered up to rest on one arm. "Not so warm," she said, touching his face and kissing.

When they broke, she crouched up and turned. "My back," she said, "can you see it?"

Richard looked. The candle glow, reflected from the walls, lit up her flesh like a painting. She was pink and blotchy and streaky all over. Her skin was cross-hatched and marked with multicoloured flower heads. They'd worked themselves in, staining into bruises.

"You're a Matisse," he said. "All colour and pattern."

Ginny grimaced, "Feels itchy. Like wearing wool."

He examined more closely. "It's the plants," he said, "they've taken to you."

Widening her eyes, she reached round to touch.

"You're a garden," he laughed.

Ginny considered. Her face had turned dreamy. "In that case," she said, "they stay."

Richard blinked. "You're going to keep them?"

She gazed into air: "As much as I can."

He checked her back again. It was textured like wallpaper. "So, how d'you – what's your plan?"

Ginny stood and gathered up her clothes. "If you hold the stems," she said slowly, "I'll dress over."

"Won't that pull them off?"

She considered, then reached down to her sack. "Not if you rub this in," she said, holding up a jar of ointment. "It's good stuff – should do the trick. After all, they're much of a muchness. A mishmash of oils and leaves and fibres. Everything should fuse into one."

Richard hesitated then smiled. "OK. It's herbal glue," he declared, hitching on his shirt before taking the jar. "Full treatment?" he asked as he levered off the top and scooped out a handful. Ginny nodded, and he began.

Working slowly, he picked off a few stems and petals, pressed in what remained, and started oiling. The colours ran, fusing and blurring to a dark-tanned flush. Her skin turned smooth and brown and richly-scented.

"Back to nature," he said, working the curves at the base of her spine.

When the mixture was absorbed she stooped, picked up her top and started dressing.

"I think we ought to show our faces," she said, as she leant against the wall, pulling on her jeans. "Otherwise they'll be wondering what's happened."

Richard hitched on his clothes, slipped on his shoes and picked up the candle. "Lead me the way," he said holding it high.

He stood beside the wall, awaiting Ginny. When she'd tightened and adjusted, he grasped her by the hand. "The candle's getting hot," he said, stepping forward.

When they'd cleared the doorway he turned and blew out. The darkness was instant.

"Kiss me," she whispered, "before we go."

He put down the candle and they embraced. The chamber now was visible: dark and unreal, outlined in grey. The closeness of her body made it seem both bright and shadowy.

Hearing her words repeating in his head, Richard squeezed. Ginny squeezed back, and their mouths came together.

When they left the mound, the weather had changed. The afternoon had closed up. The air was colder and a few light stipples of rain were drifting through the trees.

Richard held out his hand. "We'd better get back," he said.

Inside himself, he was still in the chamber. The rain didn't touch him. A calm soft glow and shield of warmth lay between him and Ginny.

"I smell like a potpourri," she laughed, allowing him to lead her.

Richard sniffed. He could make out – though only faintly – a soft light skin smell, a mix between body and oil. The scent, which was watery, came and went. Already the rain was damping it down.

"Look out," he said. The forest had darkened and the path was uneven. As they sidestepped rocks and skirted hollows the rain picked up.

Bending forward, he caught a whiff of plant. It set off a picture of colours on flesh. Somehow they were greyed-out and faded.

"It's getting worse," he added. The air became thick and damp. There were side-drifts and gusts and water-splashing falls, followed by gaps.

"And worse," Ginny called out.

They sheltered for a while, crouched beneath an oak, until the wind got under, making them shiver.

The rain intensified as they passed beyond the trees and climbed uphill. It fell in sheets, bathing their heads and soaking their clothes. They were half-running now, shouting to each other. By the time they reached the ridgepath the wind was in their faces and the air was thick with flying water.

"Oh shit," cried Richard, pushing on.

As they neared the observation point he could just make out the flat-topped hill: it was bare and grey and blurred round the edges. He peered across the fields, aware of something odd. Suddenly he realised. The gulley round the hill had changed. The grass had vanished beneath a grey-white ring of standing water.

"There's an underground feed," cried Ginny. "It gets cut off."

Richard frowned. "You mean...?" He peered through the rain: "Remember, the path's at the back."

"I'm sure—"

"They could be still around."

The downpour continued. Now it was relentless, soaking in and spreading, working into everything.

"Look," said Richard suddenly. He was pointing to a corner where some figures were emerging, stepping through water. "It's them," he said, waving.

The group, who were tightly bunched, cleared the water and pushed uphill. Richard descended with Ginny at his shoulder, closing the gap. They moved with difficulty, calling out warnings. When they met, the rain kept them head down and purposeful. Their clothes were running and their legs were stained with water.

"You all right?" Richard asked the children who were hand in hand with their mother and Lorna. The rain eased off, allowing conversation.

"We need to get them back," Vanessa countered.

Charlotte and Stephan, who were shivering violently, looked the other way.

"How come you stayed out? Didn't you realise?"

Vanessa bridled. "Realise what?"

"When it started. You needed to leave."

She scowled. "No thanks to you."

Lance, at her shoulder, looked startled.

Richard glowered. He fell in behind, muttering.

As they passed through the gate, Stephan slipped and fell against his mother, crying.

Richard flared. "This is stupid," he snapped.

"Tai toi," called Vanessa, speaking into air.

"What did you say?"

"Richard," she called warningly.

"Come on. Tell me."

Vanessa repeated his name.

"Don't *Richard* me. Tell me what you said."

"Shush. It was nothing."

"Bloody—"

"Richard!"

"Bloody, bloody…"

"Tai toi."

"What?"

"Tai toi."

"You mean that?"

She nodded.

He bridled. "No. No. You don't have the right…"

"Tai toi."

170

"No. You shut it. *You* bloody shut it now."

The rain cut him off. It returned full-force, falling on the path, on the earth and on the grass. Beating and drumming it hit full-on, drowning out his words, his thoughts, his feelings. The rain ran things together, beat upon their skin, their hair, their clothes, went in deep and slowed their movements; it filled up their eyes, gusted into ears and trickled into mouths. Deluge-like it spread and covered everything.

The picnic was over.

CHAPTER ELEVEN

Afterwards, when Vanessa looked back (following a week of silence in the house) she could see how all their recent efforts – their talk about open support and wider structures – hadn't really worked. They'd returned to how it was: Richard on piano, pedal-down, late-night, repeating the same tune (deaf to her interests and muttering darkly about what he called 'crap') – while she took photos and kept up with news and latest developments. She felt the disjunction. They'd hardened and they'd drawn lines. Not only hardened but taken on a slowness, a dead stop feel, a kind of stasis where both sides ignored, digging into corners and building themselves up.

Because the outing and its argument had brought back what she called The Block.

The Block was on everything. It was in the silence, the edge behind his words, the eyes without interest and unresponsive gestures. It concealed itself in quiet and unintended look-arounds, it charged up the breaks, the feel between actions, and introduced a cut-off, a shortness of avoidance, which leaked into everything and affected all they did.

So they functioned. Carried out their tasks in a head down fashion, taking things in turns, holding their ground, remaining separate.

And then, quite suddenly, after a session with Ruth and a late-night phone chat with her old friend Bess, Vanessa decided. Something had to give. What it needed was a different agenda. Time out and space, she said, to get a sense of purpose and find a different way.

"You want a break?" asked Richard standing in the doorway after bedding down the children. His words, as they came out, sounded awkward. There was a rawness there and a blunt-voiced challenge, which wouldn't let things go.

"A chance to catch up," said Vanessa, speaking slowly, "and find out what we want." She was sitting, reading a newspaper article, wedged between cushions on the front room sofa. Every so often she angled forward to take in herbal tea.

"How d'y' mean?"

"We need to know where we stand."

Richard looked doubtful. "Isn't that about talking – or not talking?"

She grimaced: "Maybe. Maybe not. We'll have to see."

The silence returned. Vanessa eyed her article, while Richard leaned out, detaching from the doorway.

"It's up to us," he said flatly, stepping into the lounge, "*we* have to talk."

She sipped more tea: "Does that *we* mean me or both of us?"

"I think you know the answer to that."

Vanessa raised her eyebrows, "I do?"

"Well, if you don't—"

"Who does?" she cut in. "Is that what you think?"

He frowned. "I don't get your point."

"The point is…" she began with a sigh, then switched. "It's how you operate. Everything's decided from the start. Whatever it is – even what I'm saying now – you've made up your mind beforehand. It's all slam-bam: cut and dried and fitted into categories. You *assume* all the time."

"Ah, I see. Ain't what you say but the way you say it, eh?"

Vanessa shook her head. "It's true. You don't talk, you give out."

"Well, if that's what you believe…" he moved towards the door, "then I can only suggest we get someone…"

"In any case," she continued, "talk has to be equal. It's not a one-way street."

"Absolutely." He stared her in the face. "Absolutely so."

Vanessa flushed, "What are you suggesting?"

Richard shrugged. "We need help."

"We?"

"Yes, we."

She considered. "So, in your opinion, what should *we* be thinking of?"

"A counsellor."

She pressed one hand against her article. "Ah, I see. But it wasn't that long ago…"

Richard shifted slightly. He narrowed his eyes and considered.

Reaching for her tea, Vanessa drained her cup. She turned in his direction and space-gazed thoughtfully: "You want to go back to that woman? What was her name – Chris? You called her The Q and A Woman. The one who kept asking how we felt."

"Someone new would be better."

She blinked: "What makes you say that?"

Richard considered. "Partly money. She got *us* to do all the talking, then charged for it. But also outcomes, I suppose. She didn't do much."

"That's one way of looking at it."

"It seems to me that kind of counselling is a con. It's all about dodging and staying on the surface. Don't rock the boat and don't, whatever you do, get too close to the problem."

She nodded.

"You agree?"

She nodded again.

"So we need a different counsellor."

"Seems so."

He paused, examining her carefully. "So who's going to look for this person?"

Vanessa thought it over. When he repeated his question, she made to say something then sighed. It seemed she needed coaxing.

"Do you want me to?" he asked, more gently.

"Would you?"

"You want that?"

A third time, she nodded.

Richard smiled. "So in this case *we* means me – correct?"

Vanessa confirmed. Picking up her cup and paper, she rose from the sofa. She walked out kitchen-wards, shifting her grip.

"We means me," she repeated, depositing her cup and returning to the hallway.

Richard, who had stood quietly waiting, nodded.

She said it again, using it as a password, and once more as a catch-phrase, as they climbed to the stair-head past the kids' bedrooms and (after taking soundings on dates they might arrange) up to the bathroom, the second-flight landing, and their curtained front bedroom.

They arrived at the counsellor's house just before 2.00. Leaving the car, Richard led across a green surrounded on three sides by yellow-and-grey blocks. At the main road he'd paused, crossed between trees, checking off numbers to arrive at the building.

It was low and set back from the road. Last but one in a long terraced row, it had steps with railings, casement windows and a paved front garden. Richard checked the time then pressed the bell, while Vanessa stared vaguely down at the basement.

As they waited Richard remained focused. Whatever was happening (or not happening) they'd been here before…

The door was answered by a short ginger-haired woman wearing a blue sequinned dress and red, ballet-shaped pumps. She was pale-skinned, with soft expressive eyes and a small round face. Her eyes and lips were lightly made-up. Vanessa judged her to be nearing 40.

"Please come in." Her voice was warm, upbeat and slightly playful. Richard noticed her Home Counties' accent.

They entered a hallway with dado and features. There were glimpses through doors of wall-to-wall bookshelves and period furniture. The house smelt of polish and flowers.

Their host led forward, directing to some stairs, a quarter-flight left, then stepped back to watch. "I consult in the lounge," she said, pointing, "up there." The arm she raised displayed a thick gold bracelet.

She followed as they climbed. Already, it seemed, she had them reckoned up.

They entered the room at a midway point. It was softly furnished with a key-pattern carpet, gold-flecked curtains and abstracts on the wall. Their host called out: "If you'd care to sit – sofa, chairs – on the floor if you like."

They settled, with Vanessa in an armchair and Richard on the couch. Between them, positioned at the centre of a low glass table, was a water jug and glasses.

The counsellor asked about jackets, mentioned the loo, then drew up a chair. She placed it at an angle, facing both. It was high-backed and wooden with a small central cushion. She perched there, watching. "So, introductions..." she said, smiling. Her tone had become ultra-bright and unequivocal.

She poured herself a glass of water then, dividing her gaze evenly between clients, began. "I am, as I think you know, Laetitia Cauldwell. I've been a fully accredited counsellor for fifteen years. My background is interdisciplinary, but my main approach is encounter – which I'd say is more direct than most." Pausing to consider, she adjusted her dress, sending small light-flecks dancing across the carpet. When she resumed – mentioning fees and initial assessments – Richard found himself drifting slightly. He was (of course) registering, giving full attention, taking it in... but behind that were the feelings, the loose ends and tangles, the tensions going back.

Because there'd been those other sessions. A number of attempts, hour-long and circular. Bids to clear the air. Slow-spoken 'explorations' in which they'd talked and talked — but not made progress. The first, as he recalled, happening quite early. It had come about as a result of battles they were having. They'd crossed a line – a row, quite shouty, followed by days not speaking – had found themselves 'stuck' (a word used in summary, appearing often in later sessions) and everything fell apart.

But the talk hadn't worked. He remembered the counsellor (mouse-man he'd called him) asking *them* to speak, offering little nods, repeating his formula. A still-life man, observing, receiving, allowing things to drift. A man of no qualities, agreeing all the time, leading from behind.

"And I may set you tasks," concluded Laetitia. "Homework, you might call it."

She smiled. A reassuring smile, torch-beam-directed, taking them both in. It was as if she was preparing them for a part.

No one answered.

"In that case," said Laetitia, "let's talk."

She began with Vanessa, asking facts: how long they'd been together, children, status, employment, interests shared, and what they did together.

"You mean films, meals out, that sort of thing?"

"Anything. Activities in common. Shared space, visits, chats, television programmes. What you both enjoy."

Vanessa pulled a face, "There's not much we *enjoy*."

Laetitia fixed her gaze on her client. Her hands were in her lap, little-girl style, and her features had rounded.

"So tell me," she said innocently, "what really *happens* between you."

In the silence that followed Vanessa sighed.

"How would you sum up your marriage?"

"Oh, I don't know. Disappointing."

"Anything else?"

"Not much."

"Tell me how it disappoints."

Vanessa laughed, harshly. "It's full of problems. Too many to name."

"But if I asked you to name them…"

"What, all of them? You want that?"

"As many as you can. It's important."

Vanessa looked down, studying the carpet. "Well, lack of communication, that's one. Assumptions, that's another. An attachment to being right – that's all the time. Sometimes intolerance. Sometimes hype. And a certain relentlessness. Male stuff, really."

"And what do you *want* out of relationships?"

The counsellor's question, delivered softly, filled up the room.

Vanessa shifted in her seat, gazing into space. "A bit of peace and calm, I suppose, and care if you like. A different approach, where things happen slowly, so there's a chance to relax and not feel pressured. And enough time and space to feel there's someone there listening."

"And how about you?" Laetitia asked, switching to Richard. Her gaze was direct and challenging.

He paused. "It has to match," he answered slowly.

"I see. So what's involved in a *match*?"

Richard glanced over at Vanessa. "I suppose," he said, "it's all about overlapping circles. Getting the right fit. Not too much, not too little." His voice flattened to a stop.

"I see. Anything more?"

"Not really," he answered, "except that we don't."

Laetitia leaned to one side, watching him closely. "So. What you're saying is you don't have any shared interests. None at all. Is that right?"

"None that work."

"But you did have some in the past?"

He hesitated, then nodded almost imperceptibly.

She swung round in her chair. "And if I asked you both, you could name them?" Her tone now was light and upbeat. She was speaking into air, addressing an audience. It was as if she was chairing a debate.

Both her clients stared, saying nothing.

"In that case," she continued, standing and pushing back her chair, "I'd like us to try an experiment, downstairs."

Vanessa frowned. She raised one hand halfway to her cheek, then allowed it to fall. Richard, who was smiling, remained attentive.

"It's OK," Laetitia said, addressing Vanessa, "I do this with lots of clients."

She walked to the door, "So, if you'd like to come this way."

She positioned herself within view, outside on the landing. Window-lit from above, the sequins on her dress glittered. Her face was moon-soft, rounded and inviting.

Her clients hesitated then, when Laetitia repeated, they looked in both directions (as if to check the traffic) and rose to join her.

"This way... this way," she called, leading down the steps and turning left through a pair of double doors.

They followed, saying nothing.

Inside was an oblong area with whitewashed walls and a bare wooden floor. It was barred to one side, with ropes in the corner, coiled like snakes. The other side was cluttered with balls in nets, a collection of sticks and a heaped-up pile of rubberised mats. "The games room," Laetitia called, walking to the centre.

Glancing round, her clients joined her.

She examined them carefully. Her face was bland, but attentive. "But for us," she said, "it's an area where we step outside ourselves."

Vanessa inclined her head to one side.

"Don't worry," said Laetitia, "it's simple. I'll show you."

By way of explanation she pointed to a line drawn across the floor. It was white and glossy and blurred around the edges. It divided off an area close to the far wall.

"We're going to play. But it's more than a game," she said. "It may change how you think."

Richard and Vanessa stood looking.

"You know *what's the time Mr Wolf?*" she asked, widening her eyes.

Richard nodded.

"You know it also?" she checked, staring at Vanessa.

The yes she received sounded slightly nasal.

Addressing them both, Laetitia developed her thoughts briefing-style, as if she was their trainer. "You sneak up from there," she said, waving to the line. "While I'm Mrs Wolf, up there," she said, indicating the door end. "Now when I call out a time, three o'clock, four o'clock etc, you take that number of steps. But if I turn around – freeze."

"And if you call dinner time..." prompted a deadpan Richard.

"Then scoot. Get behind the line before I catch you."

179

She had to repeat, fielding questions from a doubtful-looking Vanessa. After a short trial with Richard as wolf (during which he broke out repeatedly without proper cueing), she invited comment. Receiving none, she placed them behind the line and, moving watchfully, retreated to the door end. "Anyone cheats, you tell me," she called sharply, turning her back.

Her clients exchanged glances.

"So... Can I hear you – your words, please – now."

Richard grinned. "What's the time Mrs Wolf?" he called, projecting slightly.

"One o'clock."

They both took a step forward. Richard, a big one; Vanessa, a shuffle.

"What's the time Mrs Wolf?" – his voice, leading; Vanessa's joining in.

"Two o'clock."

Two more steps, all middling.

"What's the time Mrs Wolf?" – a duo now, one loud, one soft.

"Four o'clock."

Again, they advanced. By now they were two yards distant: Richard leading, Vanessa close behind.

"What's the time Mrs Wolf?"

"One o'clock."

Richard took a small stride then stopped dead as the counsellor whipped round. "You're moving," she said, pointing.

"He's not," Vanessa volunteered.

Richard's eyes widened. He made to say something, then froze. Neutral was best.

Laetitia stared suspiciously. Her eyes were tight and her mouth was squared-up. "Tongue and lips," she said, quickly.

Vanessa shook her head: "It's only feet that count."

"I see. And that's the rule?"

"It is," countered Richard.

Laetitia, looking hawkish, turned her back. "Your call," she said.

"What's the time—"

Before they could finish she was round and staring. "Dinner time!" she laughed, lunging forward.

Richard skipped off and away. He reverse-spun, dodging Laetitia's outstretched hand, and scampered back. "Behind the line!" he sang out as she made a final grab.

Vanessa, who had flattened to the wall, scrambled her way back, side-gripping the bars. "Off the floor!" she cried when Laetitia tagged her.

"Over the line anyway," Richard put in.

Laetitia drew back. "Very well," she said, laughing. "We begin again."

She returned to her post. This time she answered all their calls in ones and twos, spinning round sharply at unexpected moments. Realising her tactic, Richard slowed his approach, inching forward and stopping often when he sensed movement. Vanessa stayed with him, advancing warily. Occasionally they rushed, sometimes they stood still. When Laetitia called *dinner time* they flung themselves backwards, twisting out of reach. And in the end, after several rushes and a number of freezes (with a couple of send-backs by a sharp-eyed Laetitia), it was Vanessa who reached out and successfully tagged her.

"Well done," Laetitia called. "Now, let us conclude."

They followed her to the lounge where they took their seats. She watched and waited for her moment as their breathing slowed. Her eyes flicked round like a medic taking observations. "So how do you feel?" she asked them in turn. Richard volunteered his surprise. "But quite stimulated," he added. Vanessa gestured into air without saying anything.

Laetitia drew out an A4-sized whiteboard which she displayed, poster-like, then propped against the chair leg. "And this," she declared, holding up a pen, "is my magic marker." She leaned down and up, uniting the two. "And from today," she continued, demonstrating a tab which rubbed out words, "do we have anything to put down – anything you *can* do together?"

"Counselling," said Richard dryly.

"True," she said, printing his comment. "Anything else?"

"Children's games," said Vanessa.

"Yes. Anything more?"

"Working against you," Richard replied quietly.

"And?"

Vanessa pursed her lips, "Running?"

"That's so," put in Richard, pulling a face.

Laetitia transcribed the comments. She asked Richard to hold up the board and stepped back, appraisingly. She was measuring it carefully like a prospective purchase. "One more," she said.

"Another?" said Richard, returning the board. "There are five?"

Laetitia nodded.

He locked his fingers together, "I think you mean when you challenged us."

"Go on."

Vanessa leaned forward, wrinkling up her nose. "It's like Vaughan."

Laetitia blinked, "Explain."

"My cousin. He's not easy, but likes adventure."

"So, number five?"

"Risk taking."

Their counsellor copied out. The board now was full of neatly-printed words.

Richard unlocked his fingers. "I've two more," he said. "Six and seven."

The two women stared.

"I'd like to write them up," he said.

Laetitia smiled, offering him the pen.

Approaching the board, he looked round quickly then crouched down and pulled the tab, erasing to a blank.

"They cover all the rest," he said, by way of explanation.

Raising the pen, he drew circles in air. "When you challenged us," he said, "I thought of this. It's political, of course."

He paused and focused then, ignoring the women, wrote slowly and awkwardly in a badly formed scrawl: *1. Backing up*. After it, in brackets, he wrote *each other*. Finally, after some

hesitation he raised the marker again and added, in capitals, arranged vertically beside the number 2: *FINDING*
A
MATCH.

He paused then repeated it, using identical capitals, columned to one side.

"And," he said, half-circling both statements, "there's the question of overlap." He completed the circles, creating two sickle-shaped, printed areas on either side with an aperture between. "It's in here," he added quietly, pointed to the space in the centre, "where we don't ever go – that's the place."

"Don't ever?" asked Laetitia.

"Don't usually," corrected Vanessa.

"But maybe we've been there today?" Richard put in.

"In theory, yes."

Laetitia nodded. "And that's where we'll be next week," she concluded. "looking in detail. Point by point, seeing what you share. Or could do if you tried."

She stood with a flourish, inviting them door-wards. Her manner now was braced up and vigorous.

Richard paid in cash. Vanessa checked her diary and booked in the next session. Adjusting their expressions they filed out through the door with Laetitia behind them.

"So your homework," she said, "which you can do individually or together, is listing what you share."

She watched them to the road. As they reached the pavement she stepped back to her door. Outlined against the building she paused there, smoothing her hair and adjusting her dress. As they left she raised one hand to wave them off. "Next time: the overlap," she called out smiling, and turned towards the door.

As she turned her hair coloured up, the sequins on her dress shone and sparkled, and her bracelet gleamed gold in the afternoon sun.

CHAPTER TWELVE

When school began in September, Richard and Vanessa took it in their stride. There were all the usual problems – photocopier break-downs, books gone missing, rooming clashes and too few chairs – and a long list of duties: new groups to organise, tasks to dish out, lessons to plan and (of course), issues of control. There were meetings to attend and timetable changes and grades to set and incident reports – but Vanessa and Richard knew by now how best to play it, when to step out, when to delay, and how to hold direction. It was, after all, a route they knew well. And whatever the difficulties, it kept them together. It held them to a line, a shared intention. Because by now they'd found a formula, a position they took in relation to teaching. They were chalk-face veterans, known to the staff as activists and accepted by the kids as 'OK teachers' who understood the score. It seemed they'd registered. And they'd developed their own style: a blend of cool-talk and immediate come-backs, a liberal approach based on fairness, where they stayed in charge but showed themselves willing to fit where necessary.

For Richard it was an act – a well-practised scenario where he put up and gave out and signalled what he wanted. So when he walked into classrooms he felt himself framing, taking on a character, a kind of second self. He called it 'swanning through'. In he came, and laid out his terms. He did what he did, put out the story, gave order and direction without a pause for thought. He was upfront and centred, simple as that.

For Vanessa it was a struggle. A fragile, thin-lipped battle against school rules and procedures which made each lesson feel like an exam. There were books and extracts and equipment and worksheets and tasks to give out, all of which involved detailed preparation (like entertaining family or setting up an art show) and talking pupils through. Because behind what she did was so much hand-holding and childminding and jollying-along. It relied on makeshift: on fallback plans and things saved up. ("You carry the whole lot with you," she once told Ruth, "a bagful of supplies – pens, pencils, paper, rulers, rubbers – whatever they've forgotten – usually everything – you'd better have it all.")

So school, with its codes and assumptions and all-too familiar problems, kept them together.

But it also pushed them back – by contrast and reversal. They'd other things to do, some pressing, some political and some just intended – but also things private, the needs they didn't talk about, what moved them and touched them and obsessed them and underpinned their lives.

For Richard it was the lack. The emptiness behind everything, the gap and the fall-off, the sense of missing out, of a life not lived. He knew it and felt it and called it his *otherness* (his past and present self as Richard-the-boy and Richard-with-Ginny, concealed behind the teacher he glimpsed in the mirror). And though he could block it out (keeping upside, always busy, always sorting through) he wished for something firmer, a deep-state connection, an expressive link or hook or line in to who he was.

For Vanessa it was practical. She'd rather, she said wryly, find something less demanding. Teaching was a bore, it didn't come easily or allow for other business. What should be a job had turned into a calling – an imposition really – so that everything else was pushed into background. It felt too much like a setup, and a burden.

And then Lorna rang up. She had, she said, a proposal. What she offered came as a surprise.

"A women's exhibition," Vanessa told Richard afterwards, "with friends."

Richard blinked. "That's great," he said, smiling.

"You're pleased?"

"Absolutely."

She gave him details: a large joint show – old and new, mixed media – run, she said, in a warehouse.

He acknowledged. Already he could see them stepping clean through the door to an art space. He imagined it as wide-open, a kind of chamber or walk-through with graffiti-ed walls and improvised furniture. An arena people occupied in whatever way they could. A punk-art-emporium where those with attitude came to make their mark.

He asked about arrangements.

Vanessa beamed: "It's soon. Next month. Lorna's got the contacts and they want me near the entrance. They call it *Seeing Red*."

"So it's political?"

"Yes. Also arty, I think."

"And you've got enough photos?"

"Mostly. A few to finish."

He nodded. "Perhaps I can help," he said quietly, "transport, setting up, that sort of thing."

"Well, that's kind…" She paused, meeting his gaze for a second.

"Doug could be useful as well."

Vanessa's eyes widened: "Ah, you mean removals – Jones and co, man with van."

Her words took him back. He remembered the move-in and the outing that followed with its swing-seat episode – and how absurd they'd been. He remembered, too, how they'd made it their story, grinning and pulling faces when they told it to friends. It had been, he supposed, a convenient joke: an incident, a prank and something to talk about – a youthful absurdity.

He laughed. "Well, not the exact vehicle. But in principle, much the same thing."

"Very well," she replied, "in principle, yes."

During the exhibition run-up, Doug and Richard DIY-ed the show. They first checked the building – a hangar-like shed with strip lights and pillars and skid-marked floors – then brought in display boards (old doors and palettes which they filled and panelled out, building upward and extending with hardboard). Finding floor-holes, they screwed in supports, constructing what looked like a makeshift compound. Inside was a central display with space all around and irregular, crenulated walls (which they filled and made good with rough-mix, sanded, and various compounds). During construction, Vanessa cleaned the surfaces, which were then joined and levelled and hooked up for display.

As they worked they were visited by the organisers – two flat-faced mid-thirties women, one wearing denim with badges all over, the other in dark glasses. Speaking sweetly, they introduced themselves as Sophie and Lanya.

Moving closer, they examined Vanessa's pictures, which she'd taken from wallets and spread, newspaper-like, across the floor.

"Important stuff," murmured Sophie.

"Political – right?" asked Lanya.

"Left," put in her friend.

"Dead right, if you ask me."

Vanessa, who was clip-framing pictures, paused to look up, saying nothing.

The two women continued their exchange.

"Not centre. Definitely not centre."

"Oh God, no. Anything but."

In the background the men were busy fitting supports to a doorframe.

"In any case, not *just* left."

"Or right."

"Or even centre."

As Vanessa's eyes widened, Sophie stepped back. "It's broad front art," she called out triumphantly.

"But vanguard."

"Yes, avante guard."

"And important."

"A woman's eye."

Dropping silent, they both caught the eye of the woman with artwork.

Sophie smiled hard: "Oh, welcome to the woman's show…" she said, tightly. "Your pictures are important, very important to us."

Lanya joined in, nodding and repeating as they turned and walked off.

Their last words were upbeat, and gestural. They were sweet and bright, and echoed round the warehouse. They were out there, up there, on it, intended to be heard.

For them this was art.

It was Richard who planned the opening. At first he'd not offered. A women's event – even one where he'd looked after children and constructed the area – well, it needed careful handling. There were politics involved. A man who stepped in, even as a gap-fill, was a ready-made target.

But then, as the date drew closer and Vanessa didn't seem to register, impatience took over.

"What do you want?" he asked her twice daily (at least).

She responded vaguely and withdrew to her studio.

"Is there anything you need?" he asked, sounding uppity, when she appeared downstairs and hovered round the phone.

"Only a title," she said. "Something that says it all. A programme header."

He made various suggestions, offered phrases, quick thoughts and pointers, but nothing seemed to fit.

Vanessa simply smiled or looked without interest or turned the other way.

"So it's all right if I do what I like for the opening?"

Vanessa nodded, ignoring the edge.

When he switched, trying to talk it over, she said she'd be happy whatever he did.

"You mean that?"

Vanessa confirmed.

"In practice as well as theory?"

Vanessa frowned, then offered a theoretic formula. She called it *additionality*. It meant, she said, his efforts added value.

"All right. I take that to mean *go ahead*…"

And go ahead he did, producing an invite and circulating everyone, then following up with calls and reminders and messages left, then typing out a makeshift programme and commandeering tables (recovered from the basement then stripped and polished) and working with Doug to haul them into corners, cover them with cloth and lay on refreshments.

On the day, Vanessa was glacial. She'd abstracted herself to a blank-faced distance, an eye round, a smile and a well turned-out greeting. She was there to play hostess. Dressed full-length in white in a close-fitting dress, she welcomed all-comers.

Lance appeared first.

"You're early," she said avoiding his gaze.

"This is right? It is the opening?" he asked, sounding hoarse. He stared round short-sightedly, as if he'd just landed.

Richard laughed. He was crouched on the floor shoring up a corner where the walls had slumped. Doug, who was with him, was gripping hard round a cross-ply tool. He was driving in screws to a link-plate.

"Ask a stupid question," Richard said quietly, keeping his head down.

Vanessa, sensing something, turned and stared. "Did you say you wanted to view?" she asked, addressing Lance.

"A tour would be helpful," he said, nodding to himself.

She walked him round the pillar. On each side her photos were arranged in clip-framed batches, pinned up like posters. One wall showed incidents (demos and meetings and people giving speeches), another was of graffiti, the third wall held portraits (activists, mainly, holding up banners or selling papers), the fourth was a collage of faces and gestures and lined-up bodies – all female, all smiling, all ages.

Lance wanted details. Looking and asking, he circled the pictures. His questions, delivered quietly, seemed closed: he needed information, clear lines and specifics, something to hold on to.

Speaking slowly, Vanessa responded. At first she engaged, trotting out names, then (in answer to further questions) adding in places and incidental details – but soon she pulled back. She was registering quietly, gazing into air. When he pressed her, pointing to a photo of faces on a beach, she shrugged, claimed it didn't matter and quietly turned away. And when more guests arrived she excused herself, citing other business, and left to look around.

The area filled up. The collective appeared, arriving as a group, minus Ginny. They were debating a case which had come up at conference (with Lorna incensed, backed by Caroline, and the men all vowing action).

Ruth came next carrying a card and bottle which she presented to Vanessa. She was followed by a suited Frank, accompanied by Jackie who walked him round the pictures. "Unless it's about teaching," she joked, "he needs it explaining. ABC and first guide. Says he doesn't understand."

"You mean he's a nervous boy?" Ruth called out.

"Pretty much," put in Frank. "Failed my art exam. Bottom of the class."

The organisers showed up, debating between themselves, and ignoring the photos. Other guests arrived, including friends and colleagues, fellow ex-graduates and long-term contacts – all admiring, all giving out.

For Vanessa and Richard it offered added value.

"The show's a success," was Richard's verdict when he caught up with Vanessa halfway through.

She smiled. "My parents still haven't seen it," she said, checking her watch.

He shrugged. "No problem. Remind them it's family, then they'll approve."

"I shouldn't count on it." Her eyes met his. "But I do understand," she said suddenly. "And I know you're being helpful. It's just this exhibition means a lot to me, and I want them to approve."

"Don't worry," said Richard, "I'll talk them up. They'll like it."

"I do hope—" she began, then cut off suddenly.

"Just watch me," he said, lowering his voice. He was half-turned to the entrance, where Felicity and Derek had appeared, hand in hand with the children.

Charlotte and Stephan ran to their mother. Calling loudly, they surrounded her with talk. While Vanessa shushed them,

Richard stepped forward, greeting politely and offering to show round.

"You're so kind," said Felicity, gazing 180°. She was dressed in a grey-flecked suit with light blue trimmings and padded shoulders. Her chin was high and her colour was up. Beside her, Derek appeared to be awaiting orders.

She both-cheek-kissed Vanessa, then scanned the pictures. "My dear, you've done well," she said. "You must have worked ever so hard."

Vanessa acknowledged. "It was all a bit last minute," she said, "but in the end we got it up. Everyone's been very kind."

Her mother lowered her voice, glancing round: "Now, please don't let us interrupt you. I imagine you are busy-busy; there must be lots of people here you really *have* talk to."

Vanessa was about to deny when Lanya, who was talking to a man with a camera, called her over.

Richard stared. "Do you think it's the press?" he asked.

"I believe so," Vanessa replied. "I was told they might appear."

"Well, it looks like they want you," he said. "Now." He gestured and turned to the parents, explaining quickly.

"Oh indeed, you must go," called Felicity. "Carpe diem."

As Vanessa slipped off, Richard took over. Pointing to the photos and pitching up his voice, showman-style, he invited them to view.

"Are you sure it's all suitable?" Felicity asked, nodding towards the children.

"The highlights tour, yes," responded Richard. He gestured: "Please. If you'd care to, just step this way."

Children and grandparents were led to a collection of black-and-white photos. Arranged in sequence, they showed a woman cycling. The lines around her limbs were blurred, giving the impression that her body was in action. She seemed self-absorbed. Her pose was head down, doubled on herself, with elbows protruding.

"The name's Rhiannon," Richard said. "She's a colleague. Teaches sport."

Felicity smiled. "She certainly looks the part. I suppose she's a typical modern woman."

"In which case…" Derek began, then halted himself.

Richard, ignoring, pressed on with the tour.

They moved to a display of cityscapes and skylines. It was spread across the top half of a double-sided panel. There were friezes and verticals and wide-angle sweeps with large-print pictures and joined-together views. On the bottom (presented in circles and seen through arches) were close-ups of flowers and borders in full bloom. The horticultural images spread up and round to a third, much larger panel where the colours blended.

"Different landscapes," said Richard, pointing both ways.

Derek stepped closer. "Interesting," he said, peering at the joins. "It's all very carefully done."

Richard's mind flashed back to the upstairs train sets.

They stood as a group, regarding. It seemed they were audience sharing an experience. Even the children were aware of occasion.

"It's an awful lot of pictures," Felicity said glancing round, and Derek nodded.

Richard waited (judging the dynamic: when best to move them on) then led past clip-framed photos hung on wood, arriving at an end point. Here the walls gave out, leaving a hole. The gap between, which was narrow, was blocked by a heavy wooden table. "Vanessa's worktop," he said. "Taken from her studio."

He stepped back to view. A collection of photos stood on the desktop. They were propped on wedges, printed on card and had black and gold borders. At the front there were life-size portraits of Stephan and Charlotte with, between them, pictures of the children in parks and gardens, escorted by their grandparents. Behind there were pictures displaying younger versions of Vanessa and Richard.

Derek coloured. He was staring blankly at the picture of himself. "I didn't expect this," he said.

Felicity said his name, warningly.

"I really don't think…" he added, shaking his head.

Richard frowned: "You're not happy?"

The other man shifted his stance, not saying anything.

"I thought you'd be pleased."

"Well—"

"It's meant as a tribute," Richard offered.

"If I'd wanted…"

Felicity intervened again, cautioning.

"I do think we should have been asked."

"What do *you* think?" she responded, turning to the children.

"Grandpa looks nice," Charlotte responded quickly.

Stephan backed her up.

"And the pictures of yourselves?"

Charlotte grinned. "Oh, we've seen those before."

"But what about the show? Your mother's photographs. Do you like them?"

The children nodded.

"But one day…" put in Richard.

"One day," echoed Stephan.

"One day," called his sister, who was standing next to a portrait of Vanessa, "she'll be famous and *I'll* take pictures."

"Are you sure of that?" her grandmother laughed.

Stephan protested. It was meant to be him. That was the truth.

"Both of you," Richard said quietly. "You can both be in the pictures *and* take them." He reached forward to the table, turned a handle and flicked open a drawer. Inside was a camera.

"I thought so," he said, drawing it out. "It's an instant."

He examined and declared it ready, then checked another drawer. His search produced a few small unused frames which he propped to one side.

"And now," he said, "starting with Stephan, *we'll* take photos while *you* – if that's all right –" here he turned and indicated the grandparents, "take centre stage."

Felicity was charmed, Derek averse, but the children insisted. Richard took charge, on the one side grouping (finding that Derek preferred, for reasons of height, to be upfront with Charlotte while Felicity stood behind) – and on the other side demonstrating: guiding to viewfinder, flash, and red-button-press.

The children took pics, the grandparents smiled and no one walked between. Richard kept them up, talking and cajoling and feeding with positives. Even Derek was persuaded.

Soon they'd several prints, rolled out slowly, dried on paper and spread across wood.

"The children must choose," said Richard crouching to their level. "Two each."

Four were selected. After checking with grandparents and adding a couple more, Richard placed them, one to a frame, grouped round the portraits.

"So now you're up there," he said, standing back, "playing your part."

He smiled. The grandparents nodded. The children laughed. Suddenly they were together, centred by the camera, with nothing held back.

It reminded Richard of himself and Vanessa pictured at the zoo. Embracing to camera. Even now he could hear the shutter click. Could hear it and sense it, set on automatic. And the words he'd used – laughing, expressive, holding her to him – that he'd bloody well make it work.

When Ginny arrived it was late, the parents had gone, and the gallery was empty except for the organisers and a few remaining women who had gathered round Vanessa.

"I brought you these," Ginny said, colouring, as she presented Vanessa with a large bunch of chrysanthemums.

Vanessa's eyes widened. "Oh, they're lovely," she said, raising the blooms to eye-level. She examined them closely like a photographic subject.

They were rust-red, brown-yellow, and flecked with blue. Below they were green, above that orange, and from centre to petal tip they shaded: light to dark, red through purple.

"Sorry, I would have been here earlier," said Ginny, "but the meeting dragged on." She waved an arm towards the pictures: "Did the opening go well?"

Vanessa glanced round. Beside her Ruth and Bess offered their support. They talked as if the show was a contest and Vanessa was in the lead.

"Everyone loved it," said Ruth. "She's our own up-and-coming. Star of the show."

Vanessa blushed. "I think it was appreciated," she said, addressing her bouquet.

"And you've seen all this?" said Ruth, pointing to the walls: "We call it the farm."

Ginny laughed. "Why the farm?"

Ruth shrugged, "It's all bits and pieces. Overnight stuff, cobbled together."

"It wasn't here already?"

Ruth shook her head.

"So somebody built it."

"True." Ruth bared her teeth: "It's like all these things, there were bodies. We're deeply indebted to Doug Jones and Richard Lawrence."

"They put it up? It must've kept them busy."

"Ah, but you should have seen us supervising. Flat out we were, keeping them on task."

Ginny considered, frowning slightly. Her gaze returned to Vanessa. "They could do with some water," she said, glancing at the flowers.

Ruth laughed. She moved to a table and picked up two nearly-full bottles. Finding a jug, she poured in the contents. "I'll deal with that," she said. "Just give me the bunch."

She took from Vanessa and held them aloft. "So lovely, aren't they," she said, beaming. "You're special," she continued, addressing the bouquet, "very, very special."

Fixing her eyes on the flower heads, she smiled. "And you deserve only the best. The very best," she said with relish, lowering the stems into the jug.

For a moment there was silence.

Vanessa's eyebrows shot up. "That's wine," she said quietly, looking round.

"That's so," her friend shot back.

"But is it—"

"Suitable? Harmful? Probably not."

"Plants can filter," said Ginny. "They'll take what they need, leave the rest."

"Sounds like my kids," Ruth returned, "picking out the veg from anything you give 'em."

Vanessa laughed, "I suppose if *they* can survive on sweets and Shreddies…"

"In any case," said Ginny quietly, "chrysanths are strong – they can live on, for weeks or months, even. They're toughies."

"Flower power, eh?" quipped Ruth. "I'll buy that."

Vanessa sighed, then slowly straightened. "I think I've got it," she said, reaching down to produce a camera, which she held up like a find.

"She's really got it," sang Ruth, inconsequentially.

Vanessa ducked into the strap and directed her eye to the flowers. "Hmm, that's right," she said, pointing the lens at various angles while circling her subject.

"Yes, yes," she continued, clicking.

"That's it," she said, leaning in to get a few close-ups.

Ruth, inspecting, asked what *it* was.

"What I was looking for."

"Which is?"

"These," said Vanessa, pointing to the flowers.

"Yes…"

"They're the point."

"Explain please, Vanessa my dear."

"They're my title."

Before Ruth could speak, Vanessa continued: "The programme header," she said, putting down her camera. "Named."

"Ah, I see."

"Flowers," said Vanessa, lifting the jug as if it was a trophy. Two-handed, she held it high: "And drink," she added.

"Yes, flowers with wine," she called, turning with her trophy: "Flowers with wine. A woman's view."

In reply, Ruth and Ginny grinned.

196

"I believe it fits. A classic still life," said Richard the next day.

He was examining a poster-length shot of a jug with chrysanthemums on a stand-up board at the entrance to the show. Headed in red by *Flowers with wine*, the picture was signed in blue, with a black-lined caption announcing: *Vanessa Lawrence, a woman's view.*

"You like it?" asked Doug, who was crouched behind the board. He was fixing the stand to a floor hole.

"I think it's…" Richard paused, glancing round the empty warehouse, "…effective and eye-catching. All good stuff, I suppose."

Doug grunted, leaning hard on a screw head. "You mean OK." He straightened, keeping his eyes fixed on the stand, "but lacking?"

Richard considered. Behind him the jug with flowers was standing on its table. Switching from subject to photo, Richard frowned. "Well, possibly rather conventional," he added.

He knew what Doug meant. Throughout the period of erecting walls and hanging photos he'd been aware of his own reservations. His underlying doubts. Of course, in the rush to put up he'd kept them to a minimum. But now he'd a sense that it might be better if he stepped back, levelled, and examined what he saw.

"Though, if they *are* like that…" he began, then stopped.

"Then what?"

"Well, I don't know. It feels like a letdown."

The conversation dropped. Richard began a tour, studying photos. Varying his angle, he paused in front of some, passed by others, switched between displays. Of course he knew them well – which made them (he realised) all-too familiar. It was, he supposed, like looking in a mirror.

"So *you* think *I* think," he called, "they're not much to write home about."

Doug came across and they both gazed in silence. They were facing a line of political portraits. "They're all smiling," he said evenly.

Richard looked: "Which is more than I'm doing."

"Well, it is politics."

"You mean the show, or how I'm supposed to react?"

Doug shrugged, "Both. But don't tell the women."

"Or men. Just think of Justin and Ken."

Doug nodded.

"I imagine," added Richard quietly, "it's the effort of being right – all the time."

"The art of *having something important to say*."

"Which they call agit-prop."

Doug pointed to the portraits: "So you're not impressed?"

"Well, I do admit, they feel rather *meant*."

"But you liked them only yesterday."

"That was when I thought—"

Richard cut off. He knew his next words. *It might lead somewhere.* Somewhere for her, somewhere for him. A chance to go places, and duck out perhaps, a kind of special pleading.

"I'd hoped," he shrugged.

Doug stood back. He returned to the entrance, checked board and poster, then sniffed the flowers. "I hadn't realised," he said, wrinkling up his nose. "They're strong."

"Chrysanths don't usually smell much."

"These do. Try them."

Richard advanced. Stooping, he sampled: "Yes. A sweet-smelling offering."

"I'd say pissed."

"Certainly. They're jolly."

"Over the limit."

"Just merry, I'd say."

"Rank, sozzled, smashed."

Richard grinned, "Flowers enjoying themselves." He picked out a stem and held it up by the poster. "You never know. This might go big. Something like the water lilies."

He brandished the stems. "O happy hour flower," he called, twirling. "Icon for our times." He was grinning and declaiming with one elbow out, crooked like a waiter. Suddenly his hand slipped and the flower head twisted. His grin became fixed as the stem sprayed wine. A line of dark red spots slewed across the photo.

Realising, he froze. "Oh shit," he said. The photo surface had already softened and half greyed-out. The wine spots had started to trickle. Richard applied a finger, then dabbed one-handed with his cuff, but the smears remained.

"It's a mess," said Doug, pulling a hangdog expression. Both men laughed.

"And may not go down well."

"True."

"Vanessa won't like it."

"I expect Ruth'll have something to say."

"I imagine."

"So, quo vadis?"

"Wherever," said Richard, returning the stem to the jug. "Preferably another planet."

"Better stand your ground."

"You mean take the road to Rome, face the consequences?"

"Get it over with."

"True," Richard laughed, "let's go greet the women's army." He laughed again: "You're in for this?"

Doug nodded.

"One for all?"

"All for one."

The story, when delivered to Vanessa, was offered straight. Richard told it, backed by Doug who corroborated detail with grunts and asides and confirmatory nods. The men agreed that the damage, though visible, wasn't too extensive.

Vanessa responded with a few curt questions, then set her gaze forward. It was almost as if she'd expected, or known all along. But she wanted (she said quietly) Richard to show her, and she needed Ruth to be there.

Doug took the children while they drove round to the show.

They arrived, unlocked the warehouse, and entered in silence. The women, it seemed, were here to pronounce.

The photo that faced them looked like a cross between a painting and a map. The surface stains had deepened. Soft grey run-spots had developed round the edges.

"Did you do this?" asked Ruth.

Richard objected.

"But did you?"

Silence.

Ruth softened her tone. This sort of thing, she said, wasn't good.

Richard scratched his head. "It's certainly not a pretty sight," he said. "No doubt about that."

She suggested cleaning.

"I've tried that already."

"The problem is," put in Vanessa, "it's first thing you see, as you come in."

Richard acknowledged.

"And people go by that."

He used and repeated the word *accident*; he was speaking low, shaking his head. It seemed he'd accepted.

Ruth, who was circling, touched the surface. She set her jaw forward and stared towards Vanessa. Her colour was up.

"It's bad," she said, addressing herself. She was finger-dabbing the corners and pulling faces. "Really bad," she repeated, shuddering.

Richard looked, saying nothing.

"I can't believe that happened," she said, sucking in her cheeks. "It's horrible."

"What you suggesting?" Richard asked, frowning.

"You messed."

He eyed her: "Say again."

"Messed."

His mouth set hard.

"Badly."

"So you say."

"No use wriggling. You did it."

"Yes, and put up everything else. The whole lot."

Ruth grimaced: "I don't see how that makes any difference."

200

"No. You wouldn't."

Vanessa intervened, talking down. What's done was done, she said. The real point was how to fix it.

"Or *who's* going to fix it," called Ruth.

Richard coloured: "You offering?"

His adversary laughed: "You joking?" she countered. "Look at this," she said, fingering the picture. "Isn't it disgusting? How does *anyone* make a mess like that?"

"It's easy." Richard's fingers closed round a corner of the photo, "you just set your mind to it—"

"Richard!"

"Watch him do it," Ruth sneered.

He smiled. His fingers tightened. "I know what you think," he said grimly, "but I wouldn't give you the satisfaction." Dropping his grip, he walked away. "But who the hell cares anyway?" he called out from the exit, "because it's OK this show... it's good enough." He turned in the doorway, facing Vanessa: "It's conventional. Safe, political and MOR. And that's about it."

That evening, when Vanessa returned home, she found an unsealed envelope positioned on the mat. Stooping, she picked it up. After checking on the children, she took it to the kitchen where she laid it on the table while she brewed up tea. This, she realised, might take time. Bracing herself, she sat, pulled out the letter and began reading. At first she wasn't sure. With each sip of tea, her mindset shifted. Although he said sorry, his words seemed forced. She'd a sense of something hidden, a level of intention, as if it was an act. But as she read on, the line became clear. An apology, unconditional, his comments withdrawn, and a wish to make amends. It seemed he'd thought better.

But also, while reading, part of her avoided. She'd rather not go there. On the surface there were words: small-voiced intentions, clicks and shifts and give-aways — but behind that there was nothing: a word here, a word there; a phrase, a pop-up, a pause between breaths.

So she read, or sampled, in a state of indecision, skimming out content while sipping at her tea.

When she'd finished, Vanessa put aside the letter and stood to face the garden. While she'd been reading a feeling had developed. Richard, she suspected, was closer than she thought.

Opening the back door, she peered into the dark. At first she saw only a strip of concrete, lit from the kitchen, and a path leading off. Beyond that were outlines, fence-tops and light-streaks behind glass. Low dark clouds covered the horizon.

She switched out the light. Like water in a lock, the light levels equalised. She could make out a tree, some trelliswork, a few low bushes.

Stepping out, she adjusted. The path led forward, grey and shadowy, past a lawn and flowerbeds to arrive at bare earth. Peering ahead, Vanessa followed. As she cleared the house the light levels rose and the path became wider. Checking to the end, she could make out a figure, seated.

"Richard?" she called, approaching.

The outline shifted. "Here," he said, sounding hoarse.

"What are you doing?"

"Not much. Thinking."

She stood, staring into darkness. There were images both ways: lines and glows, windows lit up, overshadowed gardens.

"I read your letter."

Silence. Richard shifted forward: "So what did you think?"

"I'm still taking it in."

He stood. "What I said…" he began, staring round, "wasn't right."

Vanessa took a breath. The air was coolly calm and still. She wondered what might follow. Something, she supposed, where he'd find a line, a shift in his favour, a way of turning round. It was all about angle.

"It's politics I'm sick of," he said suddenly.

Inwardly, she registered. This, she recognised, was his latest theory.

"It's all so one-dimensional," he continued, "and full of people with no person skills, no understanding. They judge by rhetoric and voting record, nothing else."

"Well, it's practical." she answered, breathing calmly. "A matter of action and getting things done."

"And as for soul—"

She turned her head to stare across the fence. Greys and grey-blues played across darkness. The gardens were hard to make out.

Richard shook his head: "Politics is full of know-alls. They smile and decide, but never listen."

"You think so?"

"People who all reckon they know better."

She shrugged. "Those people try. It's not easy. They do their best."

"The activist tendency. They do and they do. It blocks out thought."

"OK, it's a struggle. But progress is made."

He snorted. "I imagine *that's* what's called a Marxist analysis."

Suddenly she felt weary. A picture was pressing, a lifestyle composition, an angle on them both. They spent their lives arguing. On and on, finding difference, crossing each other. Every day, the neighbours could hear them.

"I think you're missing the point," she said, stepping back from the fence.

Richard took her place, staring down the gardens. "I don't know about that," he said, quietly.

"Whatever you say," Vanessa countered, "politics *is* important. However difficult or unpleasant, somebody has to do it."

"Ah, the dirty hands argument."

"Politics is like that. You can't magic it away."

"You mean like rows between couples: however bad they are, you have to live with 'em."

She measured him with a look: "Maybe. But people still have choices."

Richard leaned forward. He was propping himself, spectator-like, on the fence. His face was set hard and abstracted; she could see he wasn't finished. "Marriage is what you make it, eh? I'm sure Samuel Smiles would agree."

A picture flashed through her head of a university seminar. She could see Richard talking, adopting positions, building up a case.

"I mean it's in our hands," she returned.

"Precisely. Which is why we don't need political ideologies."

"So what's the alternative? The Übermensch or something?"

He straightened, frowning: "The alternative is people, as they are. Outside the box. And bugger the theory."

Vanessa returned herself to quiet. She didn't want his language, not here, not in the garden.

"Well," she said, "that's one way of putting it."

"You don't like it?"

"Not much."

"So it offends."

"Some might say so."

He laughed: "That's the difference between us. I say it, you go round the houses."

"That's your view."

"It's true. You're like your mother, all airs and graces. A cut above."

"And that's personal."

He shrugged: "Well, as they say, the personal is political."

Flowers in wine opened to the public the next day. During the morning, after seeing off Vanessa (who left without a word) and walking the children to school, Richard practised his scales, wrote a few lines then rang Ginny. He described the accident, the photo at the entrance, mentioned arguments – lightly, in passing, without too much detail – then asked for ideas. Ginny, after talking round the problem, reckoned she could help. "I can meet you there in half an hour," she said. "And I'll bring my toolkit."

Asked what she meant, she laughed. "You'll see," she said. "Ms Fixit, on the way."

Richard arrived first. The warehouse was empty except for Lanya who was sitting in attendance, and a red-faced Sophie who was pacing the floor. They were both in a fret, exchanging comments about a journalist who'd promised, and when they'd get a write-up. They were unhappy... It didn't seem fair that a man like him... In any case there were suspicions... When Richard appeared they greeted without interest and retreated to the end.

Ginny, when she showed, was well weighed down. She entered, grinning, walking with purpose. She'd a sack on her back, a pouch-belt round her waist and a bag in each hand.

"Looks like you mean business," he said, helping to unload.

She laughed: "I've brought the lot: paints, cleaner, cloth, patch-up materials, first aid for everything. This is the full, every-which-way, all singing and dancing photo doctor."

Their hands touched briefly and he smiled.

She crouched by the picture, studying the surface. As she checked she hummed. Applying one finger, she dabbed lightly, examined the results from above, then stood back and straightened. "It's nowhere near as bad as it looks," she called, "I think a repair will be possible."

Richard watched her as she pulled out some thick glass paint pots, a soft cloth and a collection of brushes. Unscrewing the lids, she dipped and tested, then applied.

"Best begin in the middle," she said, shading carefully then stopping to change brush. She flicked and dabbed, extending slowly, filling in the surface.

When she'd finished she stood back, inviting comment.

"It's much improved," said Richard. He squinted forward: "I don't think anyone who didn't know could tell."

Ginny, who was clearing and packing up, frowned. "It'll do," she said, pausing to examine. "As long as it lasts out the exhibition."

"You're not satisfied?"

"It's how Vanessa feels. That's what counts."

"Even more so, Ruth."

Her eyebrows shot up: "Is it like that?"

Richard considered. "She's what's called an opinion former."

"Like Justin, you mean?"

He laughed. "Justin and Ruth. Leaders in their field. I can just see that."

Ginny finished packing.

"You've done a wonderful job," he said, shifting position. "Wherever you look from, it's great."

They stepped outside, with Richard carrying her bagged-up paints. "Don't worry," he said, checking his watch, "I shall give you a lift." When she made to argue, he opened the car door and deposited the bags. "More, please," he said, nodding to her sack.

They drove back to her house and unloaded. "No call out charge, then?" he asked, standing in the hallway.

Ginny smiled. "Friday's your payday," she replied. "But I'll take a small deposit," she added, offering her mouth.

He lip-touched, lightly, then closed to a kiss.

"I'm in your debt," he said afterwards, laughing.

She gazed at him closely. Her expression was fixed. She was involved in something far off and yet immediate and deeply personal.

"How long's Vanessa's exhibition?" she asked.

"Ten days."

"That short?"

"I believe it's to do with the rent."

Her look remained attentive. She was watching him like an artwork. "I think you had hopes from this show. A different focus. Maybe a change in direction?"

"You realised?"

She nodded.

"I'd not thought it was that obvious."

"But why? Is it something you have to hide?"

Richard considered. "I don't want to be Mr Leech Man, living through Vanessa, hoping for an out."

"So you think her exhibition might go somewhere?"

He shrugged: "Maybe. Who knows."

"And you've an idea that if that happens it might benefit you…"

He blushed: "Absurd isn't it, I thought it might be helpful. A kind of escape, or even a main chance – I know that sounds stupid but we all believe in it." He sighed and dropped his shoulders: "It's all about keeping busy, looking the other way, so you don't have to think. Putting off, and then putting off… And behind it all you're a child, still secretly believing that somehow, without any effort, everything will change."

"Ah, the fairy godmother story."

"You still think there's a reward for being good."

"As if—"

"Or at least for showing willing."

"Which there isn't."

"Or you believe in fair-dos."

"Which *would* be very nice…"

"But doesn't ever happen…"

Ginny eyed him warily. She was closing now, drawing herself up. "What you're talking about is experience. You go into it feeling you've got the measure of things, know how they work, can handle anything, anybody – then you find out."

Richard snorted. "Yes. It's more of a closing down. The dreams you had, the silly lost causes, even the smallest, stupidest inclination: it all becomes you, the last little bit left standing." He threw out a hand: "You hear it in your mind, repeating, *stay 'n' alive*. Suddenly all that trivia and indulgence and messiness takes on a different feel. You want it back, whatever it was, want to throw life up in a spin, go for broke, run off somewhere and never come back…"

Ginny laughed. "True," she said fiercely. "Too true. And one day we'll do it."

CHAPTER THIRTEEN

Vanessa decided, before the exhibition ended, that she'd like to go away.

From the first day of visitors she'd put in the time, done everything possible and now she needed space. During the show she'd existed in what she called 'all-go mode': a space without sleep where everything was a whirl. People had wanted, and she had to deliver. It was all about presence, the organisers told her: about making connections, about face and impression and putting yourself round. Later, in the second week, she'd started to wonder if Richard's comments (despite the letter and his poster-fixing) were to some extent true. Suddenly it seemed no one was interested. The pattern had changed. The space was empty, the pictures seemed flat, and there were no smiley faces. When she looked at her photos a voice in her head pushed in with questions. Was it as he'd said? *Safe, political and MOR*? Or just so dull that nobody cared? And she wondered if his help was an act of condescension, a sop he'd offered to keep her in her place.

When the ten days ended Doug and Richard appeared again. Working systematically, they collapsed the walls and removed the show, as if they were roadies, and did it every day. But their efforts had a downside. She knew they were saying things – if not straight out then by implication, signalling and suggesting as part of how they worked. Particularly Richard whose actions were reminders and whose verbals were designed, she felt, to open up a distance, put him in the clear. *He* was considerate, knew his code of practice (something he'd perfected, a laid-back rightness which served him well), while *she* was the spoiler, the one who had it all.

Then there were the words, the ones on stand-by, used in disagreement, book terms and theories and what he called 'definers': quirks and tics and talk of repression and other people's issues. He knew about syndromes, saw through denial, accounted for background, displacement, projection and hostile formulations.

"I'm feeling overrun," was how she put it when rehearsing in her mind for the next week's counselling. In the head-talk that followed she ran through various formulae, imagining rejoinders, offering defences and practising what she'd say.

It seemed she'd had enough.

"A complete change," she told Ruth, "where one doesn't really *have to* – a kind of health-farm break-out, that's what I need."

"Women-only," she added, smiling.

With Lance she was cool. She needed to take stock, challenge how she did things, find another way – which might, she warned, affect their Fridays.

With Richard she spoke quietly, proposing that he and Ginny spent time with the children.

With Lorna she was upbeat. "What *was* that place," she asked on the phone, "for women-only weekends?"

With herself (after picking a date and ringing round) she was happy, grateful for the break and pleased to be with friends. She would go there for a rest, a recharge, and spend more time with women she could bond with. Together they were strong.

They left on a Friday, soon after school, five in a car, with Caroline driving, Ruth looking out, Lorna singing, her cousin on maps and Vanessa herself calling directions. The house they arrived at was a short drive south and longer westwards. After searching for an entrance, then bumping slowly down a potholed track, they drew up at twilight. Standing alone in rolling hills it was steep-roofed and quirky with arch-shaped windows and a door round the side. A sign on a bush said *Welcome to The Hen House*.

They were met at the door by an ample, round-faced woman with pale enquiring eyes and a smattering of freckles. She was wearing a round-brimmed cap, set at an angle, and paint-streaked overalls. Ushering them in, she conducted to the hall which was full of bicycles. After closing the door, she introduced herself:

"Hermione would like to say," she called out, "how pleased she is to see you."

Staring above their heads, she pointed and directed: to the right, a door to where they'd eat; behind, a passageway; and above, a dark oak staircase. "But first, you get to settle," she said, advancing to the stairs. They were shown to their rooms – small and compartment-like, all opening from a landing just above the hall – then invited downstairs to gather in the lounge. On the way back she pointed out a wall map, a horse brass, a key on a hook, then led in to a soft-furnished space that linked, through an arch, with a dining room. "Supper," she called, waving to a spread arranged on a heavy wooden table. It was piled up, scented and garnished on top, full of strange mixtures and spread on paper plates. Here Hermione, promising return, went off on business. She left them to Victoria, a willowy, dark-eyed woman wearing a green silk scarf and two-tone jacket. Victoria had style. She stood high and tall with an air of engagement. With her shoulders back and long S-shaped spine she looked like a dancer. "Welcome," she said, "I've prepared a beanfeast. I believe it will surprise." She delivered her words with lightness and uplift, smiling quietly as she waved them to their chairs. When everyone was seated she took them round the table, naming dishes. "Be bold," she said, "and don't be afraid to try things."

While they ate she asked them their names, took an interest in backgrounds, talked and listened with measured attention, nodded and encouraged, without too much pressure. Low-key but alert, she offered tasteful guidance. Vanessa recognised in her what her mother called *je ne sais quoi*.

Afterwards, when they'd helped her to clear up, Victoria suggested they went in search of Hermione.

They found her in the hall, fixing bikes.

"Herm has been in struggle," she told them brightly. "One woman, many machines."

The guests exchanged looks.

"Hermione would also like," she continued, standing tall, "to show you the workshop. Where the battle began." In proof she held up her hands, which were child-round and grubby.

The women followed, smiling, to a hole in the back wall. A step down, and they entered a shed-like room littered with broken appliances. There were backless televisions, eviscerated hoovers, doorless fridges, clocks in pieces and a corner full of broken mowers and fragments of what looked like agricultural machinery.

"It's the local rescue centre," Hermione said, wiping her hands on a pile of torn-up sheets, "for reassembly and rehabilitation."

They gazed round blankly, holding themselves in. What she showed they examined, nodding and looking where she pointed. "There's more outside," she said, waving towards a dirty French window with a view out to blackness.

"So this is how you live?" asked Vanessa, pointing to a leaflet featuring imaginary plants and a Rousseau-like drawing of the house. The picture had a women-symbol border and, appearing Santa-Claus-style on the roof, a fish on a bicycle. It advertised *Hen House Repairs.*

Hermione smiled. "Come," she said, directing their return to the hall, "and be shown." She led to a door set beneath the stairs. It opened to a flight of steps dropping into darkness. Flicking on a light she invited them to enter.

Vanessa was first. A faint, slightly chemical smell met her. The aroma strengthened as she descended to the cellar. "Well, well," she said quietly, half-addressing Ruth, "this is what you might call la grande cave."

The area was large and white and tiled like a bathroom. Low-ceilinged and divided by pillars, it was clean, surprisingly warm and lit by fairy lights. Near where she entered, racks of bottles lined the walls; as her gaze adjusted she made out bell jars with valves and some large plastic vats, while in the centre, which was larger, there was what looked like a giant hip bath. It was filled with a dark aromatic mixture which she realised from the smell was fermenting grapes.

"Beautiful spot," said Hermione, inhaling. In the silence round her voice Vanessa could hear the slow pop and bubble of aerated water.

"What's in the middle?" Ruth asked, pointing to the hip bath.

Their host smiled, "That's where Hermione treads."

"Lightly?" asked Vanessa, walking forward.

Ruth joined her, peering at the mixture. "You tread the grapes?" she asked, sniffing.

The other woman confirmed, adding they'd a vineyard just behind the house. "And now," she said loudly, taking off her shoes and removing her overall, "Herm will demonstrate."

She crossed the central area to a footstool and a bench set into brickwork beside a floor-level sink. Here she ran the taps, tested with her fingers, then perched on the seat to soap her feet. When she'd paddled briefly she invited them to admire, then drained the basin and pulled down a towel. After drying, she stood. "Everyone now," she said leaning on a tap which gushed out cold water. "Everyone," she repeated, mixing from the hot, then called them again. "Footwash, everyone. Footwash."

The women approached, Ruth first, followed by the others. They removed their shoes and bared their legs, piling their clothes on the bench end. Some were smiley and some seemed edgy, but they lined up as required. Encouraged by Hermione, they dipped and splashed and rubbed themselves down, then gathered in the centre. "Treading is an art," she called, reaching round to a grape-filled basket which she turned into the mix. It swished and frothed like sherbet.

"And best done in twos." Leaning forward, she took Ruth's hand and led her to the edge, where they stood like children, looking down. Hermione counted then stepped up and in, staggering slightly. She took Ruth with her.

"Hey-hey! That's squelchy," Ruth called as the liquid flowed up to her ankles. She leaned into her host as they promenaded round, circling once, twice, then a third time, separate. Their legs now were red: wine-splashed and streaked all over. "Come on in!" called Ruth, waving to the women. "Step up, my lovelies. You'll enjoy it." She caught on to Vanessa and conducted her in, one arm raised.

The two women laughed as the liquid began to bubble, frothing round their calves. "It's alive," said Vanessa as the surface peaked like whipped meringue.

Ruth giggled: "It tickles your toes."

Behind them, Hermione swung heavily to the floor, drip-staining the tiles. She rounded on the women: "In, in, in, in, in," she insisted.

They all began to move, stepping up and over, entering the bath. As their feet touched bottom the surface rocked and shuddered. The mixture swirled and spattered their legs. "Oh," cried Lorna who was holding onto Caroline's arm, "it's like treading jelly."

"Or frogspawn," put in Vanessa, grinning.

The other women laughed. They had filled up the bath and now were holding each other, shuffling round in short half-circles. Guided by Hermione they turned in step, covering the whole area. Ruth made quacking noises as they waddled back and forth.

First out was Vanessa, followed by Ruth. They sat by the basin, examining their legs. "Like wearing coloured tights," laughed Ruth, wiggling her toes. She was bright red round the sole, pink to the ankles and red-tinged above.

"Reminds me," said Vanessa, "of childhood, jumping in mud."

"Or worse."

"Worse?"

Ruth considered: "Ink or paints." She ran her hands up and down her calves: "Or blood – when you gashed your leg."

Vanessa nodded, "I think a few childhood games…" She broke off when Hermione, who had cleaned herself up, called to the women, inviting them to wash.

"But first, it's best if we can…" she said, fingering a tap.

Ruth, smiling, began washing down: "*I* think a few childhood games would be good. A whole weekend of 'em."

The water in the sink ran red to pink. It thinned and spread, turning pearl-grey to silver.

"We'll make a list."

Vanessa smiled. The water now was clear and colourless.

"And work out the rules."

Vanessa echoed back, turning off the flow. Together they began drying.

"And we'll do it together."

"Yes. Because it's a change."

"And time out."

"And fun."

"And itzy witzy spider-ish."

"And character building," concluded Vanessa, stepping dry and refreshed from the tiles into her shoes.

The first game next morning was I-spy. They played outdoors, exploring round the garden, the vineyard and the road they'd come by. They tried it with variations, sometimes by last letter and sometimes by syllables. When they'd spied a few abstracts and began to repeat, Ruth held up a hand, calling time. "We'll rename," she said, smiling. "I used to do that, pretty much all the time."

"Rename?" asked Vanessa. "What's that?"

They were standing by the back gate, looking out across hills. To one side was a fence and a farm track, in front was a grass-slope leading to a wood, while to the left, and curving right round was a brown-green patch of staked-up grapes.

Ruth pointed upwards: "It's custard," she said, "lovely custard."

"The sky?" Vanessa asked, blinking. "Grey and cloudy, if you ask me."

"Yellow, in a bowl. Custard."

Vanessa raised an admonishing finger: "I name you grey sky: custard."

"And that," said Ruth, pointing to the ground, "is flimflam."

Her friend narrowed her eyes. "Whereas that?" she asked, pointing to a bush.

Ruth tore off a leaf and sniffed. "Fool's gold," she said, pursing her lips.

214

They advanced to the vineyard edge, looking down the rows. There were unpicked grapes, visible in clusters, and staked-up branches twisted into wire. The ground underneath dropped off sharply.

Vanessa waved an arm: "I call this land Cockaigne."

Ruth laughed, "I've heard that somewhere. Isn't it a *Sir Richard* word?"

Vanessa dropped silent. She flashed back to their talks. Then and now, it seemed Ruth knew.

"Is it?" she said, feeling vaguely blocked. It was as if Richard was present, asking awkward questions. Suddenly she was weary, caught out (it seemed) by thoughts she'd hoped to sidestep. The game was over.

"Did I say the wrong thing?"

"I don't know. Maybe. It's certainly *his* sort of word."

She looked down the slope. The vines bulged out; they were thick-leaved and tangled and snaked all over. Beneath their mass, the earth was stone-dry and furrowed.

"What, him? The enough-man?"

Vanessa shook her head: "Don't remind me."

Ruth returned to her game, picking out the house and calling it cake. She continued pointing and renaming, taking in the gate, the fence, the farm track and the wood. When she'd worked round the view, she turned back and smiled. "See me," she said, dropping her eyes, "putting on an act, trying to sound jolly."

"It's like that?"

"Yes indeed. Rah, rah, rah, to keep from thinking."

The two women looked out. The hills were map-lined and patterned; with their crop rows and fencings and farm tracks leading off, they seemed artificial.

"That's a bit like teaching," said Vanessa, narrowing her eyes. "Keeping up to keep them down."

"Now that's one thing," Ruth returned, "I'm thankful I didn't stick with." She began to saunter along the field edge, kicking at dust.

Vanessa joined her. "What it is to serve," she said, glancing down the valley.

Ruth led on. "Well, you managed," she answered. "Give yourself credit. I couldn't possibly have done it." She was humming now, stepping side to side.

"Let's say you saw it coming. Take it from me, teaching's one of those jobs where you have to stay on top. You can't duck anything. Every day, it's pure front line." She laughed: "In a way, it's like a marriage. Nothing comes easily, you can't dodge, you can't bluff, and every mistake comes back to haunt you."

"Ah but Vanessa… no regrets, ma cherie…" Ruth leaned back and raised one arm across her brow. She began to sing, offering a croaky, half-audible imitation of Edith Piaf. As she sang her eyes part-closed and she drifted into something low-key and quirky. She was swaying back and forth, gazing round like a drunk at a party.

"You have to believe," she said, "even if it never seems to happen."

Vanessa laughed: "Is that another line from a song?"

"Could be. It certainly feels that way."

"Hmm, I think I know what you're saying."

"Love love love love love," Ruth half-sang, half-chanted, "that's what I want."

"Love and affection?"

The other nodded.

"We do need something." Vanessa turned to face the view: "Maybe it's out there somewhere. Somebody's got an answer, only they're keeping it very, very quiet."

Ruth's face stilled and concentrated. She moved up shoulder to shoulder with her friend. They were on curtain call, looking out together. "And that was another childhood game," she said, slowly.

Vanessa blinked. The sun was showing through. A flock of hill sheep had spread across the field below. They looked like scattered stones.

"And what was that?" she asked.

"Staying quiet. Holding your breath so long no one could see you."

"Ah yes, I played that."

Ruth took her friend's hand. "Shhh now," she said, raising their clasped hands towards the wood. "Let's go down there, playing it. Absolute silence. Walk not talk."

Vanessa put a finger to her lips, stepping forward. She nodded and they started off. They were hand in hand and wordless.

At first the slope was gentle and they followed a sheep track, swinging their joint arm through a 20° arc. The sun came out and a skylark sang. It climbed and climbed, carolling wildly, then cut off altogether. Silence followed, as a light breeze fluttered the grass stalks. A sheep baa-ed and a horsefly circled. As they descended further the ground fell away, the track gave out and they unhanded. But the quiet still held them. It was as if they were attached, roped together by an invisible cord.

When they reached the wood the silence changed. It deepened and closed up. The leaves and branches acted as a wall; inside were whispers, light-plays, tonals. Their footsteps were cushioned, advancing softly, measuring earth. At one point a squirrel scrambled up a branch and disappeared into leaves. After its departure the branch continued shaking. As they ducked past an elderberry, a blackbird clacked a warning.

They pushed on through stillness, brushing against ferns. In the gaps there were light spots and patches, with birdcalls, leaf-shifts and insects circling. Where the wood closed up, the quiet returned. They walked through calm, following the path. Where the track divided they paused, gestured both ways, then set off side by side. Still they were silent, feeling the strangeness, the all-surrounding hush. The air was pure thought, it had its own medium, a long-held quality of persistence and delay.

As they circled back, Vanessa found herself watching. It was as if she was taking pictures, recording life. There were tree trunks and leaf tips, webs between bushes, a ditch, a fence-strip then the sky around the wood edge. On the climb uphill she took in the field, the footpath, the view round to the vineyard and, close to the top, the gate towards the farm. When they reached the house, she turned to look out.

"Well, I reckon that's it," said Ruth, breaking the silence, "game, set and match."

Vanessa continued to stare across the hills. Her face was pale and slightly abstracted. Something inside her wanted to stay dumb.

"You all right?" asked Ruth, raising one eyebrow.

"Fine."

"Sure?"

Vanessa nodded.

"I think the game has had an effect."

"The walk did, certainly."

Ruth laughed: "Ah, Vanessa's taken her vow. I can see it in her eyes. The notice says: *do not disturb*."

A wry smile touched Vanessa's lips. "But what's behind the notice?"

"What indeed. That's the biggie. The Mona Lisa question."

Vanessa hesitated. She was gazing thoughtfully at the landscape. "I used to think life was all about style. Almost like a stage show. As long as you delivered, then that was OK. And I believed I had style – or the words and the outfits. So I convinced myself, kept up a front, made it work, at least on the surface."

"Yes. Seems funny when you look back now. We all thought we could strut our way through."

The women exchanged glances. Their expressions had set to a long-term kind of puzzlement. They looked like jurors weighing up a case.

"I think we're getting in deep," said Ruth. "And I'm feeling hungry."

"But I know there was *something*," said Vanessa, "about that walk."

"And the silence?"

"Well, yes. Definitely that."

Ruth shrugged: "Silence is golden."

"Maybe. But not in the way I remember that being said."

"Ah yes. Girls, button your lips. The double standard."

Vanessa stood back. She was clear-eyed, attentive, half turned to Ruth, half towards the view. It seemed she was gazing down a path, a route into being which led both ways.

"But it's still important," she said. "The game, and then the silence. However you look at it, that meant something."

"So you're still back there, with the birds and bees?"

Vanessa nodded.

Ruth laughed. "Well, I have to admit it *was* an experience. Something you don't forget easily. Spooky if you ask me."

"True, you don't forget. Though what exactly it was about…" She frowned, glancing down the slope, "But I suppose, with time…"

Ruth laughed again, "In the mean*time*," she said, "I need to grab a bite to eat."

Vanessa made to say something then, thinking better, turned towards the house. Peering at her friend she blinked, then offered her arm. Seeing her readiness, Ruth linked in and they proceeded down the garden. "Well, we'll see what we can nosh," she said. "Love, silence or whatever it takes." And they went in together, with an eager-eyed Ruth humming *yummy yummy yummy I got love in my tummy* and a tall and silent Vanessa smiling to herself.

That evening, at Hermione's bidding, the group gathered for supper in the front room. When they entered, the furniture had been pushed back, the table removed and the floor had been spread with coconut matting. A large, patchwork cloth, fitted round the edges of an oval-shaped base, occupied the centre of the dining room. The cloth had been painted with two large starey eyes and an O-shaped mouth. Piled up with fruit bowls, leaf-shaped plates, flower-patterned cups and bottles of wine, it looked like an Arcimboldo.

"Fruit and wine," said Victoria quietly. "Please partake."

With Hermione's encouragement the group filled their plates and topped up their cups. They sat around on cushions talking, laughing and sharing jokes, returning to the spread to collect further helpings.

"Home brew and handpicked," called Caroline, licking her lips.

"Drink up, fill up," cried Hermione.

"…And let yourself go," added Lorna, draining her cup.

"A bacchanal supper," said Vanessa, thoughtfully.

"A woman's right to booze," laughed Ruth.

As the evening progressed the women warmed up. At first they exchanged remarks, offering little teases and observational comments (life-talk mainly, reporting on relationships and things said between couples), for a while they swapped anecdotes – friends and upbringings and events they had in common – later they took sides, debating strategies and movements and historic shifts – at one point they sang, swaying and grinning and shouting out rhymes – in the end they tired, drifting into sleep-chat, platitudes and private conversations.

And when a red-faced Lorna dozed off in a corner, it seemed (at least to Caroline who'd returned with coffee and found her looking ill) they'd best turn in.

Vanessa, after seeing Ruth to bed, found she couldn't sleep. Part of her felt what her mother would call squiffy. Well-done or merry, she'd certainly had enough. But another part was wakeful. Locked up in the dark. She could almost hear her thoughts – or at least she was aware, in private, and had touched on what mattered. She'd a sense, a feel and persuasion rising in her head, that something important had happened.

After some time lying, sitting up reading, then peering from the window, she descended to the hallway. Entering the front room she came across Hermione, spread across the sofa. She was examining the label on a green glass bottle. "Herm's brew – and still plenty left," she said, offering. "Drink deep. Enjoy."

Vanessa smiled. A familiar song passed through her head. For a moment she was floaty, clear-eyed and detached. "That's very kind," she said, squatting on a cushion, "but I think I'm happy as I am."

Hermione tut-tutted. "The truth my dear. Swear to tell the whole truth, nothing but."

Vanessa frowned. "I'm not sure I'm with you."

Hermione held up one finger like a baton. "Wait," she said as she rocked forward to lean across the spread. "There's a lesson to be learned," she said, selecting two large apples for close examination. She stowed one in her lap and side-rubbed the other on a corner of the cloth. "Take," she said, examining what she'd polished. "You don't have to eat."

Vanessa accepted.

"In the story," said Herm, holding up her apple, "it stands for what you might see in the mirror."

Vanessa, who was watching at an angle, replied with a nod. Her words, when they came, were directed to the floor: "Well, if that's how…"

"No, it's simple," cut in Hermione, "the truth's in there. If you can bear to look." She was gazing pointedly at her apple. "Observe: it's the Atlanta factor. Stoop to pick up and you'll lose the race."

"I mean," she added quickly, turning on her guest, "I can tell, it's written all over. E for ego, my dear, ego. You came here to escape, thought you could beat it, but it – or you – can't let go."

Vanessa's eyes widened: "I don't know… Well, I'm not really sure." She met Hermione's gaze: it was pale, unsettled and directed at her.

"You have a problem – domestic – and you must let go," Herm continued. "Allow what happens, don't hold on."

Vanessa thinned her lips. It seemed for a moment as if she'd been spotted, approached by a stranger and taken into confidence.

"I have to admit, it's much as you say," she said. "There's a major business. Long-standing, and rather messy. What I call a sore."

"Concerning?"

"It's a question," she answered, "of two people fighting, and if there's a solution – how's it to be done."

Her host nodded quietly. "Ah, the old old story," she said, "over and over. You must make it yours."

In the pause that followed Vanessa flashed back to her wood walk with Ruth. That, she knew, was important.

Hermione sighed. She raised her apple like a toast. It was red and green and polished to a shine. "You as well," she said, touching Vanessa's elbow.

Two arms went up, each grasping fruit.

"Now eat," said Hermione.

Both bit in. As they chewed and swallowed the apple-flesh appeared. It was white and uneven and soft round the edges.

Pausing between mouthfuls, Hermione laughed. "The apple of your eye," she said, "that's what you want."

On the next day, their last, it was Ruth's idea to end their stay with selected party games.

"We'll play them as a send off," she said, "goodbye and all that."

At her insistence (after a morning doing nothing, existing on aspirins, glassfuls of water and large cups of coffee) the women came together, grouped around the lounge. They were cushioned at odd angles, sitting on arm rests and squatted on the floor. Ruth, who was positioned at the centre, acted as MC.

She began with twenty questions. "Animal, vegetable, mineral?" she asked, turning on her panellists, fielding their suggestions and returning yes-no answers. When they paused she grinned, when they guessed she answered tongue in cheek, when they ran out of chances she awarded extra tries. She kept them going, speaking slowly, stringing out the process, switching into deadpan when the next round began.

When she'd challenged and teased and stirred them to interest, she changed games without warning. "For this one," she said with a wide-eyed expression, turning to Victoria, "we have paper and pens to give out – for everyone."

The women looked round, seeking confirmation. They were grouped now in a rough half-circle. Ruth was moving round the area that remained, turning on her heel and leaning forward, camera-like, to fix on listeners.

"We're playing consequences," she announced, supervising the distribution of materials. "All the normal rules. So you write an answer when I call out, fold down, pass on. The same for the second round – and so on – but no peeking answers!" She paused, checking round the faces: "*Except*, there is a twist: I'll also ask for some to be read out."

An objection was raised. It was a white-faced Lorna, speaking out; there were, she said, contradictions. Points that needed sorting (which she called out, finger-listed, then summarised as sexist). Caroline chipped in – she thought the point valid – but Vanessa backed her friend. The room fell silent when Herm shushed them all.

"Ready?" called Ruth, ignoring.

"That's right," said Hermione. "You go ahead."

"OK. The man's name. Write it," Ruth called. "The man's name, now."

Six pens moved across paper.

After some seconds watching, Ruth leaned forward. "And your answer?" she asked Lorna, pointing.

The other woman shrugged, saying nothing.

"I know what," cried Hermione. "Her answer's Larry the Lamb."

"Continue," smiled Ruth, "now write the woman who Larry meets. Her name."

The pens moved again.

"So, when Larry the Lamb met who?" asked Ruth, nodding to Victoria.

"Salome."

A few eyes widened. Ruth herself laughed.

"Now then, location," she called. "Where did they meet?" She looked round the room inviting answers. "Don't bother writing," she added, "just say. The spot."

"Larry the Lamb met Salome at a selection meeting," called Vanessa.

Ruth pushed her jaw out and blinked: "Right. That's good. Now you all know the rest: he said, she said, the consequences, the world said. So let's have your answers. Firstly, he said…"

"You're so baaaad," cried a sheep-eyed Hermione, hunching forward.

"She said…"

"Heads I win," called Victoria.

"The consequences were…"

"A gynocracy," said Lorna.

"And the world said…"

Raising her voice, Vanessa smiled round the group: "It just goes to prove that women can get ahead."

"While men," put in Victoria, "are headless chickens."

Hermione began clucking, ducking forward and back.

Ruth clapped her hands. "Great stuff," she cried, "Now forget what we've just said. We're going for a second round. This time on paper with no calling out. So, let's begin with the woman's name. Female and first. *Her* name, please…"

They left soon afterwards, calling their goodbyes and waving off. They'd shared addresses, thanked their hosts, passed over money (a decent-sized whip round, presented by Vanessa) and climbed in smiling. It had been, said Caroline, a busy weekend. On the car drive back they caught up on sleep. Ruth took the wheel, stopping frequently and swapping with Caroline, Lorna and her cousin dozed in a corner, propping each other up, while Vanessa slumped sideways, nose against glass.

During the journey the sky darkened, the wind got up and rain began to fall.

As they entered the suburbs Ruth began to hum. Her voice rose and fell, hovering between notes, then moved onto words. She settled on a tune, a chorus, repeated, with long-held phrases and a catchy format. At each repeat the refrain lost a word. Gradually it became clearer as the words reduced and the voice tone coarsened. When she got down to two and the words fused together, she stopped, then resumed da capo.

The wind, which had intensified, blew streak-lines and splashes against glass.

In the back Vanessa, who was dozing, heard or imagined a song sound going round. Blurred or buzzy, it circled and stuck, repeating in a jingle. It was harsh and vigorous, full of mockery and inscrutable laughter. She heard or caught snatches, took in the words, one by one, as if she was a stranger hearing from a distance. Though asleep she could hear it, up close and jumpy, dinning in its pattern, matching its rhythm to the wind-blown rain.

Oh Sir Richard do not touch me,
Oh Sir Richard do not touch
Oh Sir Richard do not
Oh Sir Richard do...

Over the weekend, while Vanessa was away, Richard kept busy. He received Ginny (who stayed and helped, then went off to see family), he took the children on outings, dealt with domestics, fielded telephone calls (mainly Vanessa's: political enquiries and follow-ups to her show), then, when the kids had been bedded, searched through his drawers, pulled out his notebooks and sat up late, reading.

The notebooks were numbered. All small and blue-bound, they went back years. Their pages were full of small thoughts and sketches, accounts of feelings, mindsets and reflections and what read like a logbook – a blow-by-blow record of struggles at work, over children and in their relationship. More about the relationship as the notebooks continued. A kind of you-versus-me running commentary. Episode after episode, with key words and thought-chains and diary-like reflections on things done and said.

Reading, he could see it all, laid out like a book.

There were thoughts about separation. First as an adjective: how they needed separate space, came from separate families, were separate in views, in lifestyle (keeping very different hours, liking different friends) and separate or different as teachers and parents. Secondly as adverb: separately (and distinctly, independently) in things done and felt. Thirdly as noun – a line drawn, a walkaway – and verb, intransitive, with clean break and cut-off, ending in a split.

Also, and related, what they called their own. Their own distinct areas, their own rooms and possessions, their own thoughts and theories, own time, own needs and own clear space.

His on the patio and practising the piano. Hers in the studio, talking on the telephone and in bed with the children.

The man obsessive, the woman walking off.

Both with opinions, refusing to back down.

Then there were the statements, dialogues and exchanges, words that stayed with him, both those on paper and those suggested. He read them as callouts, word-shots and pop-ups, things said (or imagined), floating in his head.

We're basically territorial.

Opposites attract – but we're out of touch.

We bounce off each other.

Whatever one does, the other contradicts.

It was reactive stuff.

Reading round the entries (some short, some bright, others more questioning, a few with footnotes and parentheses and additions in the margin), he came across a notebook with some A4 paper inserts.

Four sheets together, with black and red writing.

Map-like and creased and quarter-folded.

Picking them apart, he looked.

RELATIONSHIP PRIMER the top sheet said, with a list underneath of terms and definitions (one he guessed, from the wine-stained edges, he'd written on the patio). The list continued over all four pages with numbered headings, in capitals, each with its definition and named example.

Turning to the end, he examined what he'd written.

Recent (and familiar), point by point.

Nametags, labels and one-off formulations.

Looking like this:

1. <u>POWER-PLAYS</u>

These include:

a) Saying nothing, or a minimum. Giving f. all away. Helps force the issue. Whoever holds back can't be in the wrong. Example: most counsellors.

b) Saying EVERYTHING, or pretending to. Straight from the shoulder to demonstrate ultra-honesty – and mislead (self-fooling, especially). Eg Justin.

c) Compartmentalisation. Different person, different places. Everything in boxes. Has to be Ken.

2. PROCESS-WATCHERS
Those who obsess over how an action/decision was arrived at, ignoring purpose or outcome. Definitely V.

3. BIGSWITCHERS
Ego-driven, hot-cold swingers. 'Now I like you, now I don't' playground-types. Fits Lorna.

4. BLACK BOOK
A comprehensive, permanent mental record of a partner's (or rival's) past errors, omissions and offensive remarks. Colours everything. Cannot be erased. Possibly Ginny towards L.

5. PAINTING INTO CORNERS
The process (usually unconscious) where one partner takes up extreme positions, forcing the other to take up contrary (and equally entrenched) positions. Anything you can do I can do... Quick on the draw. Yours truly, pretty much 24/7 + V.

When he'd read all four sheets he folded, replaced the paper, closed the notebook and – reflecting on the self found in those entries – moved to the back room.

As he entered there were feelings: grey thoughts, mindmaps, pictures pressing. A mirror showed his image: thin-faced, eye-sharp, a man looking round. Positioned by a wall, the piano was waiting. With lid up and keys, and spot-lamp above. He could see himself practising: scales and arpeggios, then finger-drilling pieces. Bent over exercises, hours at the keyboard. In dream appearance: entering, bowing, delivering his solo.

His obsession, she called it.

His nothing-else-matters.

A way of blocking out.

He switched on the lamp. Sitting, he adjusted. Music, seat height, one pedal down, the other hooked under. As he gauged his own mood – tired but alert, focused forward – a pause occurred. He was gathered and set...

And then he was listening.

Heard in his head, a voice cut in. It was Laetitia, objecting. Like learning the piano, she said, if you wanted a relationship you had to give it all.

100% effort.

Over and over.

Level best and more.

Working the hard parts.

When the music started he was head down, focused – nodding and counting while holding down the pedal. As he played he felt the notes, circling quietly. They were hushed-in, breath-light, and slowly repeating. They seemed, like his thoughts, to be strangely and calmly (almost beautifully) persistent – soft, nocturnal and high in the register – and determined by events from a long way off.

CHAPTER FOURTEEN

"I think we should speak," Vanessa said after supper, with the children upstairs.

It was her first Friday back and they'd got through the week, surviving by keeping themselves busy, playing down differences and being what she called *spare*. By spare she meant slimmed down, separate, contained within themselves – almost economical. She also meant selective, choosing what they did and how (as well as where) they functioned.

Richard, who was preparing to leave, looked doubtful. "When's Lance due?" he asked.

Vanessa shook her head: "He's not."

"Has something happened?"

"Yes, things do happen."

"But what?"

She shrugged and took a seat, saying nothing.

He put down his sack and stared. "Is there something wrong?"

"Not really. I just decided it wasn't working. He said he wasn't happy and needed more. In a way, it's a bit of a relief."

Richard sat down opposite. He watched her carefully with his hands spread in pianist position. "Does that mean it's over?"

Vanessa nodded. In her eyes was an artificial brightness. Something about her was close to crying out.

"So he won't be around anymore?"

She straightened and frowned. Somewhere, at a distance, there was a struggle going on. "That's right. But no one knows yet. So keep it quiet."

"Well I can't say I'm—"

"Sorry or surprised?"

"No. Just not clear. About what happens next."

"Nothing really. You go, I'll be here. The usual arrangement."

He waited. It was as if he was counting bars in his head.

"Do you want me to stay?"

Her eyebrows shot up: "I certainly wasn't expecting. You go."

"But it does need to be balanced. We always said that."

She smiled. The words seemed to prompt her. An imagined conversation came back into her head. "I don't think that now," she said.

Richard shifted, placing both hands palm down on the table.

"Is that," he said, squaring slightly, "a new theoretic development?"

"Something like, if that's how you want to label it."

He glanced up and round, taking in his hands, the table, her tight-eyed expression. "So you've had some thoughts?"

She looked towards the hallway. A child's voice was raised, carrying down the stairs. "I want us to try something," she said slowly, "when you get back."

Richard considered. His first-off speculations seemed unlikely. "Well, whatever it is I'd rather know. Otherwise I'm going to imagine all sorts of things…"

Vanessa half-rose, blushing slightly: "Oh, it's nothing big. Just a walk, by ourselves. That's all."

When Richard didn't answer, she waved towards the door. "You can go now. Really, it's all right, go."

As he reached for his sack she dropped her voice slightly: "And don't worry about the walk: it can wait. But ask Ginny when she can take the children. Tomorrow, if she's free."

His answer was cut off by another childish call. Vanessa rose as the cry came again. It persisted, imitating itself. Perfectly balanced between song and dispute, it was blithe, repeated and slightly plaintive.

When Richard arrived, Ginny was watching from the window. The street was in shadow, the sun had set and the skyline had hardened. The pavement was empty, and the air was still. She could see right down the terrace, outlined against grey. It was dark and light and spot-bright in places. Like a model, it didn't seem real.

Sensing his approach, she descended to the hall where she slung on her backpack and stepped outside, locking the front door. "Welcome, stranger," she said as he parked and climbed out. They hugged and kissed, then held position. They were watching each other like long-lost relatives. His breath felt warm on her cheek.

"Could we drive?" she asked.

"Yes, whenever you want."

"Now, if possible."

"Bien sûr. Where to?"

"You know, the playspace."

Richard nodded and returned to the car. "The same route as before?" he asked as they both took their seats.

"That would be best," she said, "if you're happy with it."

He manoeuvred out and off, switching on the headlights. The road opened before them, joining others as it skirted an estate. After reaching a carriageway he drove several miles through mock-Tudor semis and the odd tower block, then cut off at a junction. Here they took a ring road. The traffic was light and Ginny kept her hand resting on his shoulder. While driving they talked, exchanging news, recapping feelings and checking directions. In the dark they were united, progressing forward.

A mile down the ring road they turned into a lane sloping uphill. It led to a village with half-timbered houses and spaces between.

"You know which way to go?" she asked.

"I remember," he replied.

At a bend by a church they forked left and began a gradual ascent. The road was narrower, holed in places, and Richard switched to full beam. On both sides there were woods.

"Here," said Ginny when they reached a P-sign with a metal-arched entrance and a clearing behind. "It looks different in the dark," she added, reaching for her sack as they turned in and bumped across potholes and parked. As he switched off the headlights Ginny shifted forward. She was talking to herself. Something about her tone suggested distance. Their arrival had changed things.

Stepping outside, they took in the silence, the emptiness, and the dark perimeter wood. "Yours," she said flatly, pulling out a black plastic torch with red-yellow flashes. She passed it over, pulling out another which she beamed in an arc.

"They're headlights," he said, aligning his torch beam with hers. Ahead was a track, leading forward through rows of silver birch.

"When I first came here," she said, leading off, "these hadn't been planted." An echo in her voice made it sound unreal.

They followed the track through wood-twists and silence. The torch beams flashed white, catching on bark. The trunks, it seemed, were peeling from within.

Ginny led on, passing a pool, a fenced-off dip where the forest darkened, and a meeting of paths with a deeply rutted area and a moss-bank to one side. Ahead the torch beams cut avenues through air.

"So, we've reached the castle," said Ginny, directing her torch towards a sprawling wooden construction with ropes and ladders at the centre of a clearing. They approached across grass, flashing their lights round and up.

Richard played his beam on a board to one side. It was head-high on a pole, bordered with metal and looked like a traffic sign. The words 'Adventure Playground' were cut into wood.

"Let's try the swings," said Ginny, pausing for a second as if she'd been blocked. She pointed to some paint-sprayed tyres chain-hung from a bar.

They approached, using the torches to guide to their seats. The chains rattled and clattered as they took their places.

"Ready for off?" asked Richard. Ginny nodded and they switched off their lights.

At first the blackness held them. It was dead-still, close-up and all-surrounding.

"Can you see anything?" he asked.

"Depends," she said, grasping her chain and leaning back. "It's different if you look up."

The sky above was grey-lined and patchy. The moon was faint, only half-visible, hazed by cloud and softened to a glow.

Richard sat still, adjusting slowly. The wood edge appeared, then the planks and walls of the playground construction. When he looked down his feet were there: side by side, and planted.

He swung gently back, leaning with the arc to work the swing higher. As Ginny joined in the chain began to creak and the frame shuddered slightly.

"Did you swing here as a kid?" he called as they passed in the air.

Ginny confirmed. Her words came in snatches. She was struggling not to show.

"With friends?"

She didn't think so.

"But not at night, surely?"

That, she said, might surprise him.

He continued throwing out questions. Ginny replied, calling as they crossed. Their remarks remained hanging, repeating in the dark. They were like balls thrown up for practice.

They allowed their swings to run free. Their words tailed off, becoming more gestural as the oscillations shortened. The clouds had pulled back and the moon, which was high and large, was fully visible.

Richard was first off, landing on grass. He moved to one side, stretched out his hand and helped Ginny down. She descended in silence, then walked round like a guard, flashing her torch all over.

The main part of the playground was built like a stockade. Vertical outside, it was cross-beamed and ribbed and buttressed at the corners. Inside went up in ramps and walkways and step-laddered blocks, rising to a flat-roofed platform with nets either side. It looked like the house that Jack built.

They entered by ducking down and groping their way through a large metal pipe. The pipe was holed from the sides and above; it smelt of sand and water.

Emerging, Richard looked up. He was standing in a narrow walled-in forecourt with the stars now in view. Three sides were blocked, the other, to the right, sloped up towards a hole in a wall. This, he realised, could be an outtake from a film.

Ginny joined him, panting slightly, and they began their exploration. The hole led through to an open-topped passageway which forked and twisted and doubled back repeatedly.

"Did you come as far as this last time?" she asked, taking the lead. Behind her words, a gap had opened up.

"Not sure," he replied, "I do remember there being a maze." He was aware of her back, shadowy in darkness, and the need to keep up. Suddenly it struck him that he needed guidance. If she left him here—

"It's a simple route," she said, "as long I don't think."

Richard gave an uneasy laugh. "Eyes closed is best."

Ginny laughed too, but there was strain there, hidden. He could hear her breathing hard. She was all head and shoulders, moving at a shuffle, seeking out a route. It seemed they were infantry, manoeuvring under cover, approaching the front line.

"Blind man's buff," he added, searching for words to settle down his thoughts.

"Or hide and seek."

She led, he followed, and soon they reached a clearing with a pole at centre and a ladder to one side. It went up in stages, leading to a platform.

"The eye," she said, turning her torch and flashing round. The walls here were bamboo, strapped in by wire and slung between stays hammered into fence posts. They bunched around the corners, were split in places and gleamed like wheat in the glancing torch light.

"Up," she instructed, shining towards the ladder. "You first."

Richard stepped forward, following the beam. With his hands on the steps he paused, glancing back, as if he was posing for a photo.

"Go on," she urged him, "it leads to the top."

Her voice tone registered. It all seemed so simple, a cut and dried matter. She was speaking from a distance, giving out direction, talking herself up.

When they reached the top, she paced out the platform, flashing her light. It ran one side of the playground, raised up like a gallery. The wooden floor beneath shook and flexed and shuddered like scaffolding. "I'm on guard," she cried. "Up above them all, treading the boards."

Richard stood back, observing her pacing. She was humming now, skipping her hand along the top of the railing, contained in something private. Every so often she turned on her heel and threw back her head, muttering oddly. As she moved back and forth Richard had the impression that she'd come here for a purpose.

And he wondered for a moment whether she'd notice if he cut his losses, ducked out quietly and slipped off in the dark.

Ginny turned suddenly. "Don't mind me," she called, "I'm playing *let's pretend*." She gestured out towards the clearing: "I was a child-crazy – still am, really." She laughed: "I could do anyone: doctors and patients, cops and crooks, neighbours, vicars, TV characters, anyone I'd heard, taking all the parts."

In the silence that followed the air remained still. The moon shone clear and pale and whitely opalescent. Its glow touched the tree tops.

Realising what she'd said, Richard stepped forward. Her words, heard once, blended with the moonlight, the tree line, the bare earth clearing; they were private, slightly edgy and quite unexpected.

"You should have told me," he said. "Then I'd have known…"

"But you might not have come."

"Or I might have insisted – would have, without a doubt." He threw back his head: "So now it's a double act."

Suddenly the positions were reversed. Richard was in movement, fingering the railing, gesturing, pronouncing into air.

Ginny stepped forward, switching off her torch. "OK, let's pretend," she called. "We can do it together. You be the teacher and I'll play nurse."

Richard snorted. "So I get to be myself, is that the idea?"

"Yourself, yes," she said quietly. "You do that well."

He laughed, she looked up, and the clouds returned. They veiled across the moon, toning and softening to a buff-yellow blur.

"The man in the moon's winking," he said, remembering her words, naked in the park.

"Or woman," she corrected.

The sky remained grey. It was silver-grey, sheeted and haloed round the moon. Dark and light, it seemed to overreach them; it was sea-like, shadowy and expansive. They watched, looking up, then led each other round, partner-style, to the railing and the view.

"Time for the show," said Ginny, grinning.

"Right, let's pretend…"

"Mad stuff, eh?"

"Anything goes."

"Crazy, and how."

"Bonkers."

She laughed: "Completely cracked, barmy, loco…"

"Looney," he ended, glancing at the moon.

Later in the night, after playing let's pretend and doing various voices (mainly pastiche, a series of domestics and classroom knockabouts, ending with a double exit) Ginny and Richard returned to the car. As they walked back they were silent. They'd had their time, made their statement and now were taking stock. It was as if they'd been on holiday, had been there, done it, and this was their return.

As they drove back to the city the sky began to brighten; there were breaks at the edge, the fields were visible and the roof-lines showed. Following the carriageway, they cut their way through illuminated signs and lamp-lit spaces to enter between houses, turning into side streets where the sky-view returned. The breaks had now moved up. In the east there were cloud-shifts, above there were flushes, everywhere was getting lighter.

The journey passed with yawns both sides, occasional time checks, directional talk, remarks about weather. Things came and went, and a blur took over. Both were tired and needed to keep low.

Arriving at Ginny's, they filled up on biscuits, downed some tea and climbed to the bedroom, where they quickly fell asleep.

An hour later the alarm clock sounded. It jarred against wood, whirring and jangling like a broken toy.

"Ouch. That hurts," said Ginny, clapping her hand on the top red button.

Yawning and grunting, they rose, washed down and dressed.

Ginny made coffee and they stood by the window watching the weather and exchanging comments on respective relationships.

Their talk was episodic, offhand at times, turning edgy as they sketched out feelings and the collective came up. Richard, after sharing updates (including Vanessa/Lance, which didn't surprise Ginny), asked about Ken.

Ginny snorted. Her eyebrows narrowed and her gaze became fixed. It seemed she was hurting. "He's been dumped," she said. "I've got him all to myself. It's back to coupling – all because Lorna half-wit Bell *has* to be monogamous."

Richard sipped carefully at his handheld coffee. His role was to question.

"She does? So where does that put Justin?"

She stared intently at the grey-blue sky.

"He's vowed eternal love. It's the greatest story told – for at least a week."

"But what about the girlfriends?"

Ginny rolled her eyes: "Oh, they're just happy for everyone else. I call 'em glad-abouts: glad to be with you, glad without. You know the type…" here she snapped her fingers, "*nice* political groupies."

Richard smiled thinly, examining the clouds and the spaces in between. "But what about Ken? How's he taking it?"

Ginny shook her head. Putting down her cup, she flattened her expression. She seemed to be addressing an imaginary audience: "*He* says he's heartbroken. End of everything. It's like he's living on death row."

"You think he's overreacting?"

"It's her playing games that I object to." She paused, glowering. "Because in the end it's me who picks up the pieces. Every time, I have to deal with her mess. Get him into shape. Do what I can."

"So it's business as usual. The ups and downs and round each other's houses…"

Ginny laughed dryly. "And they call it women's power," she said. "I call it farce."

As she stepped back, frowning, Richard checked the time then mentioned Vanessa. Remembering their talk, he relayed her request and suggested ringing home.

"She wants to walk?"

He confirmed.

"And you?"

"I'm up for it, as long you don't mind taking the children."

"Do you know where she wants to go?"

Richard shook his head.

Ginny brightened. She picked up an apple from a handmade bowl: "OK, tell her I can come round – now if she likes. Then you two can go off… as long as you want."

When Richard rang, Vanessa answered calmly, as if she was expecting. Her voice on the line sounded assured. What was said registered (verbatim, he noticed, without too much delay), he was asked how long, cautioned about rushing, questioned about food, offered time to wash, to change, and warned that the children might need some settling. She also thanked Ginny – through Richard and directly – asked what she needed, called to the children (room to room, urging them to dress) and invited Ginny round as soon as she was ready.

Ginny handed back and Richard wrapped up, checking on timings.

"Allow forty-*ish*," she said, then excused herself.

When they arrived, the curtains had been opened and the TV was off.

Charlotte was getting washed.

Stephan was in his bedroom.

The kitchen smelt of coffee and Vanessa was clearing up.

A deal was in place.

There had been some happy families – this time on the couch – involving a Charlotte story (featuring her as beauty and Stephan as beast), followed by talk about likings, all round cuddles and an agreement to get dressed. The deal had filled a gap, a channel-hop break and hole in the schedules with job-talk and markets and all four channels broadcasting news. It had been helped (thought Vanessa) by talking and listening, taking things steadily and not inflating issues. Problems, conflicts, any kind of rivalry – and she'd quickly moved things on.

And this particular Saturday, perhaps to make a point (almost by magic, as if they'd decided that now they had the choice they would rise to the challenge and show what they could do), the children had been good. They'd taken turns, waited for the bathroom, not called out, and now were busy dressing.

When their father appeared he asked where they were, then climbed to the landing.

Downstairs was handover.

The women talking.

Details, things practical.

An update, and exchange.

Mostly it was simple. Reassurance first ("I've told them you're here and we're going out," smiled Vanessa. "They seem to be pleased."). Then guidance – tips and reminders with the odd quiet warning. Followed by thanks – repeated – and one or two pointers on health and moods. If she was worried, Vanessa tried not to show. Or say. After all, the kids might pick up. But it soon became clear, as the children emerged and Ginny greeted, that she knew which foods, had a good idea of programmes, was quick to spot problems, had a knack of being jokey and likeable, and didn't talk down.

"Are you sure you'll both be all right?" Vanessa asked Charlotte.

Yes.

Yes, yes.

Oh, *Mum*.

Vanessa kissed, Richard waved off, and they set out together.
> In the game of relationships they were searching,
> looking round for routes, trying to find a way.

Q: And what did Vanessa think?

A: Not much. She didn't want a struggle. If there was agenda or points score or too much programme, then walls would go up. She'd rather just pace out, look round, go walkabout. For her it was out there, and social.

They walked.

The sky had cleared and a white-yellow sun hung low across the buildings. A bird sang from an apple tree as they turned out into the street. On both sides there were parked cars, some with tinted windscreens, others with stickers, some with mascots hanging.

As they passed by Ruth's, Vanessa looked up. A large wisteria, sprawling across brickwork, had reached the guttering. The bedroom curtains were drawn.

Q: And what did Richard think?

A: He wanted to take soundings, mark down phrase and meaning, tone-judge, calibrate, speculate, know the ins and outs.

They walked to the street end and a small corner shop. It was piled to the door with batched-up newspapers and cardboard boxes. The owner, who was holding a pair of silver metal shears, appeared from inside, nodding a greeting.

Q: And what did both feel?

A: Vanessa: things floating, provisionals, the dark/light shifts and moods round the corner. Richard: puzzlement, a journey, a tone-change, and look back to what might follow.

They arrived at a junction and paused, looking north along a long straight road dotted with cherry trees. On both sides there were terraces. They were tall and Victorian, with fluted woodwork and square-patterned brick.

Q: So what about the other, the silence, the unexpressed dream?

A: Under and behind, hidden in everything, mind's eye and implicit – the ID question.

"So, we're going somewhere for a walk," prompted Richard.

Vanessa confirmed.

"Do we have a planned route?" he asked, sighting forward.

By way of reply, Vanessa pulled out an envelope from her bag. "I had this in the week," she said, passing over an A5 sheet of coloured notepaper. "It's from Vaughan," she said quietly. "He wants us to visit."

In the game of relationships this was a wild card.

He held up Vaughan's letter, examining the handwriting. It was clear and regular, perfectly formed, and neatly centred.

"I didn't know he was still around. It seems ages since his book."

"He lives in an executive suite by the river. Top floor he says."

Richard scanned the message. "So he's got in touch because of your show?"

"Seems that way."

"And you suggest we see him?"

She stood, undecided. "I get the impression he's changed. He does say any time."

In the game of choices:
crossroads, dice throws, directions off.

Richard checked the letter: "Well, I have to say, it does sound different to the book... So why not give it a try?" He looked at the address: "Harcourt Tower. That's easy – it's right by the route I used to walk."

Vanessa smiled: "Before you moved in?"

He nodded.

Her voice dropped low and her eyes looked off. She was thinking into air: "That's strange. I was remembering that."

"You were? I still take it now – in my head. It's a good route, straight into town."

"And to Vaughan's it would seem."

"Shall we go then?" he asked, imagining someone (his own voice but sharper, harder, coarsened by life) adding in a comment about how things had changed.

> Life-game passageways, back routes,
> look-arounds, journeys.

They walked along the street, beyond the terraces to an area where the houses were set back behind overgrown gardens. They were square-built and detached, brick-and-stone-faced with high sloping roofs and ornamental chimneys. As they walked, a cyclist passed by followed by cars, then an open-backed lorry carrying planks and poles. At a school with a crossing they turned left beneath a tree to enter a 30s estate. The blocks were redbrick and balconied with plants in corners, window stickers and handmade gates. Named after battles, they were linked North-South by a series of squares accessed by arches.

> City-game boxes, elements,
> bridges, openings, spaces.

Richard gestured forward and they entered. They passed by men in overalls, a runner, a cat beside a wall, and a group of workers digging up a trench. Turning out from an alleyway they followed a small row of shops with blinds across windows and paint-dripped signboards. At Jimmy's Cafe (a bare vinyl space with tight-packed tables and folded plastic chairs) they headed off through a park, a track between fences and railway arches.

Two, on promenade.

As they walked they spoke, they exchanged and they offered observations. Beginning briefly and factually, commenting on weather and season; then updating carefully (teaching, a little – children, more – lots about politics); sidetracking briefly into news of friends and speculation about Vaughan; all mixed in with thoughts and interjections and response-sounds and periods of extended silence.

Opposites, stepping out.

When they reached the river the sun had strengthened, playing clear and bright across metal and concrete.

"Harcourt Tower," he said, pointing upstream to a medium-sized block standing on its own with an external lift and smoke-blue windows.

In the relationship game

(although they didn't know it) this was home.

They approached along a walkway flanked on one side by neatly-clipped lawns, on the other side by a wall – which Richard touched occasionally, playing his hand across the heavy stone surface. Beyond was a drop, the river, and a view upstream, opposite, to a jetty extending over slow-moving water.

On foot, going forward.

They reached the block and entered an all-glass lobby with white walls, beige carpets and a matt-black desk. A heavy-built man in a uniform greeted and Vanessa explained their visit.

Frontliners.

They signed in as requested and occupied two wire mesh seats while the man called upstairs. While waiting, Richard studied a large abstract canvas, Vanessa eyed a vase. The painting and the flowers both felt artificial.

Mind space, to impress.

"Please go up. You're expected," said the man and he showed them to the lift.

The ride, and the view, seemed almost fairground: it was all air and sky and sunlit buildings. At the top, as they stepped out, a man appeared in the corridor wearing a close-fitting suit. He was tall and lithe with jet black hair and aquiline features. His eyes were fixed forward, with dream-dark irises. His forehead was wide, mouth narrow and cheeks sucked in. He looked like a cross between a Greek athlete and an El Greco saint.

"Vaughan," he said, shaking hands and inviting them in.

Officer, on lookout.

The room they entered was long and light with multicoloured windows, glass-topped tables and freestanding VDUs. It was soft-edged, floaty, part-museum, part-cinema, but also a viewpoint and a modernist apartment.

When Vaughan closed the door, the room became silent.

Hush.

Hush-hush.

Pianissimo.

They sat by an all-green window with an outlook downstream. Outside a plane passed over, traffic moved, barges and riverboats slid through water. On the pavements people moved and stood and waved and raised cameras. Taxis turned, buses lined up, trains crossed bridges. It looked like a silent movie.

"Triple-glazed," said Vaughan when asked about the sound. The room held his voice in a close-up stillness, quiet and persistent. It was as if they were swimming underwater.

Shhh.

He offered tea or coffee. Establishing preferences, he withdrew to the kitchen, moving quietly across thick-pile carpet. During his absence, Richard overviewed the city while Vanessa screen-gazed.

Vaughan returned and poured out. He moved at ease, offering, adjusting, adapting to their tastes. Speaking briefly, he updated on his life, then paused to take them in. It seemed he understood.

Listen.

Vanessa asked about the book. Had he any more planned?

Vaughan sat, saying nothing. For a while it seemed he didn't have an answer. He was looking over, observing his guests as if they were specimens.

"I decided," he said finally, "to give up the stunts." His eyes were round and deeply thoughtful.

"You mean flying blind, that sort of thing?"

He confirmed.

Richard nodded. "So it's a different life – here?" he asked, looking round.

Vaughan considered. "Let me show you," he said, standing.

Quiet.

He led to a screen where he button-flicked through a series of pictures. Each was panoramic: a bare steep drop, a seascape, treeless scrubland, mist clouds, waterfalls and jungle. Each was wildly trackless, elemental; all were unpeopled and strangely otherworldly.

"It's the silence," he said, "I wanted it to go on. On and on and on."

Vanessa blinked. "You used to be..." she began, stopping herself to stare deep into the picture.

"Different. I know."

The photo on screen was an icescape. Pure white and glistening, it stretched in ridges, sweeping back from a grey-blue sea to an all-white plateau. It was bare, blocky in places, jagged round the edges, and completely empty.

"Antarctica," he said.

Dream-space.

Wilderness.

Void.

They all looked. Vaughan pressed a button and the picture came closer. They were staring now at a raw, blasted, uneven landscape littered with snow-lumps and projecting spars. Ice cracks and fissures zigzagged across white.

"Were you alone there?" asked Richard.

"By myself, yes."

"But not alone..."

Vaughan nodded.

They continued looking as the picture closed to a grey-white blank. The screen was all off-whites, greys and silvered surface. It was ice-clear, mist-like and transparent.

Tabula rasa.

Vanessa asked a question about how long he'd stayed. Vaughan's answer came slowly. As he talked he gazed long and hard, without expression. He looked like a pilot about to take off. In a way, he said, it seemed he'd never left.

The screen they were watching dimmed out. A long shot of mountains took its place.

Unreal.

"So were you ever frightened?" asked Richard. He was thinking of Frank, and the faint sweet smell of burning flesh.

"All the time. That's what drove me."

"And the silence," added Vanessa.

Vaughan nodded. He stood back from the screen, saying nothing. His face had stilled and alerted as if he was judging distance. Pointing, he led down the room, walking the length, inspector-like, checking both sides.

Watch-spot and gallery.

They stopped to examine the tinted glass, studying each colour and peering down at the cityscape below. Each pane was a cameo, a colour-square framed, a keyhole view.

"Like scenes with different lighting," said Vanessa.

Richard nodded: "Or times of day."

Kaleidoscope.

At the end of the room they reached a different view. A door led through to a dark-walled space that ran the length of the second side of the building. It was bare, shielded by blinds and backlit by a discrete blue glow which appeared from somewhere hidden. The effect was nocturnal.

"My studio," said Vaughan.

Enter the darkroom.

The floor was wood-beam, polished; across it lay a scattered collection of stones: some large, some patterned, mostly lying flat. They were arranged in groups: a few in spirals, others in parallel lines, some heaped up, with blocks and edges and blade-like projections; others tile-like, overlapping, and several positioned upright in odd-shaped patterns and combinations.

Mindspace and thoughtbox.

Encouraged by their host, Vanessa crouched down and picked up a rock. "It's allowed?" she checked, and he nodded. She handled several more, examining front and back, remarking on shape, on colour, then returning them to their piles. On one she found a quartz streak, another a fossil, there were large stones with cracks, pebbles with curves, coagulated lumps, rock-splits and shards and hollowed-out fragments.

Handfuls.

Pick-ups.

Still lives.

Richard joined in, fingering stone. "Are they all from your travels?" he asked, imagining Vaughan trekking over desert or ridge-walking coastline. He wondered (if they did) how one man could have carried them.

"Some. Others are Victorian, from collections. Your father," here he turned to Vanessa, "provided several."

"My father, Derek?"

"He and Felicity designed the apartment."

"They did?"

He nodded.

Richard put down his stone. "Have you seen his models?"

Vaughan blinked. "I didn't know you knew."

"First time round, he showed me."

"And every time we go," Vanessa put in. "They spend hours playing upstairs."

Vaughan narrowed his eyes. "But he didn't say what he did here…"

Richard confirmed, looking puzzled.

"Come," Vaughan said, "I'll show you."

Sidestepping rocks, he moved to the gallery end. "To the balcony," he said, inspecting the edges of a heavy-framed door. When his guests had joined him he placed one hand on the handle, issued a warning, then turned and opened.

The door unsealed.

The volume upped.

A wedge of light struck into the gallery.

As they stepped outside the noise grew louder. There was a sudden shudder, an in-out rush and a whooshing sound. Plane and traffic noise filled the air. It was as if he'd opened a hatch at sea.

Vaughan took them round. The balcony was narrow, metal-barred and crammed with small plants. It overlooked long lines of roofs. Beyond, they could see arterial routes, a side branch of the river and – further out again – a large green park.

Outsiders.

Holding the railing they shuffled sideways, edging carefully between flower stems and pots. As they moved the air seemed to thin out. They were high and bright and poised above the drop.

Turning a corner, they followed Vaughan left and up. He was climbing some steps that led to the roof. At the top, reaching a wall-gap, they passed between pillars. Filing in, they arrived at a bare, open patio with paths leading off and an all round view.

Vanessa gazed forward: "Your own secret garden," she said. They were facing a cultivated area: a spare, geometric space with patterns in gravel, low box hedges and greenery in pots.

A sign in the wall said *The Hanging Garden*.

Vaughan confirmed. "Based on the golden ratio," he said quietly. He stooped to pick up a rock. "And symbolic," he added, offering it for inspection. The rock was flat, mirror-smooth and decorated. It carried two conjoined heads – one sun-rayed, one crescent-shaped. Both were relief-carved.

Find.

Talisman.

Artefact.

Richard examined, then switched back to the garden. He was remembering their outings. An ironic smile played across his lips. "Annihilating all that's made…" he said, savouring the words.

They explored the paths – which crunched and skittered and sighed beneath their feet – with Vaughan in the rear and Richard and Vanessa going forward.

The paths all led to a central, bare-walled building. It was fronted by a forecourt and approached by two steps up and a pillared entrance. Inside, light from above picked out a marble slab. It was square, waist-high, and plinth-like. Centred on top was a tall, cut-away, architectural model.

Image.

Symbol.

Prototype.

"Harcourt Tower," said Vaughan.

"By Derek?" asked Richard.

Vaughan nodded.

Vanessa circled the finely-painted copy, leaning forward to scan the floors and stretching up to check the garden. On the outside it was well-worked, full of small detail and showed, in section, the flats' interiors. In there were everyday objects: fittings, fixtures and miniaturised ornaments. It was exact, camera-like and perfectly proportioned.

Made in the likeness.

Beside it, on the table, was a numbered plaque with a key below which named various features.

She checked from plan to model. "So we're standing in the temple, looking at the 'gin," she said, reading from the plaque.

"And below is the cell," added Richard.

Vanessa looked up: "I didn't realise," she said, thinning out her cheeks.

As Richard responded she cut in with a laugh: "Are all his models like this?" she asked, pointing to the top floor interior.

Richard's expression flattened. He looked where she pointed, nodded, measured his response: "Crafted, I'd say. All of 'em. With amazing detail."

Like for like.

Vanessa looked long and hard, moving her head from side to side and making appreciative noises. "It's like finding a photo album," she said finally, "with pictures of distant relatives. Ones you've heard of but haven't ever seen."

"So. An eye-opener?"

"Definitely," she smiled to herself. "And next time home, I'm going upstairs…"

"Ah, but aren't they the product of male obsessiveness…?"

He smiled a challenge. Vanessa smiled back. "You know best," she said quietly.

"I do?" he asked, feigning innocence.

Vanessa made to answer, then curbed herself. It didn't seem necessary.

"But then, thinking about it," added Richard, "isn't male obsession what we're looking at here…" He arm-swept round, taking in the model, the three of them stood looking, then out towards the garden.

"Yes, everywhere," responded Vaughan. "Magnificent, foolish, childish, absurd."

He held up his sun-moon rock. Mirror-like, it fitted in his palm.

As she looked Vanessa thought – absurdly – of Ruth, the argument with Richard and the beer barrel coaster.

As he looked Richard thought of Ginny, the night walks, the voices, and her carved wooden sun sign suspended on a chain.

An hour later, returned to the river, Richard and Vanessa climbed the metal steps to the walkway on the bridge. The sky was light and dark, with sunlight spotting water and cloud over stone. On one side was concrete and flag poles and tree-lined promenades, on the other a road with lane-marked junctions and traffic queuing up. They passed by graffiti, paint-peeling dents in rusted metal, grime and droppings and litter caught in wire.

Reaching the middle they gazed upstream. Vaughan's block was there, looking like its model.

"You heard what he said about how his stunts began?" asked Richard. He was staring at a barge through cross-meshed girders.

"The schoolboy stuff – red flags on buildings?"

Vanessa looked out at a dome with, beside it, a column surmounted by a uniformed statue. Both were flecked white and circled by pigeons.

"But you notice who with?"

"I don't know if I heard…"

"I think it says a lot."

She looked him over quizzically: "I hope you're not going to keep this to yourself."

"We know him."

"We do?"

"Know him well."

"And the name?"

"Guess."

250

Vanessa shrugged her shoulders.

"Shall I give you a clue?"

"No games. Just the name please."

"You give up?"

"Richard—"

He laughed and shook his head. "Try again."

"Name. Now."

"You sure?"

"No more talk. Name him."

"*Justin Peters.*"

Vanessa blinked. "Surely—" she began, then turned. As she searched Richard's face a far-off shiver ran across the bridge.

"The boy is father to the man," said Richard, as the sound came closer.

Metal on metal, it advanced with a shudder.

"But in their case," he added, "one grew, one didn't. Something happened, or was there already. In the end we adapt – and that makes the difference."

The approaching noise was filling up the air. Drumming hard, the sound locked them in.

Vanessa raised her voice: "So, it could go either way – is that what you're saying?"

He nodded.

"And whatever game you play," she added, "you can never know what's round the corner…"

As Richard acknowledged, she circled her arm, taking in the bridge, the river and the advancing train. "So, it's see for yourself, stand looking out – and that's good enough…"

The noise cut her off. It was as if she was on a phone and the line had gone dead. She continued mouthing, panto-style, as the walkway shook and the noise took over. It flowed and echoed and pressed in from all sides. It advanced with a shudder, a lurch and a top-heavy beat; it closed and filled the air.

They were in the middle.

In medias res.

And then they were in deep. Inside – in the stillness – behind the sound. They were in the hush.

In there, quiet, high up, caught on playback, singing in their heads – with the long line of carriages and window faces passing – and behind that, half-heard, dreamed-of, imagined: the big booming silence of the last departing train.

CHAPTER FIFTEEN

The Hen House
10th Nov

Dear Vanessa and Richard,

After you've read this letter I'd like you to burn it. A match
to the corner, and watch as it goes. All up in smoke. And don't tell
a soul. See it as a message whispered, a voice in the head, rain
against glass.

Or you could just chuck it. Take scissors to the corner, teeth,
then fingernails, to tear and scatter, and straight down the flush.
Whatever the method, it has to be final, over and done with. I've
said my piece, and I don't want them to know.

Here are my thoughts.

Begin.

What counts is who we are. I wanted it to work, played
Simple Simon, did my doggie best. Do this. Now this. Best friend
and supporter. Speak and offer warnings. Run, run, run.

Who we are, yes. A leaf, a wind, elements from a star. I am
what I am what I am.

Let me explain.

WHO: Ginny, crazy. Ever seen those drawings of a child's
face popping up from earth? A small peepy-eyed girl appearing
like a daisy inside the lion's mouth? The child peering out from
the whale?

WHAT: Objections, contradictions... can't stand the want-it-
both-ways, about-and-about facers... Lorna, Ken, Justin, the
whole fizzing lot of 'em. Too much dancing.

WHERE and WHEN: I suppose I've walked. Backpack,
map, provisions and head for the hills. Or, to tell the truth, the
railway line at night, Belvedere Park then up and off, beginning

the grand tour, to ridgepath, hill and passage grave. Yes, if I'm missing, it's a gap I'm filling, you understand... revisiting the patch.

Where am I going? Brambles, hawthorns, gorse slopes, ditches.

WHY? Well, here goes...

When I returned to the house late Sat afternoon, there was Ken jawing on the phone.

"Lorna?" I said, though of course I knew. The white face and hands, the attempted smile. Bottom lip threatening. *This is not me*, written all over.

Afterwards we rowed. "You're *allowed* one hour," I said, "to make some sort of case?"

Excuses, evasions, talk about the struggle.

When he came back The Line had him hooked. Pink and twitching, words in the mouth. Women as vanguard, the right to decide, female and first.

The next day, on phone call. Back on the case. Some talk about Xena and Melissa, needing sitting.

"What about Justin?"

Whereabouts unknown – on *Activist* call-out, fighting the cause.

Another row and exit.

Later, more of Ken, returned again. A decision this time, everything off, a second front opened.

By now I'd reached super-cool rage. "Oh, you mean it's still all monogamous?"

Not so, apparently.

And the upshot? Two more days with Ken in the air, jaw out, shaky, short-breathed on the phone... crisis, crisis, crisis.

Surprise is a child gazing at a hill.

Disappointment is an adult looking from the top.

All became clear at Wednesday's meeting (inner circle group: Lorna, Justin, Caroline, Ken, yours truly, plus one other). Dream-attentive faces, gathered in a circle. Executive business, money, targets, *Activist* subs... then all hail and salute to welcome the new member.

Lance.

The cat that ate the cream, Georgie Porgy, Little Boy Blue, butter wouldn't melt...

And this is where it snapped, afterwards, chatting (and when you've read through this burn, burn, burn, burn), with red mist and monkey up and hot blood and up gals and at 'em.

Lance + Lorna, the latest thing.

Words used: chuck, chuck out, upchuck, big chucking yuck. The mega-stink. Knee high in gunk. Bogus, phoney, rotten apples. Nettles grow from slops.

I think you know the rest.

So I'm on migration. A late summer visitor, here to stop off. By the time this reaches you, I'll already have flown.

From where I'm heading all this is all past. See me as I go. Now high, now low. The nightwalk child. I'm in the shadows, searching for scraps. Anywhere, nowhere, everywhere.

What we do is send out a signal.

So I'm out here in the wild, somewhere, walking. In the rain-streaks and mists, dew-clouds and wet paths and grey tracks and hill drifts and wild wind journeys. OTT. Crossing over water, climbing rock, down on mud, up into fog, stepping over feelings. Poor Gin.

While it lasted it was nice.

Wants are to needs as head is to heart.

All roads lead there.

Stay 'n' alive.

Ginny xx